W9-BNF-776

Ariel

Consider Ariel Jardell, an adopted twelve-year-old girl driven by jealousy–her mother thinks–and by forces far more bizarre–as you will discern–to a precocious excursion into evil from mere mischief, to malevolence beyond compare . . .

Haunting as *The Turn of the Screw*, chilling as *The Bad Seed*, *Ariel* spins a complex web of demonic circumstance with a fascinating, terrifying child at its center, giving new definition to the age-old conflict of good and evil, sane and insane.

Also by Lawrence Block
Available from Carroll & Graf

Ariel

A NOVEL BY
Lawrence Block

CARROLL & GRAF PUBLISHERS, INC.
NEW YORK

Copyright © 1980 by Lawrence Block

All rights reserved

First Carroll & Graf edition 1997

Carroll & Graf Publishers, Inc.
260 Fifth Avenue·
New York, NY 10001

ISBN 0-7867-0385-7

Manufactured in the United States of America

For Patrick Farrelly

ONE

WAS there a noise that woke her? Roberta was never sure. The old house was full of night sounds. Floorboards creaked. Curtains rustled. Window-panes, loose in their frames, rattled at the least touch of a breeze. She had been a light sleeper all her life. Caleb had just recently taken to sleeping through the night, and she had not yet entirely adjusted to his new schedule. The slightest sound could rouse her.

Or had she dreamed a sound? There might have been music, that thin reedy music Ariel made on her flute. Roberta sat up in bed, curiously troubled, straining to hear something in the silence.

Then she saw the woman.

A dark shape hovered in the far corner of the room near the window. A woman, wrapped in a shawl, her face averted.

Roberta pressed one hand to her breast. Her heart was fluttering, her mouth dry. She thought *David*, and her other hand reached out to her side, patting at empty air.

In the other house they had shared a bed, and she had always been able to reach out and touch him in the night. Now they slept in twin beds separated by the width of a night table. She had selected the bedroom furniture and donated the old double bed to Goodwill Industries. And she had been the one who picked this house. And now David slept, his breathing audible now in the room's stillness, while this woman lurked in the corner of their bedroom.

There was a lamp on the night table. Roberta's hand left off patting the air between the two beds and groped tentatively for the lamp. Her fingers found the switch, then hesitated. She was afraid to turn the light on even as she was afraid to remain in the dark.

She closed her eyes, opened them. The woman was still there.

Then a windowpane shook in its mullions and suddenly the woman was gone. It was as if she were a creature of smoke, and as if the wind that rattled the pane had slipped into the room and dispersed her. Roberta stared, blinked her eyes.

There was no woman in the room.

But she had seen—

An illusion, of course. Some trick of lighting, some shadow cast by moonlight through the old handmade windowpanes. But how extraordinarily real it had appeared to her! And what menace the shape had seemed to hold!

Unafraid now, she switched on the bedside lamp, then flicked it off again. There had been nothing and no one in the bedroom. Some forgotten dream must have awakened her, an unpleasant dream that left her anxious and suggestible. And so she'd seen a shape where there was no shape, and her imagination had cloaked that shape in a woman's shawl and touched her with a sense of evil.

Roberta lay down, closed her eyes. After a few moments she opened them again and stared at the corner of the room where she had seen the woman.

Nothing.

She closed her eyes again and tried to summon sleep. But it wouldn't come. Her mind was racing, and every stray thought that came to her seemed to increase her anxiety and focus it upon the baby. She had seen a woman who wasn't there, and now she was worried about her son.

It was ridiculous, and she knew it was ridiculous, but she also knew that she would not be able to sleep until she had checked Caleb. And wasn't it even more ridiculous to lie awake until daybreak? She sighed, then slipped out of bed and padded barefoot across the bedroom floor. David had wanted to carpet the whole upstairs, even as the other house had been carpeted wall to wall. She'd explained as patiently as possible that you didn't buy a house almost two hundred years old and cover its random-width pine floor with Acrilan broadloom. Now, though, she could almost sympathize with his position. The floorboards were cold underfoot and she found herself setting her feet down on them with exaggerated care to lessen their creaking.

Halfway down the hall, she hesitated at the open door to Caleb's room, then entered and approached his crib. There was enough light so that she could easily see his face. He was sleeping soundly. She stood there for a long moment, listening to the night sounds and gazing down on her son.

Before returning to her own room, Roberta walked the length of the hallway and stood outside Ariel's door with her hand on the knob. Then, without turning the knob, she went back to her bedroom.

Of course there was no dark shape in the corner. She shook her head, amused at her own fear, reassured now by the sight of her sleeping infant son.

Funny what tricks the mind played . . .

David stirred in his sleep and she looked down at him. The smell of alcoholic perspiration touched her nostrils. It was a sour smell and she wrinkled her nose at it.

Odd, she thought. He was never drunk, not as far as she

could tell, but after dinner he would sit reading in his ground-floor study and during those hours he always had a glass in his hand. It didn't seem to change him—as far as she could tell it didn't do anything to or for him—but while he slept his body eliminated some of the alcohol through the pores, and in the morning his sheets were often damp with it. But he never staggered and he never slurred his words, and if he had hangovers in the morning he never mentioned them.

She got into bed, settled her head on the pillow, let her thoughts drift where they wanted. Now the night sounds comforted her—the wind in the branches of the live oak outside her window, the loose windowpanes, the occasional creak of a floorboard, the inexplicable sounds that come from within the walls of an old house, as if the house itself were breathing.

Once she thought she heard the piping of Ariel's flute. But perhaps she was already asleep by then, already dreaming.

She was up later than usual the next night. She often went to bed right after the eleven o'clock news, occasionally hanging on for the first half hour of the *Tonight* show. But something kept her in front of the television set. She watched Johnny Carson through to the end. Even then she was faintly reluctant to go upstairs, and she dawdled on the ground floor, rinsing out a couple of cups and glasses she'd have ordinarily left for morning. She checked the pilot lights of the large old six-burner gas range. There were three pilots, one for each pair of burners, and they were forever going out in the damp brick-floored kitchen. One was out now, and she took a moment to light it.

She checked both outside doors, making sure they were locked and bolted, and she found herself testing the window locks and became impatient with herself. She felt like

4

an old maid checking under the bed for burglars. What on earth was she afraid of?

She checked the children. Ariel was asleep, or pretending to be asleep. She lay on her back, her arms at her sides under the covers, her breathing deep and regular. Caleb, too, was asleep, and while Roberta stood beside his crib he stretched and made a sweet gurgling sound. Air currents in the room shook the mobile suspended over his crib, an arrangement of gaily-colored wooden fish equipped with tiny bells that sounded when the air moved them. Caleb made his gurgling sound again, as if in response to the light tinkling of the bells, and Roberta felt a rush of love in her breast. She lowered the side of the crib, bent over and kissed Caleb's forehead.

How sweet he smelled. Babies had the most delicious scent . . .

In her room, David was already sound asleep. Maybe that was what the drinking did for him, maybe it enabled him to get to sleep and sleep soundly. Maybe she should have had something herself. But that was silly—she was tired, she would sleep with no trouble, she had never needed help getting to sleep.

And indeed it wasn't that long before she slept. Nor was it too long after sleep came that she was suddenly wide awake, fearfully awake, with her heart hammering against her ribs and a pulse working in her temple.

Her eyes were open and the woman, wrapped in her shawl, was standing by the bedroom window.

"Who are you? What do you want?"

There was a gust of wind. She heard it in the live oak, rustling the leaves, tossing the bunches of Spanish moss. It rattled the window glass and seemed to blow the woman about, as if she were a bundle of old rags. But she was a woman, it was very clear that she was a woman, the same woman who had been there the night before. Her form was

5

quite distinct in the dim corner. She stood facing the window, her hip and shoulder toward Roberta, her face invisible.

Roberta reached for the bedside lamp. Her fingers rested on the switch. She thought *David*, but did not speak his name aloud.

The woman turned toward her. She had a quick impression of a pale face. And the woman was holding something in her arms. Roberta squinted, trying to focus on the woman's face, trying to see what she was holding, and even as she narrowed her gaze the woman began to fade away, to merge with the shadows.

She switched on the light. The woman was gone.

She couldn't seem to catch her breath. She was drained, exhausted, and for several minutes all she could do was remain where she was, breathing raggedly, willing her heartbeat to return to normal. David slept on. She checked the time on the alarm clock, something she hadn't thought to do the night before. It was a quarter to four.

She told herself to go to sleep. She turned off the light and tried to lie still but it was impossible. She had to get up, had to check the baby.

She hurried down the hall. Caleb was sleeping like a lamb. The sight of him was evidently all she needed. She sighed with relief and tiptoed out of his room, returning to her own room without bothering to check Ariel.

In her own bed, she had a sudden impulse to go downstairs again, to check the doors and windows, to make sure none of the pilot lights had gone out. But she resisted the urge and sleep came to her with surprising swiftness.

When she awoke a light rain was falling. She changed Caleb and fed him, then went downstairs. David had made his own toast and coffee and was sitting behind the morning paper. Ariel had helped herself to orange juice and a bowl of sugared cereal. Roberta joined them at the table with a cup of black coffee and a cigarette.

No one spoke during breakfast. Twice Roberta was on the point of mentioning what she'd seen in the room the past night, but both times she repressed the impulse. The sentences she tested in her mind proved inadequate. *"I had the strangest dream last night."* But had it been a dream, last night and the night before? If so, it was unlike any dream she'd ever experienced before. *"I thought there was someone in the room last night."* But it was more than that, more than a trick of lighting and shadow. She'd sensed a menacing presence, had seen the woman turn to her before disappearing. *"There was someone in our bedroom last night."* But was there? Or was her own mind conjuring up images?

David was the first to leave. They chatted briefly, perfunctorily. Then he carried his briefcase to the car while she poured a second cup of coffee and lit a third cigarette and picked up the newspaper he'd abandoned. As usual, it told her precious little about what was new in the world and rather more than she needed to know about Charleston. She scanned an article about plans for the next Spoleto festival, skimmed a report on activity in the state legislature at Columbia, and read wire service pieces on arms-limitation talks and congressional maneuvering without really taking them in. She turned with some relief to Ann Landers and immersed herself in other people's problems. A secretary found her boss's wife domineering, a man felt guilty about putting his old mother in a home, and an adolescent girl felt unloved, unwanted, and singularly unpopular. Ann told her to make a list of all the positive things in her life.

"Time for school, isn't it?"

Ariel nodded, rose from the table, carried her dishes to the sink. How pale the child was, Roberta thought. Pale skin, pale blue eyes. Expressionless eyes—looking into them gave her a feeling that verged on vertigo, as though one could fall through the child's eyes into a bottomless abyss.

"Have a good day, Ariel."

"Thank you. I will."

"You'll be home afterward?"

"Where would I go?"

Where indeed? The child didn't seem to have any friends. She spent all her time alone, reading or doing homework or playing her horrible flute. Had she been as isolated when they lived in the suburban split-level? It seemed to Roberta that Ariel had been less thoroughly alone, that she'd had a playmate or two, but it was hard for her to be certain. That had been before Caleb's birth and so many things had been different.

But she was always a solitary child, Roberta thought. She seemed most content that way, as if she required solitude as other children required companionship.

The door closed. Roberta hesitated a moment, then went to the front room and drew the drapes a few inches apart. She stood at the window long enough to watch Ariel walk to the end of the block and turn the corner, disappearing from view. Then she opened the drapes all the way.

Back in the kitchen, she rinsed the dishes and thought about Ann Landers' column. Perhaps she ought to make a list of all the positive things in her life. Well, there was the man she'd married, the daughter they'd adopted, and the son she had recently borne. And there was this house, historic and well-preserved, on one of the best blocks in the Old Charleston section south of Tradd.

An impressive list. So what if the marriage had turned loveless? So what if there was something strange, almost frightening, about Ariel? So what if the house made sounds in the night, and the pilot lights wouldn't stay lit, and the damp was so pronounced you could grow mushrooms on the kitchen's worn brick floor? So what if sleep was interrupted by nightmares, or visions, or whatever had possessed her two nights running?

Caleb fussed in his crib, demanding her attention. "I'm coming, sweetie," she called out, crushing her cigarette in the ashtray, hurrying up the stairs, grateful for the distraction from her own thoughts.

The rain stopped by late morning, and shortly after noon the sky cleared and the sun came out. Roberta gave Caleb a bottle, lunched on leftovers, then bundled the baby into his carriage and took him for a walk. She headed aimlessly up one street and down another. She never seemed to tire of walking in the neighborhood, its houses dating clear back to Colonial times, its narrow streets free of heavy traffic, its walks shaded by ancient live oak and crape myrtle and magnolia.

Soon, she thought, the leaves would be turning. It was her favorite season, autumn was, a welcome relief after a summer that was invariably too hot and far too humid. Caleb had been born in the spring, and summer had been hard on both of them, but it was autumn now and autumn was a long season on the Carolina coast. Winter, when it finally came, was brief and not too bad, yielding before long to spring.

"And in the spring you'll be able to sit up in a stroller," she told Caleb, cooing the words to him. "You'll be able to see everything—dogs and children and people. You'll be a big boy in the spring."

He beamed at her and something clutched at her heart.

Around one-thirty she was seated on a green-slatted park bench at the Battery, gazing out at the ocean. Off to her left, several old men were fishing, their poles extending over the iron railing.

"They don't be catching nuffin but a cold," a voice said. Roberta turned to see an old black woman ease herself down onto the far end of the bench. She had frizzy white hair and very dark blue-black skin. She was tiny, small-boned and gaunt, and her skin clung to her bones like leather that had been soaked and left to dry in the sun.

"A million fish in the ocean but they don't be catching none of ems," the woman said. "You got a fine baby. A manchild, innit?"

"Yes."

"What do his name be?"

"Caleb."

The woman nodded, halved the distance between them, got up on her feet and peered down at Caleb. She nodded again, smacked her lips once and sat down. "You live round here," she said.

"Yes."

"One of them old houses?"

"Yes. Just a few blocks from here."

"Do there be haunts in it?"

"Pardon me?"

"Do there be haunts or ghosts?"

Roberta stared at her. "Last night," she said. "And the night before."

"You saw sumpin?"

"An old woman. She was standing by the window. And then she . . . disappeared."

The woman nodded. "A haunt," she said, satisfied. "Must be she lived and died there."

"I thought she was a real woman. And then I thought I was seeing things, and—"

"Haunts is like that. She lived there and died there. Happens sometimes a body dies and don't know it. Could be she were murdered. Killed of a sudden." She rubbed her old hands together and shivered with delight. "All them old houses has their haunts," she said. "That's what you saw."

"I was afraid."

"Only natural. Anybody be fraid. Nuffin to be fraid of, though. Haunts don't *do* nuffin. They just *be*."

"I never saw her before. And then I saw her two nights in a row."

"Maybe it be the season. Fall comin on."

"Maybe."

"Maybe it be she died this time of the year. Haunts will do that. One house I lived, long long ago, you could hear a dog. He would howl the night away. And there were no dog in that house. He were nuffin but a haunt, and you never did see him. You only did hear him."

"I think I really saw her."

"Course you did."

"I thought maybe it was a dream, or a lighting trick. But I really saw something."

"What you saw were a haunt."

"Maybe you're right."

"Haunt won't never hurt nobody," the woman said. Then her face grew animated and she was pointing. "Look at that! I said they wouldn't catch nuffin and look at that! That be a flounder." The man who'd caught him, an elderly white man in bib overalls, gripped the fish in his right hand while deliberately disengorging the hook with his left. This done, he held the fish aloft for a moment, then dropped it into a galvanized pail. "Them flatfish be good eatin," the old woman said. "Flounder be sweet clear to the bone."

Just a ghost, Roberta thought. A mere haunt. Nothing to be afraid of. An asset, really, on the house's balance sheet, like the original glass panes in the mullioned windows and the brick floor in the kitchen. An authentic touch of pre-Revolutionary Charleston.

She wondered idly who the woman might be. Perhaps

she'd been around at the time of the Revolution, when Francis Marion, the old Swamp Fox himself, had harried the British with his own brand of guerrilla warfare. Perhaps she'd occupied the house in the early days of the Republic, perhaps she'd known John C. Calhoun when he was the clarion voice of South Carolina. Or was the Civil War her time? Roberta hadn't felt anything of the southern belle in her aspect. She'd seemed more like an immigrant woman in one of those sketches of nineteenth-century slum dwellers in New York, a new arrival freshly transported from Ellis Island to the Lower East Side. Huddled in upon herself, wrapped in a shawl, carrying something—

She didn't mention the woman, not at dinner or afterward. Ariel spent the evening doing homework in her room, interrupting her work now and then to pipe tuneless music that pervaded the old house. David talked with her a bit over coffee, telling her about something that had happened at the office. She kept up her end of the conversation without paying much attention to what he was saying, and in due course he withdrew to his den to smoke his pipes and drink his brandy.

But she did talk to Caleb as she readied him for bed. "We're not scared of haunts, are we?" she cooed, powdering his soft little bottom, fixing a clean diaper in place. "We're not scared of anything, Caleb." And she kissed him again and again, and Caleb gurgled and laughed.

David went to sleep early, taking himself off to bed without saying goodnight, and she was grateful to hear his heavy step upon the stairs. She had spent a solitary evening, but now she could enjoy the special solitude that came when one was the only person awake in the household. She sat in the front room with coffee and cigarettes, her coffee flavored just the tiniest bit with some of David's brandy.

Would she see the ghost again?

She hoped not. It helped, curiously enough, to think of it as a ghost, although she was by no means certain she believed in such phenomena in the first place. Believing that the house was haunted, however, seemed to be rather less threatening than believing either that the woman was a real living creature or that she, Roberta, was going quietly mad. Perhaps that was how people had come to believe in the supernatural, she thought; perhaps they were relieved to latch onto an alternative to something even less acceptable.

If there was a ghost, did that mean she had to see it every damned night?

Perhaps not. Perhaps she could sleep through the nightly appearance of the ghost, even as Caleb had learned to sleep through his two A.M. feeding. The fact that she had only just taken to seeing the ghost did not mean the ghost had never walked before. Perhaps the ghost had appeared every night for years but she'd slept through the performance until the night before last, even as David had continued to sleep on through it.

And perhaps familiarity would eventually breed some form of contempt, so that if a night sound woke her she could sit up, blink at the apparition, say *"Oh, it's only the ghost again,"* and drift calmly back to sleep.

Had Ariel seen the ghost?

The child had certainly said nothing, but would she? She was so secretive she might have witnessed the apparition nightly for weeks without seeing fit to mention it.

If Ariel encountered the ghost, she thought, it would be the ghost that ran screaming.

She giggled at the thought, then flushed with guilt. Something was happening, some change in the way she related to Ariel, and she didn't know what it was or what to do about it. She penned a quick mental letter.

13

Dear Ann Landers, / Twelve years ago my husband and I adopted a baby girl, and now I've just had a baby of my own, a son, and I don't know what to do about my daughter. She's not what I had in mind. Do you suppose there's a way I could give her back? Just sign me / Having Second Thoughts.

Her own thoughts disturbed her. She frowned, crushed out her cigarette in the ashtray, and tried to force herself to substitute thoughts from an earlier time. Images of the three of them immediately after the adoption, she and David going on long walks with Ariel, then a montage of mental family pictures over the years. Ariel growing, learning to walk and talk, developing over months and years into a person.

A person Roberta knew less with every passing day.

She gave her head an impatient shake. This would all pass, she told herself. She had a new baby now, and any negative thoughts and feelings she had toward Ariel were almost certainly part of the process of nurturing that new baby. Older children were traditionally assumed to resent infants, and it struck her that their jealousy was well-founded.

In time, when her great love for Caleb became less obsessive, when she took his presence a little more for granted, her feelings for Ariel would be what they had once been.

Or had they started to change *before* Caleb was born? Even before he'd been conceived? She *was* a strange child, curious and remote. There was no gainsaying that. Even David admitted as much, although he seemed to take delight in the very strangeness that Roberta found unsettling.

And just when had she begun to find it unsettling? Before Caleb's birth? Before his conception? Well, she'd been so unsettled herself during that stretch of time that it was hard to separate causes and effects. Twice-weekly visits to Gintzler for maintenance doses of therapy and Valium.

14

The whole business with Jeff was going on then, impossible to handle but more stimulating than the therapy and more addictive than the Valium. She could see now that she'd been skating closer to the edge than she'd ever realized. Now that she'd come back from the edge, now that she was settled again with a baby and a house and a stable daily routine, she could begin to appreciate just how unstable her life had been for a while there.

She put her cup down. Shouldn't drink coffee late at night, she thought. It made her mind race. She'd come a long way from ghosts and haunts and things that went bump in the night.

She lit another cigarette. If she just stayed up late enough, perhaps she'd sleep through the ghost's command performance.

She was dreaming. In the dream the old black woman from the park bench at the Battery was sitting on her haunches beside an enormous wicker basket filled with fresh fish. She was taking up one after another, gripping each fish in turn in one bony hand while with the other she wielded a nasty little knife, slitting the fish up the belly and expertly gutting it. While she did this she spoke of the supernatural, of ghosts and haunts and the walking dead, of voodoo curses and the power of a mojo tooth. The wicker basket gradually emptied and the pile of gutted fish at the woman's feet grew steadily.

Then she was holding not a fish but a human infant. "The manchild, he be good eatin," she said, and smacked her lips. Roberta noted for the first time that she had no teeth. Her mouth was black and bottomless.

Roberta tried to move. She was frozen, incapable of motion. She could neither act nor cry out. The old woman cackled, and the knife flashed, and Roberta sat up in bed and wrenched herself out of the dream.

It was a dream, she thought, fastening onto the thought and repeating it to herself.

Then, in the corner of the room beside the window, she saw the woman. As on the previous night, the figure was facing the window, with hip and shoulder toward Roberta. Tonight, however, her form was more completely defined, as if her presence became more concrete with each appearance.

She's a ghost, Roberta tried to tell herself. *Ghosts are harmless. You had a bad dream and now you're seeing the ghost, but dreams can't hurt you and ghosts are harmless.*

It didn't help. The dream had shaken her badly and the sight of the woman was considerably more frightening than it had been on the two previous nights, her thoughts notwithstanding. An air of evil was present in the room. The woman bore it like a perfume and it was palpable in the thick night air.

"What do you want?"

Had she spoken the words aloud? Was she talking to this apparition?

Slowly, like a statue on a revolving platform, the woman turned to face her. Roberta saw the heart-shaped face, the bloodless lips, the pale eyes burning in the pale face.

The eyes held Roberta's own eyes. Something unspoken and unspeakable passed between the woman at the window and the woman on the bed. Then, against her will, she dropped her eyes to see what the woman was holding in her arms.

A baby.

A male infant, his body swaddled in a part of the woman's shawl, only his face visible. His face was as pallid as the woman's own and his wide eyes burned with the same pale fire.

Slowly and magically, like trick photography in a television commercial, the baby's face lost flesh and turned to a gleaming skull. And the woman, too, was a bare polished skeleton wrapped in a shawl. And she drew away, the skeletal infant in her arms, floating through the closed window and out into the night.

Roberta cried out. She opened her mouth and screamed.

There was a gap, a blank space. Then she was being held, a hand patting awkwardly at the back of her head. She breathed in the smell of alcohol sweat and knew then that David was holding her, trying to comfort her.

"A dream," he was saying. "You had a bad dream. That's all."

She wanted to correct him but she couldn't, not right away, because her heart was racing and she couldn't catch her breath, and if he didn't continue to hold her very tight she felt she might shake herself apart.

Then, when she could speak, she tried to explain. She told about what she'd seen for three nights running.

"A dream," he said.

"Night after night?"

"A recurring dream. I've had one off and on for years, I'm someplace dangerously high and trying to get down from it, endless fire escapes and catwalks, and I'm frightened and I can never get back to ground level. Variations on a theme. You know about dreams, all those months with Gintzler, stretched out on his couch."

"This wasn't a dream."

"All right."

"I had a dream first, a crazy dream about a black woman cleaning fish." She hurried on, not wanting to recall the dream's ending. "Then I was awake and I saw her again. She was standing right there."

"She's not there now."

"Of course not."

"You think you saw a ghost?"

"I don't know what I saw. I don't know anything about ghosts. It was some sort of . . . some sort of spiritual presence."

"A being of another world."

"It had that feeling to it, yes."

"Why was it so frightening?"

"She was holding—I can't say it."

"What do you mean?"

"I can't make myself say it. I'm afraid."

He looked at her.

"Hell," she said. "She was holding a baby."

"So?"

"The baby died. She turned to show me the baby and I watched while the baby turned into a skeleton. Then the woman was a skeleton too, and they went out the window and disappeared."

"Jesus."

"I'm telling you what I *saw*, David."

"Now tell me why it's frightening."

"Are you crazy?"

He shook his head. "Why's it frightening to *you?* What are you scared *of*, Roberta?"

"You know."

"Tell me."

"Why do I have to say it?" She turned her eyes away. "The baby," she said.

"You're afraid of the kid she was holding?"

"You know what I mean."

"I think you should say it."

She closed her eyes, lowered her head. "Caleb," she whispered.

"What about him?"

"I'm afraid."

"Afraid of what?"

"God *damn* you!" She made a fist, struck out at his chest.

"I'm afraid my baby's dead, you son of a bitch!"

He said nothing. Her hands dropped and her shoulders sagged and she wept soundlessly, the tears streaking her cheeks. After a time the crying stopped and she wiped her tears away with the back of her hand.

"Roberta?"

"What?"

"Do you really believe—"

"I don't know what I believe. I never believed in ghosts until I saw one. Or whatever the hell I saw."

"Why don't you go check Caleb."

"Now?"

"Why not?"

"I don't—I'm afraid."

"I'll go with you."

"I'm afraid. Isn't that ridiculous? I don't know what's the matter with me."

"You had a bad dream and then you either saw something or thought you did, and maybe it amounts to the same thing. Would you like me to check him?"

"Would you?"

She sat up in bed and waited for what seemed like a very long time. He returned with a comforting smile on his face. "He's fine," he said.

"You're sure he's all right?"

"He's sleeping like a baby. Do you want to see for yourself?"

"No." She took a deep breath and let it out very slowly. "Thank you," she said. "I'm crazy tonight, I really am."

"You had a rough time there."

"Thanks for going. And thanks for making me work it out."

"You're all right now?"

"I think so." She looked at him, drawing from him a sense of strength he hadn't given her in years. His body was growing softer with the years. A sedentary life had changed his body shape, and the droop in his shoulders mirrored the quiet desperation of so many nights spent in his study with his pipes and his brandy. He was bare to the waist, his chest hair matted with perspiration, and as she looked at him now she felt an unfamiliar surge of desire.

"Well," he said. "We'd both better get to sleep."

"Could you—"

"What?"

"Could you come into my bed for a little while?"

He slipped out of his pajama bottoms and joined her under the covers. She really only wanted to be held, but when he began making love to her she was surprised by his passion and at least as surprised by her own. Afterward she held onto him but he deliberately extricated himself from her embrace and returned to his own bed.

She felt herself drifting off to sleep. She was on the edge of it when he spoke.

"When you screamed," he said. "Do you remember what you said?"

"I just . . . screamed. And then you were holding me."

"You don't remember what you said."

"No. What did I say?"

She didn't think at first that he was going to answer. Then he said, "I don't know. I was asleep. Maybe you just cried out. I thought you might remember."

"Maybe I called your name."

There was a pause. "Sure," he said at length. "That must have been it."

She heard his alarm clock when it rang. But she stayed in bed until he had showered and dressed and gone down for his breakfast. Then, reluctantly, she dragged herself out of bed. There was an emptiness within her, a hollow void, and she didn't know what it meant.

She went to Caleb's room. He was lying on his back in his crib. His eyes were wide open, rolled back in his head, and his face had a blue tinge to it. She made herself extend a hand to touch him. His skin was cool beneath her fingers.

Then she must have turned from him, because the next thing she knew she was in the doorway of his room, her back to the crib. Ariel was just emerging from the bathroom. Roberta stood still, feeling her breasts rise and fall with her breathing, as the child approached.

Ariel said, "Is something wrong? Is something the matter with Caleb?"

Roberta couldn't answer.

"That's what it is, isn't it? What's the matter with Caleb? Is he dead? Is Caleb dead?"

Roberta threw her head back and howled like a dog.

TWO

EARLY on the morning of Caleb's funeral, Roberta slipped out of the house and went for a walk by herself. She had no conscious destination in mind but wandered around as she had often done on her walks with Caleb, heading up one street and down the next. She was not surprised, though, to find herself at the Battery. Her feet had often led there in the past, and she realized now that she had been on her way to the Battery from the moment she left the house, realized in fact that she was looking for the little old black woman with whom she'd talked of ghosts on the last day of Caleb's life.

She didn't find the old woman. There were two men and a woman fishing, a handful of people sitting with newspapers, and one bum stretched full length on a bench, his overcoat serving him as a blanket, his shoes tucked under his head for a pillow. Over to her left, in the shade of an equestrian statue, two young mothers were engaged in conversation. One moved her carriage gently back and forth as she talked. The other had a child in a stroller. Roberta took in the scene at a glance and at once averted her eyes. She was careful not to look in their direction again.

She stayed in the park long enough to smoke a cigarette.

Then with an effort she got to her feet and began walking slowly back to the house.

The funeral service was held that afternoon at the Whittecombe Mortuary, a rambling one-story building of white stucco located on Edgeworth Road a mile north of the city line. The split-level house where the Jardells had lived for over ten years was within walking distance of the funeral parlor. Roberta had attended a number of funerals at Whittecombe's over the years, and when her mother had died seven years previously Whittecombe's had been the logical choice. Now, although it was no longer particularly convenient, it was the first place David had thought of.

At the time she had not objected. If there had to be a funeral it hardly mattered to her where it was held. Now, sitting in the first row, with David on her left and Ariel on her right, Roberta regretted the choice. Ever since they'd moved downtown she'd disliked even driving through their old neighborhood, and now, returning to it for this particular occasion, she felt as though Caleb's death was some bizarre punishment for their having moved in the first place.

Roberta sat stiffly, her spine perpendicular, her hands in her lap. People drifted up to offer words of sympathy. She would look at each person in turn but her eyes refused to focus on the faces in front of her, even as her ears were unable to make sense of the words they took in. *So sorry for your troubles crib death is such a mystery even in this day and age have our sympathy want to say how much certainly do hope tragedy good die young such a shame—*

Once she turned, thinking she'd spotted the old black woman out of the corner of her eye. But she'd only seen one of Horace Whittecombe's bloodless little assistants scurrying around.

She managed now and then to nod to the people who

offered their sympathy, managed to return a bit of pressure to the hands that pressed her hand. From time to time she would force herself to look beyond the faces to the tiny bronze casket. Miniaturization, she realized, transformed an ordinary casket into something curiously obscene.

At least it was closed. But it had been open earlier and she had looked inside it. Before the others had begun to arrive, when there were just she and David and Ariel, Horace Whittecombe himself had slithered across the room to ask if they would care to view the remains.

What a word—

David had not wanted her to go for that final look. As if it would be too much for her. As if she were not strong enough to bear it.

As if she could bear *not* to look.

And so they had all viewed the body, all three of them. David had held her and supported her while she stared down at Caleb's waxen face. She thought of other corpses she had viewed. Her father, who'd died in a car crash when Roberta was not much more than Ariel's age; the steering wheel had crushed his chest but the accident had left his face unmarked. Her mother, gaunt and ravaged by disease before death took her. David's father. Aunts, uncles, grandparents. A handful of others.

For all the pride morticians took in their cosmetic skills, she had never seen a corpse that had looked remotely alive. At best the dead looked dead; more often, they looked as though they had never been alive in the first place. They might have been window dummies.

But Caleb looked like a doll, like a child's doll. A wax head, a little body of stuffed rags swaddled now in a blue blanket.

She had stared dry-eyed at him for as long as she could bear. Then she had turned and ordered the casket closed.

Now she glanced down at her hands. They lay in her lap

like pieces of wax fruit on a plate. She could almost see them aging before her eyes, the skin drying and shrinking on the bone, the knuckles swelling with arthritis. Her own mother had first shown her age in her hands, and Roberta took after her mother, looked like her, shared her tastes and inclinations. Her mother's hands had grown old long before the rest of her. The woman had retained a youthful face long after she'd had an old woman's hands, and then in a rush the rest of her had caught up with her hands. She'd had lung cancer and it reached metastasis before they found it, and then the decline had been abrupt and dramatic.

Roberta looked at her own hands and thought of her mother and her mother's death and wanted a cigarette. Her mouth was dry and her hands and feet were chilled and she wanted a cigarette badly, wanted a drink of water, wanted to use the toilet. But nothing was worth the trouble, nothing was all that urgent, and she remained in her seat, staring dully ahead.

So many people offering their sympathy! True, she had lived in Charleston all her life, but she'd been an only child and David had no family here, and most of the friends of her youth had drifted away. While she and David had been socially active earlier in their marriage, they had become less so even while they still lived in the suburbs, and what social life remained had shrunk considerably since the move to the city. They had neither made new friends nor kept the old ones, and yet people kept coming, murmuring unintelligible words, patting her wax-fruit hands.

"Sorry for your trouble, Mrs. Jardell. I'm Curt Rowan, a business friend of your husband's."

She nodded, let her hand touch his.

"Mrs. Jardell? I'm Ariel's teacher, Claire Tashman. I'm so sorry."

"Roberta, what a terrible thing. I'm so deeply sorry, dear."

"I'm sorry for your trouble, Mrs. Jardell. I'm Erskine Wold, I'm Ariel's friend."

What an odd-looking little boy, she thought, certain she'd never seen him before. Trust Ariel to choose an odd child for a friend. Birds of a feather—

"Oh, Roberta, you poor darling!" An ancient friend of her mother's, her face as wrinkled as a monkey's, her name impossible to recall. Roberta had not seen her since her mother's funeral. An embrace, a powdered cheek to be kissed, and then the woman moved off and a man took her place.

She sensed his presence before she raised her eyes and saw him. She had had fleeting thoughts of him during the past two days but had refused to allow herself to entertain these thoughts.

Now her eyes took him in and she kept a tight hold on herself, not letting herself react visibly to the sight of him. Of course he had come—why shouldn't he? He'd been her friend for years, hers and David's, and he lived just a few blocks from Whittecombe's. It was a fine fall day, cloudless and cool. Perhaps he'd walked over, cutting a dashing figure in his pinstripe navy suit, striding athletically through the quiet suburban streets, his arms swinging at his sides.

Jeff Channing.

Did he know whom they were burying this lovely afternoon? Did he know who it was in the little brassbound casket?

She wanted to tell him. She wanted to tell them all. She wanted to lift the lid of the obscene little coffin and cry out at the top of her lungs, telling Jeff Channing to take a first and last look at his son.

But all she did was nod, and pretend to have heard whatever he might have said, and murmur something unintelligible in evident response. He hesitated only a moment before moving on to express his sympathy to David. He had not moved to take her hand, nor did she offer it.

She looked down at her hand, lying so still in her lap. Soon, she thought. Soon it would begin to show its age.

Ariel wished they would start it already. All of these people were driving her crazy. She didn't know who most of them were and she didn't really want to know, but instead of just leaving her alone they had to give their names.

Not the man who'd just passed, though. He hadn't called her by name nor had he supplied his own, and the funny thing was that she was pretty sure she recognized him. She'd seen him before, though not recently.

Maybe it was just that he had the kind of blank good looks you saw in magazine ads and on television. He could have been the master of ceremonies on the *Dating Game*. Maybe he was working up a new game show. The *Funeral Game*—pick the right coffin and win an all-expense paid trip for two to Forest Lawn Cemetery.

At least he hadn't bugged her. So many of them seemed to feel a need to drop some special message on her. One grayhaired woman with huge nostrils had asked her if she would miss her baby brother. That was about the most disgusting number anyone had done so far, but a lot of people had told her that she would have to be very brave and help her mother, and she felt like asking the next moron who came up with that line just what good her bravery would do Roberta.

Because it was pretty obvious that Roberta didn't give the northern half of a southbound rat whether she was brave or terrified or anything else. The only thing she could do that would make Roberta feel better would be to change places with Caleb. If it was Ariel in the little brass box instead of poor old Caleb then Roberta would jump up and down and turn handsprings.

Not that she'd fit. She was twelve, just two months short of thirteen, and although she was not particularly tall for her age she was still far too large to squeeze into Caleb's coffin. She had a sudden mental picture of herself jammed into it, legs doubled up and all scrunched together to fit, and old Roberta jumping maniacally up and down on the lid in an effort to close it.

The image struck her as hysterical and she had to fight the impulse to giggle. That, she knew, would just about tear it. Roberta hated her as it was, hated her for being adopted, hated her for being alive, and hated her for being *there*, and all it would take was one tiny little giggle and Roberta would just about strangle her. Besides, even if Roberta didn't notice, even if nobody happened to notice, the last thing she wanted was to sit around breaking herself up at Caleb's funeral.

What she really wanted to do was cry. But she couldn't do that either. She had cried all of yesterday and most of the day before, and she would almost certainly do some more crying, probably that night. But she had to be alone to cry. She just wouldn't cry in front of anybody.

The parade finally ended when a pair of ushers moved in and began steering people toward their seats. The people who worked in funeral parlors, Ariel decided, had to be about the grimmest people in the world. There was old Mr. Whittecombe, who owned the place, and who looked as though he had died years ago and had been very skillfully embalmed; they'd done such a perfect job on him that he could still walk and talk, but if you watched closely and listened carefully it became obvious that he was actually dead. Then there were his two sons, younger versions of their father, and there were three or four other young men who hovered around, and they all wore the same black suits and had the same oily voices and narrow-shouldered bodies and they were all spooky. Which only figured, because you had to be pretty spooky to decide to do things like this for a living.

And you had to be able to glide around like an efficient zombie, which wasn't likely to be a million laughs. And, speaking of laughs, you could absolutely *never* laugh. But that probably wasn't a problem for these men because they didn't look as though anything had ever struck them as funny.

The minister mounted the steps and took his position at the lectern a few steps to the right of Caleb's casket. Ariel had met him earlier that day but didn't remember his name. He wasn't their minister because they didn't have one—they didn't attend church—but David had evidently dredged him up somewhere. Maybe old Whittecombe found you a minister if you weren't able to come up with one of your own. Maybe it was all part of a package deal.

The minister started talking but she decided not to listen to him. It was easy enough to tune out things you didn't want to hear. She'd had plenty of practice over the years not listening to Roberta, and had reached a point where she could ignore just about anybody. And it didn't seem likely that the minister would say anything sensational. What could he talk about, anyway? What a great life Caleb had had and all the good things he'd done in it? She figured he would just come up with the standard crap about how God's ways are mysterious, and that wasn't anything she wanted to hear.

She wasn't sure about God. Some days she believed in Him and other days she didn't. Today she didn't, but not because Caleb had died. That could just as easily make her believe there *had* to be a God, because nothing that rotten could happen just by accident. A little baby goes to sleep at night and doesn't wake up in the morning—well, that convinced you either that there was a God or that there wasn't, depending which way your ears were pointed that particular day.

She looked at the minister, a tall man with very prominent eyebrows and dark blond hair that had gone gray at the temples. He had the same kind of unreal good looks as the man who could have been planning to emcee the *Funeral Game.* Her eyes moved from the minister to the coffin, and then she closed her eyes and tried to think of something else to think about.

She had never been to a funeral before. She'd been about five when her grandmother died and they'd left her at home with a baby sitter. Her regular sitter couldn't come that day, probably because the funeral took place during school hours, and the sitter who showed up was a plump bubbly woman with a hearty laugh who told great stories and kept her occupied nonstop from her parents' departure to their return several hours later. The woman had been a far more grandmotherly type than the woman they buried that day, whom Ariel now recalled as having always been ill, lying in bed first in a sick-smelling bedroom and later in an equally unwholesome hospital room.

Though this was her first funeral, Ariel had known what to expect. You saw enough of them on television. But she had not known what the experience would *feel* like. And she had had no idea that she would have to go stand next to the coffin and look at Caleb lying there.

Not that she had been forced to look. In fact they hadn't seemed to want her to look, but it didn't matter what they wanted. If you were supposed to go and look, then that was what she was going to do.

So she had stood there, just able to gaze over the side of the coffin, and it was the strangest feeling. It was like standing at the side of his crib and looking through the bars at him while he slept. Except that he wouldn't wake up. He wouldn't coo and make his giggle sounds, and he wouldn't raise his feet for her to play with them and make him laugh, and he wouldn't go ga-ga looking at his fish mobile. He wouldn't do any of those things, not ever again, but here she was looking down at him, and it was, well, weird.

Speaking of weird, she was surprised that Erskine had come. She had only met him when school started and she really didn't know him at all. They were in two classes together, arithmetic and social studies, and they would nod at each other when they passed in the halls, but that was the extent of it. Nobody else had come from her new school except for her homeroom teacher, Miss Tashman, and no one at all had come from her old school, and that was about what she had expected. She didn't really have any friends.

Maybe Erskine just happened to be a nut about funerals. It almost figured that he would be. He was certainly creepy enough. He was short, five or six inches shorter than she was, and he was plump. Not plump all over but just in the stomach and chest. His arms and legs were quite thin, and he had very small hands and feet. His eyes were blue and looked larger than life because he wore glasses like the bottoms of Coke bottles that magnified his eyes so they looked enormous, making Erskine look something like a Martian in the process.

His complexion, she thought, was even paler than her own, so pale it looked unhealthy. And he was almost as well-coordinated as a spastic, unable to walk through the halls without dropping at least half of what he was carrying. Sometimes he bumped into people. Sometimes he caromed off walls. Sometimes he tripped over his own feet. And his voice was high in pitch, and he tried to conceal this by talking down at the very bottom of his throat, which made him sound either like a girl trying to imitate a boy or a sparrow trying to imitate a bullfrog.

Weird.

So maybe he never misses a funeral, she thought. Which would figure. Or maybe he likes me, which would also figure, because I'm almost as unusual looking as he is. Erskine Wold and Ariel Jardell, and how's that for a corner on the weirdness market, ladies and gentlemen?

Still, it was nice of him to come.

Jeffrey Channing sat alone in the last row, where he paid no more attention than Ariel to the words the minister was saying. The room was little more than half full, and Jeff was the only person seated in any of the last five rows on either side of the center aisle. This physical gap between himself and the others intensified a feeling of detachment that had been strong to begin with.

He was thinking about crib death.

He'd spent most of the morning reading about it, first in the main public library downtown, then at the medical school library at Calhoun and Barre, where articles in pediatric journals referred to it as SIDS, the acronym representing Sudden Infant Death Syndrome. Which, it seemed to him, just accented how little was known about crib death.

Perfectly healthy babies went to sleep and didn't wake up, and no one seemed to know why. There were theories, he had learned, but they came and went with the seasons. One article he'd read suggested that SIDS might be some form of anaphylactic shock, an extreme allergic reaction of the sort that gave some individuals fatal reactions to a bee sting or a shot of penicillin. Another writer argued that the syndrome was far more common in bottle-fed babies, and reasoned that it was caused by a constitutional inability to digest the larger protein molecules in cow's milk. Yet another authority explained the phenomenon in terms of the

33

failure of the body's autoimmune system. Jeff knew that the autoimmune system was a factor in some patients' rejection of transplanted organs, but that was about all he did know about it, and he couldn't understand how it might relate to the death of Caleb Oliver Jardell.

Lord, what a handle for an infant. Caleb Oliver Jardell sounded like some grizzled captain of industry, some board chairman cloaked in respectability but with the soul of a pirate. Would the kid have grown into the name? Or would they have wound up calling him Butch or Sonny or Callie or something of the sort?

Hardly mattered. Caleb had been born and had died without Jeff's ever having seen him. Nor would Jeff see him now. The casket was closed, and soon enough it would be in the ground.

Funny how he hadn't even wanted to see the kid while he was alive. The affair with Roberta had ended, broken off abruptly at her insistence before he'd had any idea that she was pregnant. He'd been surprised by her decision, and more than a little hurt. At first he tried calling her, but her reaction made it very clear that she wanted him to keep his distance.

To hell with her, he'd decided, and he had put her out of his mind without further ado. First he'd taken his wife for a week's vacation in Bermuda, attempting to reinvigorate their marriage while dealing with his guilt over the affair. The trip was a limited success, but on his return he found himself still smarting from Roberta's rejection. He had promptly plunged into a series of brief affairs, using deliberately casual sex to cheapen whatever he and Roberta had had between them.

Then he'd found out that she was pregnant.

He had dealt with this reality by denying it. His first reaction to the discovery was the immediate assumption that she was carrying his child. David, after all, had never been capable of fathering a child. It was true that he did produce living spermatazoa, but Roberta had said that his sperm count was so low as to make his sterility a medical presumption. After several years of trying and extensive series of tests, they had adopted Ariel.

Now, more than a decade later, she was pregnant. She and David barely slept together. Jeff, on the other hand, was fiercely fertile, and they had made love frequently during the several months their affair had lasted.

They'd taken precautions, of course. This was something of a novelty for both of them; Roberta had had no need to employ birth control when she slept with her husband, and Jeff's wife Elaine had had tubal ligation after the birth of her second daughter. So they'd used condoms, which had given their lovemaking a high school lovers' lane element, and evidently one of the condoms had been unequal to its task.

Roberta had become pregnant with his child. And, on realizing as much, she had decided to terminate not the pregnancy but the relationship, returning to David and presumably convincing him that his sperm had improved with age. Which he no doubt was pleased not to question.

Then the denial mechanism had taken over. How did he know it was his child she was carrying? David might not have many sperm, but all it took was one. And a sperm count wasn't necessarily fixed. It could increase or decrease over the years. And pregnancy after the adoption of a child was such a common phenomenon as to be almost a cliché. When it happened, you didn't run to the window looking for a bright star in the East.

She was part of the past, he had decided. And the baby was probably her husband's, and if not that didn't make it Jeff's anyway, because who knew how many other clowns she'd been screwing over the months? He at least had used condoms. For all he knew she'd balled the entire Citadel football team, including the coach and the waterboys, and hadn't even made them use Saran Wrap.

So the hell with her, and the hell with the kid, and good riddance to both of them.

When the child was born his denial faded. He recognized that Caleb's sex was a factor. His own children were both girls, and although he loved them none the less for their gender, he would have liked a son as well. But Elaine had had a hard time with the second pregnancy and was determined to stop at two, and her tubal ligation was a *fait accompli* by the time Jeff learned about it. He'd been hurt by the way she'd made the decision all on her own, but it was her body, and these days women were making a lot of noise about their right to do as they wished with their own bodies, and maybe two children was enough. Maybe he was better suited to father daughters anyway, maybe he'd have been awkward with a son.

Then all at once he had a son, had him but didn't have him. And of course Caleb was his son—how had he managed to make himself believe otherwise?

Was there a resemblance? His daughters both favored Elaine, although the younger one had her father's eyes. Whom did Caleb resemble? Himself or Roberta?

Not David, he knew. Not a chance of that.

Ever since Caleb's birth, Jeff had kept his distance from Roberta and the baby without putting them out of his mind. He entertained a variety of fantasies in which he eventually got together with his son. In one of them, David and Elaine both perished in some convenient fashion; Jeff liked the idea of their being copassengers on some airliner that might fly into the side of a handy mountain.

Then, after a suitable period of mourning, he and Roberta would court and eventually marry. She would be a mother to Debbie and Greta, and he would be to Caleb what he already was biologically, and Caleb would never know the real circumstances of his conception, and—

Other fantasies were somewhat more likely to be realized at some future date. He thought he might manage to get a look at Caleb sooner or later, if only to see for himself whether a resemblance existed. When Caleb was older, he might manage to meet the boy. Someday, when the boy was old enough to handle it, maybe they could have a few beers together and the truth could come out.

Anything was possible. Especially when you kept it a fantasy.

Not now, though. Not with Caleb dead.

Why had it happened?

One of the articles he'd read that morning discussed the psychological effect of crib death on the victims' parents. Almost invariably, the mothers of those babies—and to a lesser extent the fathers as well—blamed themselves for what happened. Because there was no identifiable cause of death, because a seemingly healthy infant had died suddenly for no good reason, the parents assumed responsibility. Some viewed the baby's death as punishment, just or unjust, for their own sins. Others had a less abstract view of guilt; they felt they must have neglected the baby, that they had cared for it inadequately, that there should have been something they could have done to prevent the tragedy. If only she had checked him during the night, a mother might berate herself. If only she had given him an extra blanket, or no blanket at all, or wakened him for his feeding, or let him sleep through it, or—

And what could he have done? Forced himself into the picture during Roberta's pregnancy? Broken up her marriage and his own? Even if he'd made an effort, there was no reason to think she'd have accepted him. He'd been acceptable as a lover, but evidently she'd decided she preferred being married to David Jardell.

And suppose she'd come to him and told him of her pregnancy? Suppose she'd wanted to leave David and marry him? What would he have done then, if it were not fantasy anymore but a case of hard-edged reality?

Would he have divorced Elaine? Would he have been willing to give up custody of Debbie and Greta for the sake of a child as yet unborn? For that matter, would he have been that thrilled at the idea of marrying Roberta? She was an exciting bedmate and a stimulating companion, but how well would that kind of stimulation wear? She was sometimes brittle, she was acerbic, she was moody, she smoked too much—how quick would he have been to choose her over the comforting presence of Elaine?

And what about Ariel? He craned his neck, trying for a glimpse of her over the intervening rows. There was something odd about her, something faintly spooky, some intangible aura the kid gave off. That was the trouble with adoption, you never knew what you were getting, and if he had married Roberta, Ariel would almost certainly have been part of the package.

Pointless speculation. Caleb had been conceived and born and was now dead. Jeff had not seen him. And never would.

The damned finality of it—

It wasn't fair.

Just as the minister was hitting his stride, a joke popped into Erskine's mind. He couldn't remember where he'd read it. *Mad Magazine*, probably. It was their kind of humor.

Question: How do you make a dead baby float?
Answer: Take one dead baby, two scoops of vanilla ice cream, a little chocolate syrup, some club soda—

He felt a whoop of laughter gathering itself within him and headed it off by launching a coughing fit. A woman seated just across the aisle turned to give him a dirty look, which didn't astonish him. Adults generally gave you dirty looks.

One dead baby, two scoops of vanilla—

Classic.

He just wondered how soon it would be cool to try the joke on Ariel.

The minister was talking about the will of God. God's will, he said, had three properties. It was good, it was acceptable, and it was perfect.

The three words kept echoing in David's mind. Good, acceptable, perfect.

It was difficult to identify those properties in certain types of tragedy, like the death of an innocent infant. God's ways were a mystery to us, the man went on, but our inability to grasp his plan for us did not mean the plan did not exist.

Good, acceptable, and perfect.

How, David wondered, could it be good for a baby like Caleb to die? Well, he could see an argument. As long as the human race had existed, infant mortality had been high. Only in recent years, with the advances in medical science and the development of immunization and antibiotics, had this pattern begun to change.

And wasn't high infant mortality nature's way of culling the weaker individuals? When you planted a vegetable garden, you always sowed more seed in the rows than you could allow to grow to maturity. The little seedlings would come up shoulder to shoulder, but in order to give them room to grow you had to thin them ruthlessly, leaving only the best and strongest plants.

Why shouldn't Nature thin the crop of human seedlings?

And, with the original complement of infant diseases no longer as effective, why shouldn't a phenomenon like crib death emerge, carrying off the weak and infirm quickly and painlessly while they slept. Surely it was a gentler thinning mechanism than whooping cough or diphtheria.

But why Caleb?

Well, perhaps there was an answer to that, too. Caleb was a child who should never have been born in the first place. They had been doing fine without him, he and Roberta and Ariel. Certainly there were imperfections in their life. His job, in the traffic department at Ashley-Cooper Home Products, had evolved into a comfortable rut; fortunately his ambition had eroded even as the possibilities for job advancement shrank. His salary was adequate, his position secure, his work pleasant and undemanding. It wasn't the brilliant career he'd envisioned at twenty-one, but one's attitudes changed as one's life defined itself, and he was happy enough doing what he did.

Roberta's life, too, had had its discontents. His inability to impregnate her had been hard for her to handle, but after a frustrating couple of years they'd adopted Ariel, and that had strengthened them as a family while giving Roberta the fulfillment of motherhood. And Ariel was an endlessly interesting child, and it was exciting for David to watch the gradual evolution of her unique personality.

Caleb had disturbed the balance. Ariel, an adopted child of unknown parentage, was equally the daughter of David and Roberta.

Caleb, on the other hand, was Roberta's son.

The fact had never been discussed. He had known for some time that she was having an affair, had known it without consciously acknowledging that he knew it. But when she announced the miracle of her pregnancy he had immediately gone along with the fiction that it was indeed miraculous, that his sparse and sluggish sperm had managed an amazing increase in number and mobility, one of them actually charging through to the goal line, planting the flag on Iwo Jima.

He'd never really believed this for a moment. Nor did he think Roberta actually thought he was fooled.

When Caleb was born, David thought he might come to love the boy. He loved Ariel, wholly and without reservation, although he had not fathered her. Why shouldn't he love Caleb, whom he had not fathered either, but who at least was the child of his wife? His first sight of the baby, through the thick glass window at the hospital, was quite lacking in emotion. But that didn't necessarily mean anything. From what he'd heard, relatively few fathers were overcome with a rush of love at the first sight of their offspring.

Instead of love, what he grew to feel was resentment. Roberta was crazy about the kid, and there was no getting away from the fact that she favored him over Ariel. At first he told himself it was simple favoritism for the needier newborn, a natural maternal prejudice perhaps essential for survival. But he came to see that it was rather more than that. Roberta's attitude toward Ariel underwent a definite change. She resented the girl as David resented Caleb.

Of course they never talked about any of this. The new house lent itself to their spending time apart. His study was the immensely comfortable masculine room he'd always yearned for, and it quickly became his habit to retire there after dinner with a book and a bottle. Sometimes Ariel would come in and sit on his lap. Sometimes he would spend hours by himself until it was time to go up to bed.

The brandy helped take the sharp edges off his feelings. He would drink slowly but steadily from the time dinner ended, and by the time he left the little room on the ground floor he was generally pretty tight. He held it well, though, and he clung to this fact whenever he found himself wondering whether he was drinking an un-healthy amount. He never showed the effects of the brandy, never threw up or staggered or passed out, and if he experienced a fairly rocky morning once in a while it rarely amounted to more than a cup of black coffee and a couple of aspirins could cure.

Once or twice he'd had memory lapses. More than once or twice, if you counted the short ones. He'd wake up in the morning with no clear recollection of leaving his study. But obviously he'd been all right. He'd made it up the stairs and he'd wake up in his own bed with his cloth-ing hung neatly in the closet. If he'd done anything bi-zarre during those vacant periods he surely would have heard about it from Roberta. And if he happened to have lost the memory of a few minutes or a half hour or what-ever, what earthly difference did it make? A person's head was cluttered enough with facts and memories; one hardly needed total recall of every time one climbed a flight of stairs.

In any event, the brandy helped. It smoothed things out. Throughout, he'd been confident things would work out. Roberta would get over whatever she was going through with Ariel. He himself would work things out as far as his feelings for Caleb were concerned. And everything would be fine.

Good, acceptable and perfect.

So it was "good" that Caleb was dead. And it was "ac-ceptable," in that he was able to accept it. And it was even "perfect," because now they could go back to being the family they had been, strengthened by what they had been forced to endure, closer than ever for having passed through it.

He took his wife's hand in his and gave it a comforting squeeze.

In the limousine, seated once again between David and Ariel, Roberta turned around to count the cars lined up behind them. There were ten or a dozen of them, their headlights on, queued up to follow the hearse to the cemetery.

"It's the weather," she told David.

He asked her what she meant.

"A nice crisp bright fall afternoon," she said bitterly. "A little rain would have cut the attendance, but the weather's so good they want their money's worth."

She faced forward, looking out through the windshield at the gleaming silver hearse. Was Jeff in one of the cars behind her? Having come to the funeral, would he ride a little farther to see his son tucked into the ground?

Why not? It was, after all, a beautiful afternoon.

David was saying something, talking with Ariel, but Roberta wasn't paying any attention. There were things on her mind, things she hadn't been able to make sense of, things she'd barely permitted herself to think about since Caleb's death.

The ghost in the bedroom, for one. Obviously the ghost had come for Caleb. But was it really a ghost? Had the apparition truly existed? Contradictions in terms . . . likely her own subconscious mind had conjured up the woman, creating her out of some inner knowledge that Caleb was going to be taken away. She'd know more one way or the other if someone else had either seen or not seen the woman, but only she had been awake to witness the appearances.

The ghost had not walked on the past two nights. More accurately, Roberta had not seen it. But she couldn't swear it hadn't put in an appearance, because she herself had been so sedated she could have slept through a nuclear attack. The morning of Caleb's death David had put in a quick call to Gintzler, who immediately phoned in a prescription to

43

the drugstore. Roberta, numbed out on Valium, had made it through the days and slept as if comatose through the nights.

No Valium today. They were putting her son in the ground. If there was something to feel, she wanted to feel it.

But if the ghost came back tonight—

Worry about it when it happens, she told herself. They were approaching the cemetery. She was going to have a lot to get through in the next little while. She would just have to take it as it came, and when it was bedtime she could worry about the woman in the shawl.

The ceremony at the graveside was a brief one, with a short formal service. The minister read about ashes to ashes and dust to dust and the resurrection and the life and a lot of familiar phrases. Throughout it Ariel tried to decide whether to close her eyes when they lowered the coffin. She wound up watching the whole thing.

Erskine had come to the cemetery. That surprised her. And the man from the *Funeral Game*, he had turned up, too, standing off to one side at the rear.

Mrs. Tashman had not come. Evidently just turning up at the funeral was enough for most people, but some liked to sign on for the whole routine.

Her grandmother was buried here somewhere, and other relatives of Roberta's. Probably Roberta and David would wind up here sometime, buried along with Caleb.

And would the same thing happen to her? She couldn't be buried with her real parents, not if she didn't know who they were. Maybe she could be buried at sea. Or they could cremate her and scatter the ashes from an airplane, like that movie star they were talking about on television.

She didn't like thinking about death. But what else could you think about at a funeral?

44

The limousine returned them to the funeral parlor. Then they were in their own car and David was driving back to the city. At one point she thought they were going to drive past the house where they used to live, but they didn't.

It was a little creepy, being in the old neighborhood. She hadn't wanted to move downtown, but now she liked the new house so much better.

No one spoke while David drove. He parked finally on the street directly behind Roberta's Datsun. Houses were close together on this block, with no driveways or garages, but the house was large enough so that you could easily park both cars at the curb in front of it.

Ariel opened the back door and got out. She stood on the strip of grass between the sidewalk and the curb while David emerged from behind the wheel and walked around the back of the car to open the door for Roberta. She seemed reluctant to get out at first. Then she took his hand and let him help her out, and the two of them stood side by side, looking up at the towering red brick house with its ornamental black ironwork.

David put his arm around Roberta and she leaned against him. Ariel felt funny watching them. While they stood there, supporting each other, she scampered up the walk and mounted the steps to the front door.

THREE

THE night of the funeral Ariel was afraid to go to sleep. She knew it was crazy, but what she couldn't get out of her mind was the idea that if she actually did fall asleep she would be dead by morning. Just like Caleb.

And of course it was crazy, because she was too old for crib death, which certainly sounded as though it was limited to kids too young to sleep in a regular bed. And, since she hadn't heard anything about an outbreak of Bed Death reaching epidemic proportions in downtown Charleston, it stood to reason that she had nothing to worry about.

Knowing this wasn't terribly helpful. She went to her room after dinner, reading for a couple of hours, and then she got into pajamas and went downstairs to say goodnight to David and Roberta. David picked her up and set her on his lap and put her to work running a pipe cleaner through one of his pipes. That had been a real treat for her some years back, and evidently David hadn't figured out that she was a little old to go bananas at the opportunity to clean the tobacco spit out of a pipestem. But she did it, and pretended as much enthusiasm as possible.

David kissed her and told her to have pleasant dreams. Roberta, sitting in the kitchen with coffee and a cigarette, told her to sleep well. Ariel went upstairs with no intention of either sleeping or dreaming. She didn't care whether it made sense or not. She was going to stay awake until morning.

But it was boring just sitting there. After a long time, when she was sure both of them were sleeping, she picked up her tin flute and played it as softly as she possibly could, piping the notes tentatively. She had barely begun playing when she heard Roberta's footsteps in the hall. She put the flute down and managed to be in bed when the door opened.

"You're awake," Roberta said.

"I couldn't sleep."

"I don't want you playing that thing."

"I didn't think anybody could hear."

"I don't want to listen to that tonight. It's a matter of respect, Ariel. For Caleb."

"All right."

"And try to get some sleep."

"I will."

Alone in her room she tried to figure out how playing the flute showed a lack of respect for her dead baby brother. *I don't want you playing that thing. I don't want to listen to that tonight.* Fair enough, she thought, but why drag Caleb into it? He'd liked her flute music when he was alive and it certainly wasn't going to disturb him now. Either he was six feet deep in the suburban cemetery or he was up in Heaven with God and the angels, whichever way you wanted to figure it, and either way her flute wasn't going to put him off his feed.

Anyway, she'd been sort of playing for Caleb. And then Roberta told her to show respect by stopping.

She made a stab at reading, picking up first one of her Oz books, then a young adult novel by Sandra Scoppettone. Both were favorites, but tonight it seemed to her that she

48

had outgrown the first without having yet grown into the second. She put the books away and retrieved the flute, sitting cross-legged on the bed with the mouthpiece to her lips and her eyes closed. She fingered the notes without blowing across the mouthpiece. In this way she was able to hear the music in her head while the flute remained silent.

Eventually she put the flute back on her desk. After a while she turned off her light. She felt a chill and got under the covers. It was all right to close her eyes, she decided, so long as she didn't let herself fall asleep. For practice she closed them and lay still, counting her breaths, then snapping open her eyes and sitting up in bed on the fiftieth breath.

Perfectly safe, she told herself. That would get her through the night, little stretches of rest with her eyes closed. As long as she never stayed that way past fifty breaths she couldn't possibly fall asleep, and if she didn't fall asleep she wouldn't die in her sleep. Not that she really believed in that possibility anyway, but why take chances?

She closed her eyes again, counted fifty breaths, and opened them. She closed them a third time, and when she opened them again it was morning. She'd slept after all, and had lived through it, and she felt a little sheepish and greatly relieved.

After that she didn't have any further worries about Bed Death.

The second week after Caleb's funeral Ariel stopped at a Meeting Street drugstore on the way home from school and bought a spiral composition notebook. When she got home Roberta's car was gone and the house was empty. She let herself in and hurried up the steep staircase and down the hall to her room at the rear of the house.

Her tin flute was disassembled on her desk. She fitted the pieces together and put the instrument to her lips, holding the pose for a moment before beginning to play. Then she let herself drift into a melody, improvising, letting the flute lead her fingers to the notes it wanted to sound. She played with her eyes closed, and, as the music caught her up, a remarkable serene expression transformed her face.

She played for perhaps ten minutes. Then she put down the flute and took the new spiral notebook from her book-bag. She uncapped a green felt-tipped pen and began writing on the first page, forming the letters in a neat angular hand. The words flowed as effortlessly as the notes had poured forth from the flute.

I am Ariel, the Adopted.

"I am the beautiful stranger." I liked that book. I didn't finish it, though. I don't know why. I do that a lot, start a book and get interested in it and enjoy it and then not finish it.

Anyway, I am not the beautiful stranger. It's the beautiful part that doesn't fit. I don't hate my looks but I would never stop traffic, not unless I flung myself in front of a car and maybe not even then.

I can just about picture that, like a cartoon. Me lying dead under the wheels of a car and a crowd of fools all standing around gawking and one of them saying, "Well, poor child, she just wasn't pretty enough to stop traffic."

Sometimes it scares me, the kind of thoughts I have. All the wrong things make me laugh and none of the right ones.

I just looked in the mirror to see what it is about me that isn't beautiful. I can't exactly say because beautiful is how things all add together or how they don't. But my whole head is long and narrow and my chin comes to a point and that doesn't help a great deal. I remember one Halloween when I was young enough for that sort of thing I was got up like a witch and it could chill you how much I looked the part. It's the shape of my head that does it, and what are you going to do about that? If I were one of those Jewish girls with big noses in all those books I start but don't finish it would be simple enough. But where is the plastic surgeon that will change the shape of your head?

Plus my eyes are too small. Correction: the eyes are big enough but the irises are too small. There was an expert on the Chinese art of face-reading on Merv Griffin who said eyes like mine are a sign of a small and insignificant character. I got mad and turned the set off. Like it would teach the fool a lesson.

Roberta used to tell me I was pretty. She used to talk to me a lot even if I was never much at paying attention to her.

She hardly talks to me at all now. I don't know when it was that she decided she didn't like me anymore. Maybe she never liked me but I used to be too dumb to know the difference, and maybe as I grew up she got tired of pretending, plus I began to notice things.

She was through liking me by the time Caleb was born and now that he's dead she hates me. For being alive, I guess.

For a while I thought things were going to change. When she came into my room the night of the funeral, I thought she would say how she couldn't sleep either, and we'd wind up having one of those mother-daughter talks.

I tend to expect too much.

I never really believed her when she told me I was pretty. I knew she didn't mean it. It's something you do, you tell your little girl she's pretty. David told me the same, and when he tells me I believe it. Not that I am pretty but that he thinks I am.

I wonder who I look like. My mother or my father.

No way on earth I'm ever going to know.

I think about this a lot. When I think about my mother sometimes I'll just stand staring into the mirror over my dresser and try imagining my face the way it'll be when I'm older. Of course I don't know how old my mother was when she had me, but what I usually decide on is that she was seventeen or thereabouts, because that seems a usual age for having a baby and putting it up for adoption. This is just guessing because she could have been forty for all I know but I usually settle on seventeen. Well, I am almost thirteen now. That is just four years shy of seventeen, so the face in the mirror isn't all that different from hers when she had me.

I can just hold that thought in my head and fool with it for hours.

That's if I look like her. I could just as easy look like my father, and I don't even know where to start when I try thinking about him. He could be anyone at all, anyone in the whole world. He could be old or young or dead or alive, and no way in the world for me to know anything about it.

That gets to me sometimes. It really does. I could pass either of them on the street and never know it.

Twice in recent months Ariel had seen women on the street with faces that seemed to remind her of her own. Each time she found herself following the woman, hurrying along on the opposite side of the street trying to sneak quick peeks at her. She began working out in her mind an elaborate sequence in which she and her mother recognized one another and had a whole joyous family reunion.

Then in each case she had seen that there was really no strong resemblance after all. And if there were, what would she do about it? Just tag along until she was noticed, she supposed, and then slink off like a whipped dog.

Oh, I am not beautiful, but I am the stranger.

Well, that is obvious. I would not be writing in this book if I had anyone in the world to talk to. It isn't even a real diary. I looked in Woolworth's the day before yesterday and they had diaries but I didn't have any money with me. Then yesterday Erskine walked me home and I couldn't exactly say, "Let's stop in Woolworth's so I can buy a book to write secrets in." And by this afternoon I decided I couldn't see myself buying one of those books that say things like *My Secret Thoughts* in gold on the fake leather cover.

They have locks a baby could open with a toothpick, if a baby happened to have a toothpick, and all Roberta has to do is find a locked book called *My Secret Thoughts*. That would be like writing *Be Calm and Relaxed* on a red flag and showing it to a bull. Plus it wouldn't matter where I hid it. I could bury it six feet deep in the flower bed and she would "just happen" to dig up that particular bed and come across my diary.

Plus I'd probably just lose the key my own self.

So instead of a diary I have this notebook, and so instead of hiding it where I'd never find it but Roberta would, I'll keep it in my schoolbag with my other notebooks. Yes, like *The Purloined Letter*, which I actually read all the way through, short as it was. Roberta could never resist a diary, but who on earth would want to read a kid's dumb notebook?

My name is Ariel, the Adopted.

"My name is Ozymandias, king of kings." Names, names, names. Sometimes I think ninety percent of school is learning the names of things, whether they're cities or presidents or parts of the body or whatever they are. I wonder if it makes any difference whether you know something's name or not. Say a bird flies by and you say, "Hark, there goes a Great Crested Flycatcher." Now what have you actually said? You've only proved that you just happen to know what other people have decided to call that bird. It's not as if the bird *knows* he's a Great Crested Flycatcher. He just hangs in there catching Great Crested Flies, or whatever he does for a living.

I can just ramble on and on. I wonder does everybody have thoughts like these or am I crazy. I can just say that easy and all, or sometimes I can worry about it. Not exactly working up a sweat, but more like lying in bed at night ready to sleep and getting a chill at the thought and sitting right straight up in bed for a few minutes.

My name is Ariel and I don't know if I like it or not. Sometimes I do and sometimes I don't and I don't know which feeling generally has the upper hand.

The first thing about my name is that it is unusual. When you are a little kid that is awful because all little kids want is to be like everybody else. Anything different is bad and embarrassing. Especially your name because that is something everybody else knows about you.

Ariel.

I used to be teased about my name. Kids would all make the same stupid jokes about car aerials or TV aerials. Or they would call me Antenna. Hysterically funny. Thinking about it now I wonder why I even bothered to hate it, but I did. You tease a little kid about anything and it's going to hurt, even if the teasing doesn't make any sense.

I started to like my name about the same time I started becoming the unbeautiful stranger. I guess everything started happening in the early part of the year. We moved here and I left my old school and started in my new school and Caleb was born and I got my period and Roberta started not liking me anymore and I started turning into a private person.

I don't think I became a different person, exactly. I changed by becoming more completely the person I really was all along. As if I was *always* a stranger but never knew it before.

Ariel the strange stranger.

What I like about the name Ariel is partly what I used to hate about it, namely that it is different. It is just fitting that I should have an unusual and uncommon name. Plus it makes me think of flying, soaring high in the sky above the ordinary people, gliding effortlessly like a hawk in the autumn sky, just floating on air currents and having a great old time.

There is a book of poems called *Ariel* by a crazy woman who killed herself as soon as she was done writing them. I found the book in the public library over the summer. My heart jumped when I saw it. I had never heard of it and there was my name on the cover of a book. It was the oddest sensation seeing it like that, as if the book had been put there just for me to notice it.

I was almost afraid to touch it, but I'd no more not pick it up than Roberta would pass up a book that calls itself *My Secret Thoughts.* I sat at one of the long reading tables with it and my first reaction was to be disappointed because it was poetry. I like poems but I guess I thought the book would be about me and tell me who I was or some such silly thing, and then it was poems.

Before I ever tried to read them I read on the book cover about Sylvia Plath, who wrote them, and how she kept writing her poetry and thinking about suicide until finally she stuck her head in the gas oven.

And I got so *mad!* I don't know if I was ever so mad before or since. Because I thought they named me Ariel after that book of poems, named me after somebody putting her head in an oven and turning on the gas, and I thought, God, what a hateful thing to do to a baby!

That book was published *after* I was adopted. I checked the dates. They just went and named me Ariel. Maybe Crazy Sylvia named her book after me.

Oh, who cares? She was crazy and her poems are crazy,

or at least I can't make head or tail out of them. Anyway I don't *want* to make head or tail out of them. They make me feel all cramped, all that hate and blood and anger, all that screaming without any noise.

I wonder who picked the name. David or Roberta?

I guess they like unusual names. Their names are ordinary ones but they picked Ariel and Caleb for their children. Caleb Oliver Jardell. I wonder if Caleb would have liked his name, or if they would have teased him about it.

My middle name is Emily. For David's mother. I hate it.

I liked Caleb's name. The sound of it, and the way it looks on the page when you write it. It looks like *Cable* with the letters switched around, and once you see that you keep switching letters and trying for other words, but all you get is gibberish.

Elbac.

Laceb.

Blace.

Oh, please don't let me think about Caleb. I feel terrible when I think about him.

I don't care for the name Roberta. I don't like women's names that you get by tacking an ending onto a man's name. Pauline, Georgette. There's a girl in my geography class called Davida and I really feel sorry for her. It's as if her parents are telling the whole world right out that they wanted a boy so much they couldn't be bothered thinking of a girl's name.

I wonder what my real name is.

That sentence looks so weird I decided to leave plenty of space around it. But I know what it means and it makes sense to me.

I have thought about this a lot. How when my mother was pregnant with me she decided to put me up for adoption. Maybe she had no choice. I don't know anything about that.

But she carried me for nine months, unless I was premature (which I probably was, just to be different), and during that time she must have done some thinking. In the hospital, waiting to give birth to me, she must have had thoughts. Even knowing she was putting me up for adoption, even knowing that she would never set eyes on me, she would have been wondering if I would be a boy or a girl.

And she would have picked out names. She might not have wanted to, knowing it would just hurt her, knowing it would make it that much harder to give me up, but I honestly don't see how she could have helped herself. Oh, I myself will sometimes think up names for kids, and I am only twelve years old and not pregnant, nor likely to be, thank you all the same! But I will now and then imagine myself married and with children, which I can imagine easily enough, and I'll think, well, I would call the boy Ethelbert and the girl Davida, or whatever names I am crazy about that particular day.

Now she must have done this. So she had a name in mind for me. So in a sense that is my real name and Ariel is just what they call me.

They call me Ariel, the Adopted.

I don't have a nickname. Back when she used to like me Roberta would sometimes call me Honey or Darling but they were never specific names for me, just all-purpose pet names that she used. And David used to call me Little Pooch. I don't know where he got the name from. Now that I think about it, I don't guess it's awfully flattering. But I used to like the idea that he had a special name for me.

Now he generally calls me Ariel, like everybody else.

There was a girl, Linda Goodenow, who was sort of my best friend two years ago, but not quite. I didn't have anyone I liked better but I never felt close enough to Linda to call her a best friend. Anyway, the point is that she used to call me Airy. She didn't ask if I wanted to be called that. She just one day called me Airy and went on with it.

I hated it. Thinking back, I don't know why I didn't ask her not to call me Airy. How was she to know I hated it if I never said anything? But I never did and she went right on calling me Airy, probably because it made her feel more like best friends to be the only person to call me by that name. Some best friend to be the only person in the world calling me by a name I hated!

But then her father got transferred and they moved. All the way to California. She wrote me four letters. I answered the first one and it took me forever to think of enough things to write to fill a page, even writing large. Then I didn't answer the next three letters and I guess she took the hint. She doesn't even have my new address since we moved. I guess if she wrote to the old one they would forward it.

Linda called her parents Jack and Rita. She said that was what they taught her to do. She called them that from the time she was a little kid, which is weird to imagine, a little kid calling out, "Hi, Jack! Hi, Rita!"

If I called Roberta Roberta I think she would shit. I don't know what David would do. Needless to say I have never called either of them by name, or even referred to them by name to other kids. I suppose I would to Erskine if we got to know each other well.

So far I only call them David and Roberta in my mind. And nobody knows what's in my mind.

Sometimes I don't even know—

Back to David and Roberta. I was just thinking. I don't really call them *anything*. I always used to call them Mommy and Daddy. Since I am going to be officially a teenager soon I suppose I ought to switch to Mother and

Father. But lately I don't use a name of any sort when I talk to them.

Sometimes it used to bother me, calling them Mommy and Daddy. I had the feeling of being disloyal to the real mother and father I had wandering around somewhere in the world. But I never got too worked up at the thought because I had brains enough to realize it's not terribly logical.

I may be crazy but I'm not stupid.

But what's hysterical is Linda Goodenow with real parents she calls by their first names, and me, adopted, calling mine Mommy and Daddy.

Call me Ariel, the Adopted.

Or call me Ishmael, if you prefer.

There's another book I didn't finish. *Moby Dick.* Twenty pages in the library was enough to convince me I didn't care all that much about whales, and what I did care about whales was that people would stop hunting them to extinction, so the last thing I wanted to read was a book about men hunting whales.

I loved that opening sentence, though. "Call me Ishmael." It really grabs you.

Imagine being the last individual of a vanishing species. Like if you were the last whale in the universe. Except how would you know you were the last one? Although whales are supposed to be super intelligent and God only knows what they know and don't know.

My Secret Thoughts, by Arnold the Whale.

I was just standing over at the window. It's been raining on and off all day. I can get mournful just from the weather. You would think the funeral would have been on a day like this one instead of a good bright day with the sun shining.

Let's think of something else.

At least it's interesting here looking out the window.

When we lived on Coteswood you could stare out the window all day and never see anything more exciting than someone mowing his lawn. Now there are always people walking around, and a lot of interesting dogs that don't have to be on leashes.

I like this house so much better. The first day we moved in I was completely at home here. It's big and it rambles and Roberta and David kept getting confused at the beginning. They would try to walk from the kitchen to the downstairs lavatory and wind up in the living room instead. But I never had this problem. As though I had a map of the inside of the house in my head before I ever saw the place.

A floorplan, I mean. Couldn't think of the word.

I think that's Roberta's car. I'll go look.

Yes it is.

I even knew what this house would look like before I saw it. I guess I must have heard them discussing it. But when we first came here and parked down the block I knew right away which house we were going to look at. I mean I just knew, as if I had seen a picture before and I was recognizing it.

I never mentioned this to them. I think they already figure I'm crazy so why make trouble?

She's on the stairs now. Roberta. *"Hello?"* But it's easier not to pay attention.

The stairs always creak when she climbs up or down them. They *never* creak when I do.

It's funny.

I've got homework, arithmetic and social studies, and I just don't feel like doing it. Of course that's what Roberta thinks I'm doing right now.

This is great. She's standing in the doorway of my room watching me and I'm pretending I don't even know she's there. She thinks I'm doing homework, writing in my spiral notebook, and I'm writing about her. This is really neat.

There. She left. Because of course she wouldn't want to disturb me when I'm busy with my work. Just another way this book has it all over *My Secret Thoughts*.

Footsteps on the stairs. Creak creak *creak!*

Homework is boring and stupid, so of course she wouldn't dream of interrupting it. But if she knew I was doing something that mattered to me, like what I'm writing now or like my music, then she'd make a point of cutting in.

Caleb used to love it when I played the flute for him. At least I think he did. I would go to his room and play for a long time and he just loved to listen.

Nobody else in this house does. They think I'm just fooling around.

I think Roberta's finally beginning to get the message that I don't want flute lessons. She says if I were to take lessons I could have a real flute. What popped into my head the first time she said that was that I don't want a real flute, I want an adopted one. Another example of the kind of thing I think is hysterical but nobody else would.

I like my flute. It's sort of tinny but I like the sounds it can make. It fits into the kind of music I want to play. As hard as it is to play, I don't think you could call it a toy.

I never heard another instrument that makes just this sound.

That's why I like it and I suppose that's why Roberta doesn't.

Oh, I'll get at my homework in a few minutes. I always do. I'm always prepared and I always do well in school and get good grades. When I switched schools they were doing completely different things in some of my classes on account of being in the City of Charleston school system. I picked it all up in the middle of the term and got good marks right from the beginning without even having to kill myself doing it.

It's how I am.

I guess I must have had intelligent parents. Even if they did manage to be stupid about one particular thing.

At least my mother decided to have me. She could have had an abortion, and then where would I be? And who would be having all these thoughts?

I wonder what she was like. I wonder about both of my parents, but I especially wonder about my mother.

I wonder if she was evil.

FOUR

TWO of the three stove-top pilot lights were out. Roberta relit them with a wooden kitchen match, then put a copper-bottomed teakettle on to boil. She measured out instant coffee and powdered chickory root and waited impatiently for the teakettle to whistle. Her mind wandered while she waited, and when the kettle whistled the sound startled her.

Nerves, she thought. She was a nervous wreck.

Why did the pilot lights go out all the time? The damp chill air of the kitchen seemed an unsatisfactory explanation. Maybe there were air currents in the room that blew out pilot lights on a whim. Maybe there was something wrong with the old stove itself, some eccentricity in the gas line that would shut off the flow of gas long enough for the flame to die.

The gas company had sent a man to check the stove and its connections. He'd found nothing wrong, assuring Roberta that she had a great old stove. "They made this baby to last," he told her. "You made a range like this today, nobody could afford to buy it. Your gas line's sound and all your fittings are tight. There's no leak anywhere."

"But the pilot lights—"

"No reason they should be going out."

He'd said this with a sullen certainty, as if implying that some unmentionable action of hers was responsible for the trouble with the pilot lights, and that was patently absurd. Air currents in the kitchen, she told herself, or perhaps an intermittent blockage in the stove's gas line, or something related to the damp in the kitchen. She didn't really understand these things, but couldn't it be that some sort of inert gas rose up from the damp brick floor, hovering in the air long enough to smother the flame of the pilot lights? Maybe such a hypothesis didn't make hard scientific sense, but wasn't it possible all the same?

In a house where ghosts walked, where healthy babies died abruptly in their sleep, wasn't almost anything possible?

She lit a cigarette and sipped her coffee. A couple of nights ago, when all three pilot lights had gone out, she'd asked David about the possibility of having the pilots shut off altogether and lighting the burners with a match. She thought it might be safer that way. The idea of gas escaping silently and invisibly from an extinguished pilot light frightened her.

He had insisted it was nothing to worry about. "There's not that much gas involved," he explained. "Just a trickle, just enough to nourish the tiniest possible flame. If it goes out it's an inconvenience but it's not a danger. The small amount of gas that escapes gets dispersed right away. It can't build up enough to cause an explosion, if that's what you're afraid of."

"But I can smell it. I walk into the room and I can smell it."

"It's not even the gas you smell. Natural gas is odorless. The manufacturers are required to add a chemical to it, and that's what you smell."

It seemed academic to her whether she smelled the gas

or a substance that had been added to the gas. If the gas were such a harmless compound, why would the law require the addition of this chemical? Gas was dangerous. It burned, it exploded, it asphyxiated people.

She drew on her cigarette, blew out a thin column of smoke. She remembered a news story from a few years ago. A town somewhere in the north, Pennsylvania or New Jersey, she couldn't remember exactly where. They had had trouble with underground gas lines freezing and thawing during the winter. Several homes had exploded, with more than a few deaths resulting.

One incident had made an indelible impression. A woman evacuated her house just minutes before it exploded. She lost all her possessions but escaped with her life. After her house blew up, she took shelter with a neighbor a couple of blocks away. Whereupon the neighbor's house exploded, killing the woman.

Roberta had thought at the time that the story was enough to make a fatalist out of anyone. If you were destined to die in a gas explosion, one house was as good as the next. God would get you wherever you ran.

It was easy enough to believe that when your involvement was limited to a few lines in the newspaper and a few minutes on the seven o'clock news. But how well did the belief hold up when the smell of gas was present in your own kitchen?

She got up, checked the pilot lights. All three were in good order.

Outside, a stout middle-aged woman in tight corduroy slacks was walking a small terrier. The dog was not on a leash. He raced on ahead of the woman, sniffed at the base of a tree, scampered back behind the woman, barked at a squirrel, then raced to keep up with the woman, who strode on at a steady pace, looking neither left nor right and paying no evident attention to the dog whatsoever.

Roberta watched them until they disappeared from view. Maybe she should get a dog, she thought. But she didn't want a dog. She'd had the one thing she wanted and it had been taken from her, and its place could not be taken by some yapping little terrier.

She reached for her cigarettes, put them down, then gave up and lit one. She'd been living on coffee and cigarettes ever since Caleb's death. She didn't know how much weight she'd lost but she could tell from the fit of her clothes that she was losing flesh.

Upstairs, Ariel sounded a few tentative notes on her tin flute. Roberta winced. There was no escaping the child's music, she thought. It didn't help to close doors. The notes slithered through walls and floorboards, penetrating to every corner of the huge old house. And she wouldn't play a proper song, something with a discernible tune to it. Instead she insisted on making up her own horrible dirges, inventing as she went along.

An image: Ariel as the Pied Piper. Slippers on her feet with turned-up toes. A peaked cap perched on her head. The tin flute at her lips. And an endless parade of rats and assorted vermin following her as she played.

Pied Piper, Act Two: Ariel with her flute, a devilish smile on her lips. Followed now not by rats but by all the town's children, the innocent children, and all of them looked like Caleb, and—

Roberta sat up straight, gave her head a violent shake to dislodge the images forming within it.

What was the matter with her? Instead of becoming increasingly able to accept Caleb's death, she remained appalled at the injustice of it. Her mind, evidently requiring someone to focus blame upon, seemed to have settled on Ariel. It didn't make sense, and she knew it didn't make sense, but there didn't seem to be anything she could do about it. There was no way to deal with the thoughts that came to mind. She couldn't seem to talk to anyone about them. She couldn't talk to Ariel at all, about anything, and she couldn't even admit her thoughts to David, and who else was there?

Gintzler? Several times she'd been on the point of calling the psychiatrist, but each time she'd resisted, feeling that she already knew what he would tell her. He'd interpret the woman who'd appeared in her bedroom as something she'd conjured up out of guilt or anxiety, and no doubt he'd come up with some interesting symbolic explanation for the apparition, but his scientific bias was such that he'd never for a moment allow the possibility that the house was somehow haunted, that the woman was a manifestation of some force present within its walls, that she'd either signaled Caleb's imminent death or actually caused it, taking him away to another plane of existence.

Gintzler would raise an eloquent eyebrow if she even dared to suggest the possibility that the apparition was real. He'd shame her out of it, and she was enough of a people-pleaser to go along with him, pretending that her thoughts were no more than an indication of the instability of her mind. And could she be sure that wasn't the case?

She couldn't be sure of anything.

She crushed out her cigarette. Ariel's flute had gone silent again, she noticed. At least if you heard the flute you knew where the child was. She'd turned into such a sneak lately, slipping around the house like a ghost herself. When she or David climbed the stairs, a board or two invariably groaned underfoot. Similarly, neither of them could walk the length of the second-floor hallway without setting the floorboards to creak. But Ariel padded silently through the house as if her feet never touched the ground. You never heard her in the hallway or on the stairs. She weighed considerably less than they did, certainly, but Roberta was convinced there was more to it than that.

It was spooky.

She'd been more and more aware of this since Caleb's death. She'd be in one room, any room, and suddenly she'd have the feeling that the child was nearby, watching her, spying on her. She would turn around, suddenly or stealthily, and never managed to catch Ariel in the act. The child seemed to be always hovering just out of sight, like a little speck dancing on the periphery of one's vision.

Lately the two of them had seemed to be playing some terribly elaborate game without rules. Just this afternoon, for example, it had been obvious to Roberta that Ariel had known she was standing in the doorway. She'd gone on writing in her notebook, pretending to be unaware of Roberta's presence, and Roberta in turn had pretended to believe Ariel didn't know she was there. And so Roberta had hesitated only for a moment before withdrawing and returning to the first floor. It had been not unlike a ritual passage in some exceedingly formal Spanish dance, and yet each of them had performed instinctively, without thought.

She was on her way to the kitchen, bearing an empty coffee cup and a full ashtray, when the phone rang. The wall phone—beige, with touchtone dialing—was mounted at eye level just to the right of the kitchen fireplace. She put down the cup and the ashtray, reached to answer the phone.

"Bobbie?"

Her hand shook. She almost dropped the phone.

"Bobbie, are you there? It's Jeff Channing."

As if he had to identify himself. As if she couldn't recognize his voice. As if more than one man had ever called her Bobbie.

"I'm here," she said.

"How are you, Bobbie?"

"I'm all right."

"Are you? I've been thinking of you ever since the funeral. I almost called several times but I stopped myself."

"And now?"

"I had to talk to you."

She stared into the fireplace. When they first looked at the house it had been one of the special touches of charm, a cozy hearth in the brick-floored kitchen. Then, after they'd bought the house and moved in, and after she'd learned that half the damp in Old Charleston seeped up through that authentic brick floor, they'd tried lighting a fire in the cozy hearth. All of the heat had gone straight up the chimney, while the kitchen itself had filled with a sour smell that rapidly permeated the entire house. It was weeks before the smell was entirely gone, and the fireplace had not been put into service since then.

"Bobbie, I want to see you."

"Oh."

"I think it's important."

"I don't know if it's a good idea, Jeff."

"Why not?"

"I—"

"We have to talk."

"About what?"

"About Caleb."

"Caleb," she said, and drew a breath and steadied herself. "Caleb is dead."

"How did he die?"

"He died in his crib. He just died, Jeff. Are you trying to torture me?"

"He was my son, wasn't he?"

"What makes you think that?"

"Don't play games with me, Bobbie."

"I—"

"We never played games with each other. Did we?"

"No."

"So let's not start now."

"All right."

"Caleb was my son."

Was the phone tapped? Was she being tricked into admitting something? She felt drawn, exhausted.

"If you say so," she said.

"Bobbie—"

"Whatever you say, Jeff."

"I have to talk to you."

"That's what we're doing, isn't it? Talking?"

"I have to see you."

"David will be home soon. Or did you want to see both of us?"

"You know I didn't."

She wished she had a cigarette. She wished she'd thought to put her shoes on before coming into the kitchen. The floor, as always, was cold underfoot. But she hadn't planned on spending any time in this room. She'd just intended on putting a fire under the kettle and dumping the ashtray. She stood on one foot now, rubbing the sole of the other foot against her pants leg for warmth.

"Tomorrow," he was saying. "You'll be home tomorrow?"

"I suppose so."

"You don't sound good, Bobbie. There's no life in your voice."

"Oh. I can't help that."

"I'll come tomorrow."

"Ariel comes home after school."

"I'll come a little after noon."

"All right."

"I want to talk to you for my own sake, Bobbie, but I have the feeling you need someone to talk to yourself."

"Maybe you're right."

"I'll be there around twelve-thirty or so."

She started to speak, then stopped herself. At that moment, standing on one foot like a flamingo, the receiver pressed tightly against her ear, she felt a sudden touch of cold air on the nape of her neck.

A shiver went through her.

She was certain, absolutely certain, that Ariel was standing behind her. She had not heard her approach. But she could feel the child's tiny eyes upon her now, pawing at her like cold damp hands. She wanted to turn around but could not will herself to move.

"Bobbie?"

She could not answer him.

"I'll see you tomorrow, then."

The phone clicked in her ear. Still she stood there, aware of everything that was touching her—the cold brick floor beneath her left foot, the pressure of the receiver against her ear, the chill gaze of the child on the back of her neck. "Yes," she said aloud to no one at all. "Yes, that's a good idea. Certainly." And she continued in that vein, muttering something noncommittal from time to time, as if it would be somehow dangerous to let the child know that the telephone conversation had ended.

She felt like a character in a play, acting out a meaningless part in simple obedience to the author who had written it for her. Her body was frozen in position. A cramp was building in the calf muscle of her bent right leg. Her left hand was braced against the fireplace mantel, helping to support her weight, while her right hand clutched the dead telephone receiver to her ear.

"Yes, I certainly agree with you," she said crisply. "Well, goodbye, then. And I'm so glad you called."

She hung up the phone. And stood now with both feet on the floor, breathing slowly and deeply.

And turned around.

She was quite alone in the kitchen.

She sighed heavily, feeling the tension drain from her body. It was all her imagination, she told herself, all an indication of the state of her nerves. Or was it? Had the child been in the room? It was certainly not impossible. She might have stolen away as silently as she had approached, or she might not have been there at all.

Maybe it was just her mood, or the particular atmosphere of the kitchen. Maybe some guilt or anxiety over her conversation with Jeff had caused her to imagine that she was being observed and her conversation overheard.

But that sudden touch of cold air on the nape of her neck? Air currents in a drafty old house? Was that sufficient? Could that account for the tangible presence she'd felt behind her?

She checked the pilot lights. All three were lit. She heated water for coffee, dumped the ashtray, returned to the living room. There she dropped to the couch and lit another cigarette.

From somewhere overhead she heard the reedy piping of the child's tin flute.

She dreamed a good deal that night, and once a dream woke her, fading out of memory even as she sat up in her bed. She stared over at the corner of the room, squinting, trying to discern the woman in the shawl. But there was nothing there. David lay on his back in the other bed, breathing heavily, and as she listened to his breathing and waited for her own to regulate itself, he moaned softly and rolled over onto his side.

Roberta lay down, closed her eyes. When sleep did not come swiftly she got out of bed and put on slippers and a robe. She left the bathroom and walked on tiptoe in the hallway. Nevertheless, certain floorboards creaked when she trod on them.

Wasn't there a way to stop floorboards from doing that? You couldn't oil them, she didn't suppose, but couldn't you sink a nail in a strategic place to eliminate a squeak? You really had to know how to do things like that when you owned an older home. There were always little things to be seen to. But she didn't know much about such matters and David was next to useless around the house.

You could be like the child, she thought, and glide soundlessly over the floors and stairs like a small pale ghost.

Ariel's door was closed, and no light was visible beneath it. That didn't mean the child was asleep. She could be reading under the covers with a flashlight, the way all children did at one time or another. Or she could be sitting up in the dark.

The brass doorknob was cool to the touch. Roberta's hand fastened upon it. After a moment she released the knob without turning it.

She walked almost the entire length of the hallway to her bedroom. Then something made her turn, and she covered half the distance again and took hold of another brass doorknob, this one on the closed door to Caleb's room. She shut her eyes in the darkened hallway and concentrated on the silence. No boards creaked now, no windowpanes rattled, no eerie flute music wailed through the walls.

A fantasy, an irresistibly tempting one, flooded over her. It was a dream, it was all a dream, the whole past two weeks had never happened, and if she turned the doorknob and entered the little room Caleb would be sleeping in his crib, and if she picked him up he would squirm and giggle and coo, and—

She knew better. But all the same she turned the knob and pushed the door inward. Her hand found the switch on the wall and flicked on the overhead fixture.

She blinked at the glare. For a moment her fantasy was reinforced by what she saw. Caleb's room was as it had been. Nothing had been changed or removed. The fish mobile still swayed over his crib. The same stuffed animals kept their stations on top of the bathinet.

But the crib was empty.

You fool, she thought. Why do you punish yourself?

She sighed, turned, slapped the switch and extinguished the overhead light. She stepped out into the hallway and drew the door shut.

Should she go downstairs? Check the windows and doors? Check the pilot lights?

She went straight to bed, and sleep was not long in coming. In the morning, when she went downstairs, there was a slight but undeniable smell of gas in the dank kitchen, and one of the pilots was out.

By mid-morning she was in a good mood.

This surprised her. She'd had a bad night and awakened from it expecting to drag herself through the day a minute at a time. Instead the morning flew by. She did the breakfast dishes, straightened the downstairs, made the beds, and observed her own spirits rising as she went along.

Around eleven she bathed and got dressed. Sitting in front of her mirror, she realized for the first time that what she felt was excitement, anticipation.

She hadn't felt this way in a long time.

The doorbell sounded at ten minutes after twelve. She hadn't heard him drive up. She felt a little anxiety on her way to the door, but by the time she opened it she was calm and collected.

He looked wonderful, she thought. Was his suit the same one he'd worn to the funeral? It might have been, but there was certainly nothing funereal about his appearance. His shirt was cream-colored broadcloth with a rounded collar, his tie a bold affair of cream and burgundy stripes.

Their eyes met and the silence stretched until he broke it. "Bobbie," he began.

"Come inside," she said. And, leading him into the living room, she said, "My happy home. A prime example of the gracious mode of living characteristic of antebellum Charleston. All the charm and refinement of the Old South is reflected in these warm and decorously appointed rooms."

He chuckled, took the chair she indicated. "It is a beautiful house," he said.

"Make me an offer and it's yours."

"You're not happy here? I'm sorry, that was a stupid question. Of course you're not happy, not after what's happened. But you're not really thinking of selling because of—"

"Because Caleb died? No, we're not thinking of selling. At least we haven't talked about it. David doesn't even know I hate it here."

"Because of what happened?"

"Maybe. I don't know." She shrugged, reached for a cigarette. He offered a light and she leaned forward to accept it. Blowing out smoke she said, "I'm not sure what it is. This place is a mausoleum. You remember those comic books? This place is like living in the pages of *Tales From The Crypt*. Do you believe in ghosts, Jeff?"

"I never gave them much thought."

"Neither did I. I never had to before I set up housekeeping in beautiful downtown Charleston."

"Is this a haunted house? I'm sorry, I don't mean to be flip—"

"I don't know, but something's driving me slightly batty. Would you consider me a flighty woman?"

"Not you, Bobbie."

"Because I always thought of myself as Stella Stable. A sort of second cousin to the Rock of Gibraltar. Now I hear things in the middle of the night, and I've got a personal grudge fight going with a gas stove, and I'm constantly being spooked by my own kid."

"Are you talking about Caleb?"

She shook her head. "Ariel. Granted, she's an intrinsically spooky kid, but I think I've been overreacting. I *hope* I've been overreacting."

"You lost a son, Bobbie. It's only natural for you to be affected by it."

She looked at him.

"Did I say something wrong?"

"No. You're the only person who ever calls me Bobbie, did you know that?"

"If you'd rather I didn't—"

"I didn't say that." She held his eyes for a moment, then lowered her own and took a quick puff on her cigarette. "I've been going nuts," she said. "But I said that before, didn't I?"

"Yes."

"I think it started *before* Caleb died. I don't know when it started. Maybe it was moving here that did it. This house. Maybe it's not the house. Maybe—hell, Jeff, I don't know what it is."

"You're just upset—"

"I'm more myself today than I've been in a long time. At least I can talk for a change. I can't remember the last time I was able to talk to my husband, and I haven't got anybody else in my life. I don't even know the neighbors. They all stay in their own houses playing solitaire and passing the time of day with their own ghosts, I suppose. So I'm afraid you're getting more than you bargained for."

"I don't mind."

"Just what *did* you bargain for, come to think of it? A

quick jump in the feathers for old time's sake?"

He colored.

"I'm sorry," she said quickly. "I'm a bitch."

"It's part of your charm."

"Is that what it is? Gintzler would tell me it's part of the wall I build to keep other people out. Thirty bucks an hour and that was the best he could manage. Seriously, why did you come?"

"To talk about Caleb. I never even managed to see him and all of a sudden he was dead."

"All of a sudden," she said, and the next thing she knew she was sobbing fitfully and he was on the couch beside her, holding her, stroking her hair.

"Go ahead," he urged her. "Go ahead and let go."

But she couldn't. She drew away, pulled herself together, crushed out her cigarette and lit a fresh one. He returned to his chair and she smoked for a moment or two in silence.

"Coffee," she said. "I didn't even offer you a cup of coffee. The ultimate hostess."

"That's all right."

"Would you like a cup?"

"I've had half a dozen cups already this morning."

"Or a drink. Would you like a drink?"

"No thanks."

"I wish I knew what to offer you."

"That's something you've always known, Bobbie."

Their eyes met. There was a dryness in the back of her throat, a pulse hammering in her right temple. She drew on her cigarette, blew out a cloud of smoke.

"I think I want to talk," she said crisply. "Could you stand that?"

"Of course. It's what I came for."

"You may get much more than you bargained for. The ravings of a female hysteric, replete with ghoulies and ghosties and long-legged beasties."

77

"And things that go bump in the night?"

"Oh, no end of things that go bump in the night. I don't think I want to stay here. Ariel will be coming home sooner or later."

"Would it matter if she saw me?"

"Probably not. David could turn up, as far as that goes. Oh, neither one'll be here for a couple of hours, but could we just go for a drive anyway? I want to get out of this house."

"Of course, Bobbie."

Outside she said, "Where's your car? I didn't hear you drive up."

"I parked on the next block."

"There's plenty of room in front. Or were you concerned about my good name?"

"I thought it would be just as easy to park down the street."

She nodded. "Well, let's take your car, okay?"

"Fine."

"Because I don't want to have to concentrate on driving. I just want to put my head back and talk a blue streak."

She talked for a long time. He drove through town, then hooked up with the Interstate and stayed on it to the second interchange. Then they were driving in the country, taking a series of back roads, passing small subsistence farms with their little plots of corn and tobacco and tomatoes and okra, some flanked by immobile house trailers, others by tarpaper shacks straight out of Tobacco Road.

Were there ghosts that walked by night in tarpaper shacks? Babies out here didn't sleep in cribs. They generally made do with a bureau drawer. Did they ever die in their sleep, just close their eyes and never wake up?

She closed her own eyes and went on talking. It had always been easy for her to talk to Jeff Channing and it was no harder now. She had the feeling she could tell him absolutely anything, and at the same time she knew he was paying close attention to every word she spoke. Now and then he would ask her to clarify a point, drawing her out on one thing or another, and rather than interrupt her train of thought it seemed to increase the flow of her words.

Finally she was through. She sat for a moment, waiting to see if there was anything else. Off to the right, two men in bib overalls were fussing over a fire fueled with ruined auto and truck tires. The air reeked of burning rubber and she asked Jeff why they didn't just throw the tires away.

He laughed. "Slaughtering time," he said.

"I don't understand."

"You burn tires when you slaughter a hog. You have to scald the hog so the bristles loosen from the skin, and to do that you have to heat a huge iron kettle, and you need a hot fire, and nothing burns hotter than rubber. You thought they were just burning the tires to get rid of them?"

"Well, I'm a city girl."

"Uh-huh. Who do you think that woman was, Bobbie?"

"In the shawl? I don't know. I don't know if she just appeared to me or what. I don't understand ghosts."

"Neither do I. Did she look like anyone?"

"I think so. But maybe it's a false memory. I didn't make the connection at the time."

"Who did she look like?"

"Can't you guess?"

"Like Ariel?"

She nodded. "I didn't want to say it. That pale face and the shape of her head. But I don't know if I saw her clearly enough for there to be a resemblance. Maybe I don't even know how her head was shaped. She was wrapped in a shawl, don't forget."

"I'm not likely to forget. I feel as though I could close my eyes and see her myself."

"Don't do that. We'd go off the road."

"I'll try to control myself. What do you think happened to Caleb, Bobbie?"

"I know what happened to him. Sudden Infant Death Syndrome. Crib death. It's even been known to happen to kids three or four years old, although it's most common in the first year."

"I know all that. I've done a little studying on the subject, as a matter of fact. But that's not what I'm talking about."

"Oh?"

"That's what you *know* happened to Caleb. But what do you *think* happened to him?"

"Oh," she said.

"Forget logic and common sense for a few minutes. Forget reality and a sane universe. Talk about what's inside of you for a change."

"All right."

"Do you think the woman in the shawl killed him?"

She worried her forehead with the tips of her fingers. "I don't think so," she said. "I feel crazy talking like this, but I see what you mean, and I'm just going to go ahead and feel crazy if I have to. The woman in the shawl—I think the woman in the shawl was some sort of spirit letting me know what was going to happen, that Caleb was going to be taken from me. I think that was her purpose in coming and that's why I haven't seen her since. The sense I have of her—well, I don't know if she's evil or not, I don't have a sense of that one way or the other, but I don't think of her as *capable* of killing someone."

"But you think someone killed Caleb."

"Someone or something."

"Who?"

She shook her head.

"You don't know what you think or you're afraid to say it out loud?"

"Maybe a little of both."

"David woke up the third time the ghost appeared, didn't he?"

"Yes, but not until she vanished. He didn't see her."

"That's not what I'm getting at. You sent him down the hall to check on Caleb."

"That's right, and he said he was all right. But he must have been already dead, don't you think? If I saw the woman taking him away he must have been dead already. Unless that's not the way ghosts do things." She laughed dryly. "I should have paid more attention when they told spooky stories around the campfire at Girl Scouts. I never realized all that lore would come in handy someday."

"You think he was dead when David checked him?"

"He must have been, wouldn't you say? Maybe he was still warm because it had just happened. Or maybe David was just humoring me. He may have opened the door and looked in, and why take a chance on waking the baby? The only reason he went in the first place was to set my mind to rest."

"So maybe he just opened the door, assumed the baby was all right, and closed it again."

"Right."

"Or maybe he went into Caleb's room, smothered the baby in his crib, and came back and told you everything was fine."

"My God."

"Don't tell me the possibility never occurred to you."

"Never." More dry laughter. "That's a sketch," she said. "Maybe I'm not as paranoid as I thought. What a crazy idea, Jeff. I wake up screaming and my loyal husband goes to check the baby, and while he's at it he has a go at infanticide. Why on earth would he do a thing like that?"

"Did David think Caleb was his son?"

She waited a moment before answering. Then she said,

"People tend to believe what they want to believe."

"Caleb *was* my son, wasn't he? No question in your mind?"

"None."

"David's not stupid by nature. Adoption sometimes triggers fertility—you adopt a kid and then have one of your own. But not after twelve years."

"No."

"Did he know about us?"

"I don't think so. But he must have assumed I was having an affair with somebody."

"Because of the pregnancy, you mean."

"Yes. I don't think he suspected anything before then. And I don't think he knows who specifically I had the affair with."

"You don't think he knows it was me?"

"No."

"Well, I'm not so sure. The look he gave me at the funeral. Of course I may have been projecting, reading things into it. I wasn't too steady myself that afternoon."

"I can't believe he would kill Caleb."

"I can't believe it myself, Bobbie, in the sense of putting any real credence in the notion. But it's not utterly impossible. I can imagine his resenting raising another man's child as his own. Then you woke up screaming, and he was half asleep still and half in the bag, too, from what you said—"

"He always has a lot to drink before he goes to sleep. The way some people take sleeping pills, I suppose. I don't know that he was drunk."

"People who drink heavily in order to sleep do it because it gets them drunk. He's probably an alcoholic, or close to it."

"Oh, I really don't think so."

He shrugged. "It's academic. Anyway, he's half asleep and about half lit, and you've just put in his head the idea that something might have happened to the baby. And because he's not entirely conscious a lot of his automatic mental defenses aren't in place. He goes into Caleb's room and the kid's sleeping soundly and the first thing he thinks is that the baby really *is* dead, and then he touches him and determines that he's warm and breathing, and then—well, it's a pretty simple matter to kill a sleeping infant. It's a lot easier than drowning kittens."

"God—"

His hand covered hers, squeezed. "Easy," he said soothingly. "I'm not saying it happened that way. I don't think it did. David never struck me as a particularly homicidal sort. But what's interesting is that it never occurred to you to suspect him."

"Why is that interesting?"

"Because it did occur to you to suspect someone else."

"Oh."

"You suspect Ariel, don't you?"

She looked at him, her face drawn. "How could I suspect her?" she demanded. "She's a child."

"Are children capable of evil?"

"I don't know."

"Do children kill?"

"I—"

"You do suspect her, don't you, Bobbie?"

"It's not a suspicion," she said doggedly. "It's a . . . feeling, I suppose. I'll tell you something. It's been driving me crazy—"

"Because you can't accept the thought and you can't get rid of it."

"That's it exactly. What kind of a mother could think such a thing about her child? That's the tape that keeps running in my head. But I can't—"

He held up a hand. "Let's try something," he suggested. "You're the prosecuting attorney and I'm the impartial judge and you're presenting evidence. Not necessarily hard evidence but whatever comes to mind. Don't worry about telling me how your feelings are really foolish. Just tell me why you think she killed her brother."

"I don't *think* she did it. I just—"

"Don't split hairs. Let's just have all the evidence against Ariel."

"It's not evidence, really. It's just—" His look stopped her in mid-sentence. "All right," she said. "All right. I think she hated him."

"Why?"

"Because I stopped loving her when he was born."

"Because she thinks it or because it's true?"

"Both. Oh, maybe I stopped loving her earlier, maybe I never loved her. God knows I tried, Jeff. I was the one who really pushed for adoption. David was a little hesitant." She laughed harshly. "He pointed out that you never know what you're getting. I didn't pay any attention. It never seemed possible to me that I could bring up a child as my own and fail to love it."

"But that's what happened?"

She hesitated, then gave a quick nod. "I tried to fake it," she said. "I denied my real feelings and played the fulfilled young mother number all the way. But when Caleb came along the old denial mechanism got short-circuited. It was just too obvious to me that what I felt for Caleb was categorically different from anything I ever felt for Ariel."

"Obvious to you, maybe. Are you sure it was obvious to her?"

"I think so. I tried to act the same as always, but—well, she's not a stupid child. She's a strange child and I sometimes have the feeling she was born on another planet, that she's just visiting from outer space. But there's nothing stupid about her."

"How did she act toward Caleb?"

"Like a loving sister."

"Always?"

"Always."

"Then—"

"That's how she *acted*. But maybe that's what it was. An act."

"Any reasons to think it might be?"

"Nothing solid. Just a vibration she gave off. She used to play her flute for him. Did I tell you about that flute of hers?"

"Yes. You've got me wondering what it sounds like."

"You're better off wondering than listening to it. Trust me. She would stand in Caleb's room and play for him." She sighed. "That doesn't sound particularly malicious, does it?"

"What else is there about her?"

"The woman in the shawl looked like her."

"That may be more of an indication of where you're coming from than hard evidence against Ariel."

"That's true. All right, here's what keeps echoing around in my head and I've never mentioned to anyone. When I went into Caleb's room and found him dead, she was waiting in the hallway when I came out. I couldn't talk. I couldn't even think straight. And she didn't have to be told. She knew he was dead—"

"You sensed this, Bobbie?"

"The hell I did. I was numb clear through, I couldn't have sensed a hot coal under my foot. She said, 'Something's wrong with Caleb, isn't it? He's dead, isn't he?' "

"Of course she could tell something was wrong. She was reading you."

"No."

"The state you must have been in—"

She shook her head. "No," she insisted. "Of course I thought of that. But I swear she already knew. Why on earth would she leap to that particular conclusion? No matter what expression I had on my face, how could she take one look at me and immediately assume her baby brother was dead."

"Unless she killed him."

"I don't like to think that. But I can't help it."

He drove for a mile or two in silence. Then he said, "There are all sorts of explanations, you know."

"Oh?"

"Maybe Ariel went into his room earlier. Not to kill him but just to see if he was awake or to play her flute or God knows why. Maybe she touched him and he was cold and wouldn't wake up and she didn't know what to do so she went back to her room. Then you discovered him for yourself and that made the whole experience real for her, and of course she knew he was dead, and that's why she reacted as she did."

"You'd make a good defense lawyer."

"It's possible, isn't it?"

"I suppose so. And it never occurred to me."

"It's not the only possibility. You woke up and saw a ghost, or whatever the hell it was that you saw. The woman in the shawl. The first two nights you didn't know what significance to attach to the sight, but the third time it happened you saw it as a threat to your son."

"Because she was holding a baby in her arms. Carrying him away with her."

"Right. What makes you think you were the only person in the house who had an experience along those lines? You've described Ariel as a spooky kind of a kid, almost of another world. From the description, she sounds as though she'd be far more likely to have an occult experience than you would. Maybe she's a little fey. Maybe she has some psychic ability. And maybe she had some sort of experience during the night, an apparition or a nightmare or God

knows what, which she interpreted as a threat to her
brother. Then, when she saw you come out of his room and
got a look at the expression on your face, she made what
wasn't such a great leap after all. If she was already worried
about Caleb, it wasn't terribly farfetched for her to intuit
that he was dead."

She lit a cigarette and smoked half of it without saying
anything, thinking over what he had said. Sitting beside
him and looking out the window at the autumn country-
side, it was easy to accept the arguments he had advanced,
easy to dismiss the feelings that had lately haunted her.

"Then you think I've been making something out of
nothing," she said at length.

"I didn't say that."

"But—"

"It wasn't conviction that had me point out to you how
David could have killed Caleb, and it wasn't conviction that
led me to defend Ariel. I just thought it might help to take
your arguments and ideas and turn them around. I don't
know what happened to Caleb, Bobbie. There's a principle
of logic that holds that, until you specifically disprove it,
the most probable explanation is likely to be true. When a
baby dies of crib death, the logical thing to believe is that
he died of crib death—that the appearance and the reality
are identical."

"And the woman with the shawl—"

"All kinds of possible explanations. Maybe you've got
some psychic ability yourself."

"It never showed up before."

"Well, maybe you've got late-blooming ESP. Maybe you
sensed Caleb was in danger, and maybe this intuition mani-
fested itself by your waking from a dream and seeing things
in the corners of the bedroom. Or, for the sake of argument,
maybe there really was a ghost and she shows up three
nights before somebody in the house dies. I remember read-

ing a lot of English novels set in lonely houses on the moors where the family dogs all howl when someone in the family's about to expire. I know it's a cliché, but it probably got to be one because it occasionally happened."

"Then you think Caleb died of natural causes."

"I think it makes a good working assumption. I think it's also *possible* that David killed him, or that Ariel killed him, or that some malignant force in the house itself killed him. I think all sorts of things are theoretically possible. Hell, they're possible in more than a theoretical way. The point is that it's impossible to know what's true and what isn't, at least for the time being."

"Where does that leave us?"

"On a county road eight or ten miles west of the Ashley River."

"You know what I mean."

"Of course I do. We haven't cleared up any mysteries, have we? Maybe I just wanted to have this conversation so I'd have a sense of doing something. But there's not really very much I can do, is there?"

"There's nothing anybody can do."

"Not to raise Caleb from the dead, no. You still have your own life to live, Bobbie."

She nodded. "This is the first day I've felt half-alive since he died."

"It's the country air."

"That's not all it is."

He had his eyes on the road. The sun was behind them. He was driving east now, and in another ten minutes they'd be crossing the bridge into Charleston. He'd drop her off. She'd be back in her own house, back in her own life.

No, she thought. No, she did not want to let go of him. Not just yet, thanks all the same.

She put her hand on his leg, just above the knee. He

turned his eyes from the road, and sexual tension sprang between them like an electrical current jumping a gap.

His response gave her a sense of power, of confidence. She moved her hand deliberately along his thigh, thrilling at his sharp intake of breath. By the time her fingers rested upon his groin, her own heart was pounding and her underarms were damp with perspiration. She rubbed him urgently, rhythmically, and felt a rush of warmth in her own loins.

"Bobbie—"

"Can you find a motel?"

"Do you think it's a good idea?"

Her fingers worked his zipper. She felt wonderfully in control, and at the same time felt herself surrendering to something more powerful than herself.

"God, Bobbie!"

She lowered her head to his lap, closed her eyes. Her mind was awash with images and fragments of sound, and for an instant all she could think of was Ariel, pale-faced Ariel, playing her magic flute.

FIVE

THEY stood at the corner, waiting for the light to change. "It'll snow pretty soon," Erskine said. "It's cold enough already. I bet it snows tonight."

"I hope so."

"You do?" He looked at her curiously. "You like snow?"

"It's pretty."

"I suppose so. I hate it myself." The light changed and they crossed the street together. "It's one block that way," he said, pointing to the left, "and half a block over."

She felt uncertain about going over to his house, and had agreed largely because she had run out of excuses. Lately he had met her every day after school and walked her as far as her house, and for the past week he had invited her to visit at his house.

"I have a short-wave radio," he'd told her. "You can hear lots of things, ham operators and stations from overseas. Most of the time the hams just talk about their rigs, the antennas and transmitters and receivers they're using and everything. It gets pretty technical. And the regular stations play a lot of music and have newscasts."

She had said that it didn't sound terribly interesting. "It isn't," he said, "but *doing* it is interesting."

It hadn't sounded all that interesting to her. Finally that afternoon she had invited him into her house.

He had hesitated. "The thing is," he said, "your mother's home. There's her car."

"So?"

"So I don't like adults very much. Especially people's parents. Of course maybe your parents are different."

"They're not."

"Well, at least my mother's liberated. In other words she works, which means I'm liberated because nobody's home. There's stuff to eat and we could listen to the radio until you get bored with it. If you want."

She hadn't much wanted to, but at that point there was no decent way out. Now, as they turned the corner into his street, she was glad she had decided to come. She liked his house the minute she saw it, a tall old house like her own but much narrower.

"It's a nice house," she said.

"I guess so," he said carelessly. "We've always lived here. It belonged to my mother's father before I was born, and he went on living with us until he died. I was about four at the time. No, I guess I was five. Not that it matters."

"Do you remember him?"

"I don't remember what he looked like, except there are pictures of him, so I *know* what he looked like. It's hard to know what you remember. He smelled funny. I don't remember just what it was about him but he had a funny smell."

"All old people do. At least my grandmother did."

"Is she alive?"

"No."

"We'll go in the front door. I'm supposed to go in the side door, so I always go in the front. If they don't like it it's just T.F.B."

"T.F.B.?"

"Too fucking bad. Well, you asked, didn't you?"

"Gross," Ariel said.

The interior of the house reminded her of her own, but there was a difference and it did not take her long to realize what the difference was. This house had been occupied by the same family for fifty years or more, and it had a settled air about it, the feeling a house develops as a result of continual occupancy by the same people. Her own house had the same sense of age, but the rugs and furniture, the pictures on the walls, all had been placed there too recently to have become part and parcel of the house that contained them.

She liked her house better than Erskine's. But she preferred the way his house *felt*.

Of course she didn't mention any of this. When you said things like that all you got was funny looks.

His room was on the third floor. They went up the stairs to the second floor together, then walked along a hallway to a door that opened onto the attic staircase. Erskine flung open the door and tore up the steep flight of stairs as if something were pursuing him. She stared after him, then followed him at a deliberately leisurely pace. He was still panting furiously by the time she reached the top.

She looked at him, thinking again what a weird kid he was. She was growing to like him more, the more time she spent with him, but he did not seem any more normal than he had at first. If anything she was simply discovering new ways in which he was weird.

The other day, for example, he had dropped the license numbers on her.

"Your mother drove past our house yesterday afternoon," he said. She had nodded, unimpressed. "I could tell by the license number," he went on. "664-AQT. The Datsun. Your father has the Ford Torino. LJK-914."

She had stared at him.

"When I'm interested in a person," he said, "I make it my business to know things. I just do a little research. That's all. Your father's in the traffic department at Ashley-Cooper Home Products. Do you happen to know his number at work?"

"His number?"

"His telephone number. It's 787-5645. His personal extension is 342."

She had been dumbfounded. Why, she had demanded, was he calling her father?

"I didn't call him. Why would I call him?"

"Then how come you know his number?"

"I know the license numbers, too, Ariel, but that doesn't mean I'm planning to steal the cars. It's just mental exercise. You stimulate the brain by giving it tasks to do, the same as exercising a muscle. I just memorized those numbers because I'm interested in you. I have taken an interest, as they say."

"What kind of an interest?"

"I'm interested in fucking you," he'd said. "I like to think about your body when I can't sleep at night."

"God, you're gross."

Except that his obscenities—and this was hardly the first time he'd spoken like that to her—were somehow not really disgusting. Because she had sensed early on that his words served some special function. He might very well have sex on the brain, it seemed to her that most boys his age did. The words, though, served as some sort of shield between himself and the world.

Well, she could understand that. She had enough shields of her own. Her music, her books and the private worlds she could slip off into when she wanted.

Now, as he was catching his breath, she asked him what was the matter.

"Nothing."

"The way you tore up the stairs."

"It's something I like to do. I used to have my room on the second floor. Then I was exploring the attic and I found this room up here. I never even knew it existed. The attic's mostly junk. My grandfather was a lawyer and all those boxes are old papers and lawbooks and different garbage. My mother keeps saying how she's going to get rid of them someday but I guess she never will. You know how old books and papers smell? Especially in a house like this where the damp gets into everything?"

Ariel wrinkled her nose.

"Anyway, I found this room. It used to be a maid's room and there were even some old *True Confessions* magazines from the forties. It's a shame the maid wasn't hooked on science fiction or something interesting. Comic books, for instance. They'd be worth a fortune, but what kind of a nerd collects old *True Confessions* magazines?"

"What did you do with them?"

"Put 'em in a box. Nothing ever gets thrown out in this house. It's against their religion or something. Do you have a religion?"

"I guess we're Protestant, but we don't go to church."

"I thought that was your minister at the funeral."

"No, he just came with the service."

"Yeah. Well, my mother was Catholic and my father was Jewish, so we're nothing. It's like breeding cats. You take a purebred Persian and a purebred Siamese and cross them and you get an alley cat. So that's what I am. Anyway, I wanted the room and they didn't want me to have it."

"Were they afraid the maid was coming back?"

It was the sort of line she thought of often and usually didn't say because all she would get would be the funny looks, or else no reaction at all, but Erskine gave her a look and then started to giggle. He let the giggle build into a laugh and then they both came up with some lines on the idea of the maid coming back for her magazines, and when it had run its course he said, "No, see, what it was is they thought I would be lonesome by myself. You know with a whole floor separating me from my darling parents." He blinked, his eyes huge behind the thick lenses, and then he turned his eyes aside. "Plus they thought it would be a lot of stairs to climb. Up to the second floor and all the way up to the third, as if it was the Washington Monument or something." He looked at her. "So I make it a point to run up the last flight," he said. "That's all. Come on, I'll show you the room."

The minute she saw the room she knew why he liked it. It was small and incompletely finished, the walls squares of unpainted fiberboard inexpertly nailed in place. There was one small window which looked out on the street. Erskine's bed was a very narrow one. There was a chest of drawers at the foot of it and, along one entire wall, a bookshelf overflowing with magazines and paperbacks.

"Science fiction," he said. "It's about the only thing I read. I still will look at a comic book once in a while, but I'm not really interested in them."

"I never got into comic books."

"They're a waste of time. You read much science fiction?" She shook her head. "I guess girls mostly don't," he said.

There were a few dozen postcards tacked to the wall over his bed, some of them showing scenes but the majority consisting of combinations of numbers and letters. She remembered how he had memorized the license numbers and asked if the cards were related to license plates.

He laughed at the idea. "They're QSL cards," he said. "Whenever I hear a shortwave station I haven't heard before I send them a postcard saying what I heard and the strength of their signal and all, and they send one of these back. If they want to take the trouble. The foreign stations send you all kinds of things, their schedules and different propaganda. Here, let me show you."

He showed her some of the cards and a whole folder of material from Radio Moscow, and then they listened to the radio while he showed her his logbook and explained how he had run an antenna wire from his window and grounded it to a telephone pole in the back yard. She had to admit that the whole radio operation was pretty impressive. What you actually heard wasn't terribly interesting, but doing it, getting involved in it as a hobby, that was more interesting than she would have thought.

At four-thirty he turned off the radio. "We could have some milk and cookies," he said. "There's usually something downstairs if you're hungry."

"Okay."

"Or we could stay up here and screw. That would probably be more exciting than milk and cookies."

"Why do you have to talk like that?"

"Why not? It's an interesting way to talk." He turned his face from her and pitched his voice deliberately low. "Besides," he said, "if we ever get around to screwing, think how exciting it'll be for you."

"For *me?*"

"Think of the suspense. I could go any minute." She couldn't see his face now. "When I was five years old I had rheumatic fever," he said. "Sometimes it can have an effect on your heart. That's why I don't take gym, in case you were wondering. Also it's why my parents were worried about the extra flight of stairs, but that's just stupid because stairs aren't that much of a strain. Sometimes I'll run up both flights one after the other and it's not a strain. I might be breathing hard afterward but so what? In fact I could take gym and it would probably be safe enough but I hate gym anyway and the teacher's a real creep so why not get out of it if I have the chance?"

"Sure."

"You just get all sweaty. That's all gym is, getting sweaty and smelling like a locker room for the rest of the day."

"That's why you run up the stairs."

"I just happen to like to run up stairs," he said. "A certain amount of exercise is good for a person."

"Sure."

"It's actually good for the heart. That's why men go out and jog. There's a man who runs past this house every morning about eight. He wears a sweatshirt and white pants and he has this dog that runs along with him. The dog's a German short-haired pointer. I don't know if you ever saw them."

"I never saw the man but there's a dog like that who comes around our street sometimes."

"It's probably the same dog. The dog looks okay but the man really looks stupid running around like an idiot. But it must be good for his heart."

"I guess so."

He looked at her. He had taken off his glasses, and without them his eyes looked normal, even attractive. "Anyway," he said, "anybody could pop off any minute. You could be lying in bed and a tree could fall on your house and crush you. Not you in particular, but you know what I mean."

She thought of Caleb.

"So if you want to screw I guess I'll take my chances, Ariel."

She gazed steadily at him. He blinked, started to avert his eyes, then met his stare.

"I was adopted," she said.

"You're late," Roberta said. "Dinner's almost ready. I was starting to worry about you."

98

Sure, she thought.

"Go wash your hands and get ready. Where were you?"

"Erskine's house."

"Do I know who that is? Is it the odd-looking little boy I've seen you walking with?"

"Yes."

"I've seen him before. Of course. He was at the funeral, wasn't he?"

"Yes."

"What did you say his name was?"

"Erskine Wold."

Roberta looked at her. "Well, at least you have a friend," she said at length.

Ariel went to the lavatory, ran water, washed her hands and face. *Well, at least you have a friend, an odd-looking little friend.* If Erskine didn't like adults in general, he'd really get a bang out of Roberta.

She thought of the conversation they'd had in his third-floor room. She could have gone on talking for another hour or more. She had told him things she'd never said to anyone but herself.

She still wasn't sure if she liked him. There were things about him that bothered her, and getting to know him didn't make him any less weird. Not that the weirdness bothered her, necessarily. But the grossness did, and all the sex talk. She was pretty sure he just did it for effect, and maybe he'd stop it as they got to know each other better.

Well, she thought, echoing Roberta, at least you have a friend.

SIX

DAVID sat in his ground-floor study, smoking a lovat-shaped Barling and watching the blue smoke rise to fill the little room. There was a bottle of brandy on one shelf of the built-in chestnut bookcases, and his eyes fixed on the bottle as they had done every few moments since he had entered the room. He wanted a drink, longed for a drink, but he had made the decision earlier not to have one. Not tonight, anyway.

It was his nighttime drinking that was becoming a problem. He never drank in the morning—only alcoholics, for God's sake, drank in the morning. He was apt to order a drink at lunch—a Bloody Mary generally, occasionally a martini—but he never had more than one drink at that time, and frequently had a sandwich at his desk or a quick bite at the Greek place down the street and passed up his noon drink without giving it a thought.

He always had a drink after work. That was ritual. His after-work drink was scotch on the rocks with a twist of lemon, Teacher's if he remembered to ask for it by brand name, otherwise whatever the bartender poured. At the Blueprint Room, just around the corner from Ashley-Cooper Home Products, the barman knew him and he didn't have to specify his brand. He'd have one drink there, or at the Cliquot Club, or at Hardesty's. Once in a while, on a Friday, say, he might have a second. Never a third.

He'd have another drink upon arriving home. Sometimes he and Roberta would have a drink together in the front room, but if she was busy or not in the mood he'd have it himself. Teacher's on the rocks, but no twist of lemon this time. And only the one drink.

And that would be it for him until after dinner. A total of three drinks, four on exceptional occasions, sometimes only two if he missed his lunchtime cocktail. Some years ago, he recalled, he and Roberta had gotten briefly into the habit of wine with dinner. They made a mini-hobby out of it, trying different wines, reading books on the subject, drinking from elegant Waterford stemware. They'd given it up because neither of them had really liked wine all that much, and he had especially disliked the way it made him sleepy. Whenever they shared a bottle he was apt to doze off in front of the television set.

Now, curiously, he drank brandy after dinner to help him get to sleep. And brandy was the worst choice for that particular purpose, as he well knew. There was something distinctly stimulating about it, and on the one occasion when he'd taken it on an empty stomach he'd been rewarded with palpitations and jangling coffee nerves. It didn't really make him sleepy; enough of it, though, and it would knock him out.

Yet it was what he wanted after dinner. Pipes to smoke and books to read (or at least turn the pages of) and brandy to sip, here in this little room that was solely his.

Well, tonight he was breaking the pattern. He'd had his Bloody Mary at lunch, his scotch at the Blueprint Room, a second scotch while he read the evening paper in the front room. And that was enough. He didn't need any more. Hell, he didn't even *want* any more.

His eyes rose again to the brandy bottle. Force of habit, he told himself, drawing on his pipe, watching the smoke rise. Force of habit, ritual, routine. It was that simple. And he would break the habit, the ritual, the routine, just as simply—by not taking the drink.

Because he felt he had the opportunity to take charge of his life, to grab hold of it and turn it around. His life, his marriage, his household—he sensed that everything was at some sort of crossroads. Things had been proceeding in a certain direction, and then Caleb had died abruptly, and now—

His pipe had gone out. He tried to relight it but there was nothing left to relight. He knocked out the dottle, ran a pipecleaner through the stem and shank. He returned the pipe to the rack, selected another one automatically, then put it back and left the little room.

In the doorway, he paused automatically for a glance at the brandy bottle, then turned his back on it and headed for the kitchen.

She was standing at the sink, a glass in her hand. Turning at his approach, she extended the glass to him and ordered him to look at it.

"What is it?"

"Just look at it."

He took it from her hand, looked down into a glass half full of a cloudy brown liquid.

"Smell it."

He did, and wrinkled his nose in distaste. It smelled of the bottom of a swamp, of something equally foul.

"It came out of the tap," she explained. "I wanted a glass of water and that's what came out of the tap. This house is driving me crazy."

He reached to turn on the taps, the cold and then the hot. The water ran clear.

"I know," she said. "It's crystal clear now. But that's what I got a minute ago."

"Well, it's an old house. Old plumbing."

"I know it's an old house."

"And maybe it has nothing to do with the house. Maybe it's the water supply. There was something in the paper not long ago, they were getting little red worms in their water up around Race and Rutledge. Maybe it'd be a good idea to let it run awhile before drinking, but—"

She shuddered, took the glass from him, poured its contents down the sink. "It's this house," she said. "And that stove, with the pilot lights going out all the damned time, and I'm forever smelling gas."

"It's not dangerous, you know."

"So I'm told, but—"

He put an arm around her, rested his hand on her shoulder. She stiffened under his touch but he left his hand there. "You're under a strain," he said.

"Is that what it is?"

"Of course, and it's understandable. Maybe it would be a good idea for you to see Gintzler again."

"I'm not going crazy and I don't need to see a psychiatrist."

"He helped you before."

"I'm not sure he helped me and I'm not sure I needed any help in the first place. I don't want to see him now."

"If you say so."

"I say so." She turned, drew away from him, and he withdrew his hand. There was a challenge in her eyes. He thought fleetingly of the bottle of brandy in his study—just a reflex thought, just a matter of habit—and then he rose to the challenge.

"This weekend," he said, "I think you ought to take Ariel for a drive."

"I beg your pardon?"

"A nice drive in the country. God knows it's the perfect season for it. Ramble around inland or take a nice leisurely drive up the coast, just the two of you."

"What are you getting at, David?"

"While you're gone, I'll clean out Caleb's room."

"While the child and I take a nice leisurely drive in the country."

"That's right."

"While we're doing this, you'll clean out his room."

He nodded.

"I don't think I understand," she said evenly. "Are you implying that Caleb's room is dirty?"

"No."

"Or disorganized? Are things out of place?"

"You know what I mean, Roberta."

"You mean you want to get rid of his things. Throw them out."

"Or give them away."

"No."

He flared. "For Christ's sake, Roberta, why are you punishing yourself? What do you want to do, make the kid's room into a national shrine? Or do you figure if you leave everything just the way it is maybe he'll come back to it, like a soldier missing in action? Is that what it is?"

"Stop!"

"I'm not trying to hurt you."

"You're doing a good job of it. What *are* you trying to do?"

"I'm trying to help you get over something."

"What? His death? Or his life?"

"I don't know what you're talking about."

"You want to erase Caleb. You want to deny he ever existed."

"And you want to deny he's dead."

"That's not true."

"Are you sure of that?"

She turned away from him. Other thoughts came to mind and he fought to keep himself from giving voice to them. There were just too many things they couldn't say to each other, too many subjects that didn't get mentioned.

She said, "The night he died—"

"What about it?"

"When I woke you—"

"Yes?"

"You went to his room to check him."

"So?"

"What did you do?"

"I checked him."

"How?"

"What do you mean?"

"Well, did you pick him up? Did you touch him? What did you do to check him?"

"I don't remember."

"You don't remember?"

"Jesus," he said. "It was the middle of the night and I just woke up out of a sound sleep. I didn't pick him up. I suppose I touched him."

"Maybe you just looked at him."

"Maybe."

"Did you put the light on?"

"I don't know."

"Oh, please. You must know."

He thought for a moment. "I didn't turn the light on. There was enough light from the window."

"And you looked at him."

"Yes."

"Was he alive?"

"Of course he was alive."

"How do you know?"

"Roberta—"

"You don't know for a fact, do you? You just looked at him to put my mind at rest. You didn't take me seriously, did you?"

"I checked him and he looked fine. What the hell's the matter with you, anyway?"

She didn't answer immediately. Then she said, "Why did my son die, David?"

"It just happened."

"You mean you can't explain it? I thought you had an answer for every question."

"Sometimes I don't even have the questions."

"But I'm sure you have a theory."

"Well—"

"I just knew you had a theory, David."

He ignored the bitchiness in her voice. "There was something that came to me at the funeral," he said. "When the minister was talking about the will of God."

"Oh?"

"I was thinking how a century ago, even more recently than that, it was commonplace for a woman to bear half a dozen children in order to raise one to maturity. That was a part of natural selection. Infancy was a very hazardous period and only a small percentage of infants survived it—"

"So?"

"So . . . it occurred to me that crib death may be nature's method of weeding out structurally weak children. Maybe a certain percentage of babies are born with constitutional defects that modern medicine isn't yet aware of. But there's some factor that makes them weak, and one night they go to sleep and don't wake up—"

"And it's just nature's way."

"That's right."

"The same as death is just nature's way of telling us to slow down."

"Roberta—"

"You filthy son of a bitch."

He took a step backward, driven off by her words, by her tone of voice.

"You bastard," she went on. "You'd like that, wouldn't you? The idea of my son being defective. So the great God of nature just took a wet rag and wiped him off the slate. You'd love to think of it that way, wouldn't you?"

"*Your* son."

She looked at him.

"Caleb was our son. Remember?"

And he thought, *You're seeing him again, aren't you? You and Channing. Don't ask me how I know. I can read it, I can sense it. You're the way you were on Coteswood Lane, before Caleb was born, before he was even conceived. The same sort of detachment, the same preoccupied air.*

It was this realization that had made him resolve to discontinue the after-dinner drinking, to clean out Caleb's room, to take charge of their lives again.

But she wasn't making it easy.

She stood still for a moment, then turned and ran water in the sink. She let it run for awhile, clear and cold, before filling a glass. She held it to the light, studied it, sniffed it, then took a sip.

"Just cold water," she said.

He didn't answer.

Without turning to look at him she said, "I'm sorry I said what I did. I've been under a strain. You know that."

"Sure."

"And that doesn't help."

"What?"

She winced. "That godawful noise. That . . . music, I suppose you'd have to call it. Don't tell me you can't hear it?"

He listened. He hadn't even been aware of it before, the reedy piping from the second floor.

"Oh," he said. "You mean the flute?"

"For lack of a better term, the flute."

"I can barely hear it. Is it bothering you?"

"It always bothers me," she said. "God, it drives me crazy. And as for just barely hearing it, I couldn't hear it more clearly if it was happening inside my skull. It goes through me like a diamond drill."

"I could tell her to stop, I suppose. It's getting late—"

"Oh, I suppose I can stand it. But you can't tell me it doesn't bother you. It *must* bother you."

"It really doesn't."

"Maybe you should have your hearing checked. I swear it's like chalk on a blackboard."

"Oh, come on," he said. "To tell you the truth, I have to say I like Ariel's music. I don't always pay attention to it, but I like it."

"You've just absolutely got to be kidding."

He shook his head. "Not at all. Oh, I'm not saying I think it's good, but it *might* be good. I don't really know enough about music to say. I know it's not ordinary."

"I'll grant you that."

"But there's something about it I like. It has a sort of pagan quality to it, don't you think? A druidic quality. Can't you picture her sitting on the limb of a sacred tree somewhere in Devon or Cornwall and piping away like that to placate the woodland spirits?"

"What an idea."

He shrugged. "Just a thought."

"If that's what they had for music in those days, then I'm glad the good old days are dead and gone."

"Oh, I've no idea what their music was like. I doubt anyone does. But that's what it ought to sound like." He chuckled. "Anyway, the music is our Ariel down to the ground. Thin and reedy and fey and pagan and a little bit weird."

"Our Ariel."

"How's that?"

She looked at him for a moment, then shook her head, dismissing the thought. "Well," she said, "I think I'll watch a little television. Maybe I won't hear that noise over the sound of the set. I appreciate your idea of a long ride in the country, but I think we'll forget about it, if you don't mind."

"It was just an idea."

"And I want Caleb's room left just the way it is. Let's agree on that, shall we?"

"If you say so."

"I do."

"I wonder what Gintzler would say about it."

"Well, that's something you can go on wondering about, because I won't have the opportunity to ask him. I don't suppose you feel like watching TV?"

"No," he said. "I don't suppose so."

Back in his study, he took a long time choosing a pipe to smoke. He kept changing his mind. As if it mattered which one he picked.

All the things they'd said to each other. All the things left unsaid.

She was seeing Channing. He knew it and hadn't mentioned it. And it was Jeff Channing who had fathered Caleb, and he knew that, too.

And hadn't mentioned that, either.

He thought now of the night she'd quizzed him about, the night of Caleb's death. Waking abruptly, hearing her babble about some ghost who was no longer to be seen. Then padding down the hall to the baby's room.

He didn't much want to relive those moments.

Because there was something she evidently didn't realize. He'd probed a little after the funeral and she didn't seem to know what she'd said. What she'd screamed, really, because it was her scream that woke him, and she had screamed a name, and it wasn't his name.

Jeff, she had screamed. *Jeff.*

His eyes went to the bottle of brandy on the bookshelf. It was almost full. He could imagine the sound of it flowing into his glass, could picture its warm glow held up to the light.

A great improvement on Roberta's glass of swamp water.

Upstairs, Ariel was playing her flute. He smiled as he listened, and then other thoughts intruded, and the smile died.

For God's sake, one little drink wouldn't hurt. There was a world of difference between watching out for overindulgence and giving up a legitimate pleasure altogether. Alcohol in moderation had a tonic effect on the system. Everyone knew that. . . .

When the bottle was a little over two-thirds empty, he switched off the lamp in the study and made his way upstairs to bed.

III

SEVEN

IN her darkened bedroom, Ariel shifted restlessly under a heavy blanket. Her breathing became rapid and shallow and her heartbeat raced. A cold hand clutched at her heart. With a single spasmodic move she hurled the covers back and thrust herself into an upright position. Her upper lip was drawn back, and her little eyes glowed like a cat's in the blackness.

A dream.

She fought to catch her breath, telling herself it was a dream and she was out of it now. But she was afraid of this kind of dream. She sensed that all she had to do was lie down and snuggle under the covers and surrender to the darkness and the dream would come back to her and the cold hand would reach again for her heart.

She threw her legs over the side of the bed and checked the radium dial of the clock on her bedside table. It was almost four-thirty. More than two hours before sunrise. Of course the sky would begin to brighten before actual sunrise, but she could not wait that long.

She switched on her lamp. The sudden brightness made her blink but she welcomed it just the same.

Only a dream.

She got out of bed. The room was cold but she scarcely noticed. She went to her schoolbag and drew out her green pen and the spiral notebook she was using as an occasional diary. She thumbed through it until she found the first blank page, uncapped the pen, and sat for just a moment chewing contemplatively on the end of the pen's plastic barrel.

Then she began to write as fast as her fingers would move.

It was a dream but I have to write it down because I can never tell anybody.

Here's how it starts. I am asleep in my bed in this room. I am me but my hair is different and I am older. My hair is golden and hangs to my waist. It is absolutely straight. Otherwise I am the same as always except that I am beautiful.

In the dream I can see myself from inside and from outside. Sometimes I am in myself and sometimes I am across the room watching me.

In the dream I wake up. I have to go to the bathroom. I have to go so bad that it hurts. I get up and put on a flowing blue-green robe the color of the sea. It sweeps around me and stays in place perfectly. I do not have to tie it.

I go out of my room and begin walking down the hallway, but it is not the hallway of this house. It is long and winding and paved with cobblestones. It is like a path outside in some old city but it is inside, in a house. I do not know how to explain this.

The part about the bathroom goes away. I just don't have to go anymore. I am walking because there is something I must do and in my hand is my flute. But it is different. It is longer and thicker and it is made of pure gold.

And there is writing on it, carved into the gold. But when I try to read it the words move around before my eyes. It is important for me to read the message but I can't read it because the letters won't stay in place.

I think maybe it's in another alphabet. But in the dream I can understand that alphabet and I would be able to read it if only the letters would hold still.

I keep on walking while I am trying to read the writing on the flute.

Then I come to the end of the hallway and there is a door. Not a door but a doorway, and it is round and low. I know what it is! It is a rathole except that it is large enough so that I can just barely fit inside. I have to put the flute in first and then I have to get on my hands and knees and squirm through like a snake.

And then I am inside, and it is Caleb's room.

Exactly like his room in this house.

There is the crib, and Caleb is in his crib playing. He is waving his hands and feet in the air and cooing to them. He is talking to his fish mobile.

He is beautiful.

And I play my flute for him.

I could hear the music in the dream. I can almost hear it now but I don't think I could play it. I am not sure. Sometimes I can hear music in my head and then play it on the flute but not always.

I might be scared to play this music.

She straightened up on her chair, capped her pen for a moment. Her breathing and heartbeat were normal now. She closed her eyes and deliberately let herself fall back into the mood of the dream, feeling herself very nearly returning to the dream. Then with an effort she opened her eyes again and resumed writing.

The music is the color of seawater turned to smoke.

I play with my eyes closed but I can see just the same. I

can see through my closed eyelids and also I can see from across the room and can see myself playing.

Caleb loves the music. His feet grow still and he puts his hands down at his sides and he just looks up at me and grooves on the music.

Then suddenly!

Everything changes.

I am the Pied Piper of Hamelin. I am still me but different. My golden hair is gone. Instead my hair is black and short and cut like Joan of Arc. And I am dressed like Robin Hood and I have leather slippers with pointed turned-up toes. And I am carrying a huge apple pie in one hand. I know that's not what Pied Piper means but when I first heard the story years ago I imagined him carrying a pie and that's how it is in the dream.

I am carrying a pie in one hand and I have my flute in my other hand and I am playing one-handed, playing fast scrambly music that keeps curving in on itself. And I am going out through the rathole door and all the little children are following me. Thousands of children.

And all of them following me. I can see from high up, I can look back over all of us, and the parade of little children goes on forever. We are going through a long tunnel that goes on and on.

The tunnel is a sewer. There is water in the tunnel and the little children are crying because they are getting wet. And I play my flute faster and faster. The pie is gone. I don't know what happened to the pie, but I am holding the flute with both hands and playing as fast as I can, faster and faster and faster, and I am dancing around in a wild little circle and my slippers have hooves on them like a goat, and I play and I dance, and the children are crying.

And then they are not crying but squealing, and I turn and look, and all of the little children have turned into mice and rats. I turned them into mice and rats with my playing.

And the water is too deep for them and they are drowning.

All of the little children are rats and they are drowning.

And I almost wake up.

In fact I think maybe I did wake up then but slipped back into the dream. I can't be sure.

Again she stopped and capped the pen. She scanned the last paragraphs, started to close the notebook, then sighed heavily and began writing again.

I might as well write the rest of it. I'm scared but I'll write it anyway. I can always tear it up later.

Just as the children were drowning and I almost woke up, suddenly I was back in the dream but I was also back in Caleb's room. I had my own hair this time and I was me.

Ariel.

I didn't have the flute anymore. I don't know what happened to it.

Caleb was sleeping in his bed. And he just looked so beautiful.

Sound asleep.

And I was Ariel and Caleb both at the same time. I was him sleeping in the crib and me looking into it.

And I can't explain this.

And my hands went in between the bars of the crib. Each hand went between a different pair of bars. And the part of me that was Caleb saw the hands even though my eyes were closed but just went on lying there.

And one of my Ariel-hands went over my Caleb-mouth.

And the other Ariel-hand went over the Caleb-nose.

And Caleb couldn't breathe and tried to struggle and tried to move and couldn't move because Ariel's hands pinched his nose shut and covered his mouth.

And it just went on forever.

And then Caleb couldn't move anymore. The Caleb part

of me just winked out like a lightbulb and there was just the Ariel part of me plus the part looking down from the ceiling and watching.

It was a *dream!*

It never happened. Nothing like this ever happened. I don't know where the dream came from. I don't know where dreams come from. They don't mean anything. Everybody has dreams and all dreams are crazy and they do not mean anything.

I had to write this down. I don't ever want to read it but I had to write it down.

I can't tell anybody about this. I couldn't tell Erskine even.

I don't know what to do. I'm scared.

No that's silly it's all right it's just a dream.

She sat there for several minutes trying to think of something else to write. But there was nothing else to write. She capped her pen and closed her notebook and returned both of them to her schoolbag.

She got into bed, pulled the covers up. She reached to extinguish the lamp, then changed her mind and left it burning. She stretched out and closed her eyes but they wouldn't stay shut. They kept opening.

EIGHT

THE announcer on ORU, the Belgian overseas station, was commenting at length on the outcome of a recent OPEC meeting in Brussels. Erskine switched off the radio and yawned theatrically. "Boring," he said, giving the word a singsong inflection. "Bow. Ring."

"Maybe I should go home."

"Maybe you should take off all your clothes, Jardell."

She looked at him, shook her head. "You just have to be gross every once in a while to prove you're alive, don't you?"

"It's not grossness, Ariel. It's the heat of passion."

"If I did take my clothes off you wouldn't know what to do."

"I'd think of something."

"Your little old rheumatic heart would conk out and I'd have to explain it to your mother."

"I told you I was willing to risk it. You could just tell my mother I ran up the stairs again."

"She'd say, 'I just knew it was a mistake to let him live in the attic.' "

"That's what she'd say. Want to give it a try?"

She sighed. "You don't even want to."

"Then why do I keep asking you?"

"Habit, probably. You started off trying to gross me out and now you're stuck in a rut. You don't really want to, do you? With me, I mean."

He started to reply, then took a moment to think. She watched his eyes through the thick lenses. "I guess not," he said at length.

"Because we're friends?"

"Right. We're friends, and we sort of know each other, and all that. I know who I'd like to screw."

"Who? Wait, let me guess. Carol Bahnsen."

"Ugh."

"Oh, I know. Veronica, right?"

"How'd you know?"

"Veronica Doughty. I just knew it."

"How?"

"Woman's intuition. Suppose you got to be friends with her first?"

"I wouldn't get to be friends with her. (A) she doesn't like me and (B) she's stupid. But you're right, I'd like to do it to her."

"I knew she was the one."

"And afterward I'd have to kill her."

' Why?"

"Oh, because she's so stupid, Ariel. And because she's stuck up and a snot."

"She's a snot, all right."

"And to keep her from telling anybody. I'm just talking. I wouldn't really kill her."

"But you'd like to."

"Sure."

"Does it bother you?"

"What?"

"Thinking about killing people."

He shook his head. "I wouldn't *really* kill anybody. But

there are a lot that I'd like to kill. Sometimes it's fun to think about it."

"Who would you like to kill?"

"Well, Veronica."

"Who else?"

"Maybe Mrs. Tashman."

"Tashman? Why her?"

"I don't know. Sometimes she's like my mother. The way she talks. You know, so sincere that you know she's not really sincere."

"I think she's nice. She came to Caleb's funeral."

"Okay, then we'll let her live. I'll tell you who I'd like to kill. Graham Littlefield."

"Why Graham?"

"Because he's tall and strong and athletic and popular and stupid. He's really stupid."

"He's not that stupid."

"I think he's stupid."

"You're jealous."

"I don't get jealous of stupid people, Jardell."

"Veronica likes him."

"So I'll kill both of them. This is a stupid conversation, speaking of stupidity. Who do you want to kill?"

"Oh, nobody," she said airily. "I love the whole world."

"Come on, play the game."

"Roberta."

"Your mother? Why?"

"Because she's not my mother. Because she hates me. Because she thinks—"

"Thinks what?"

"Nothing."

"What were you going to say, Ariel?"

She shook her head. "Nothing," she said. "This is a stupid conversation, anyway. I'm sick of it."

"Well, let's talk about something else, then. Sex and killing are out. How about the OPEC conference in Brussels? There's a thrilling topic."

"Do you ever have dreams?"

"Dreams? Why?"

"I was just wondering."

"I sometimes dream that I'm naked and people are looking at me. It's not the same dream each time. The people'll be different from one dream to the next, and the scenes, but I don't have any clothes on and they're staring at me. It's stupid."

"Do you ever have dreams that you're afraid of?"

"It's not much fun, dreaming you're naked and people are staring and pointing. I don't have the dream too often."

"That's not what I mean."

He took off his glasses and squinted at her. "Something's bothering you," he said.

"No."

"You had a bad dream, right?"

She shrugged.

"Last night?"

"A few nights ago."

"Tell me about it."

"I don't remember it," she said. "It was just frightening, that's all. I don't remember any of what happened in it."

"Maybe you'll dream it again."

She gave him a sharp look, then shrugged again. "Maybe," she said. "Anyway, it's no big deal. It's just a dream."

There was a strong wind blowing when she left Erskine's house. She zipped her jacket all the way up and turned up the collar, then walked along briskly with her hands plunged into her jacket pockets. She thought of how she and Erskine had killed people in their conversation. And about her dream.

She wasn't sure how much she could tell him, how much she *wanted* to tell him. He was weird, and had crazy thoughts of his own, and maybe this would make him capable of accepting the kind of thoughts she found herself having. And they were friends, and that certainly made a difference.

But at the same time she wasn't a hundred percent sure of him. They were friends, true, but sometimes she had the feeling that all the people in the world, herself included, were interesting specimens as far as Erskine was concerned. He was a scientist, cool and detached, watching them all through a microscope.

Maybe it was the thick glasses that did it, she thought. They kept him remote and a ways apart. When he took them off he looked vulnerable.

She turned the corner, felt the full force of the wind, drew her shoulders together in defense. Maybe there was nothing to tell him to begin with. Maybe what she'd said at the end was true enough, maybe dreams really didn't mean anything.

And what could the dream mean, anyway?

That she had wanted to kill Caleb? That was crazy, because she loved Caleb. Of course it was possible that a part of her mind had hated him or been jealous of him or something like that. It was common for kids to resent younger brothers and sisters out of jealousy. She knew that. And it was possible to have that kind of thought buried inside you and not even know it was there. She knew that, too.

So? If nothing had happened to Caleb, the thought wouldn't have been worth rooting out and thinking about. But Caleb was dead, and that made her worry about the thought, and feel guilty about it, as if the thought had killed him. But thoughts didn't have magic powers. Thinking never killed anybody. If she had wanted Caleb to die, in some hidden secret chamber of her mind, the desire hadn't had anything to do with his actual death.

She thought of the game she and Erskine had played. He could talk about killing Veronica, or Graham Littlefield, and it didn't mean anything. It was just talk. If one of them died tomorrow, hit by a car or struck by lightning or perishing mysteriously of that rare ailment, Bed Death, it still didn't mean it was Erskine's fault or that he should blame himself for what he'd said.

And as far as Caleb was concerned, she hadn't said anything, or even had a conscious thought on the subject. All she'd had was a dream, and nobody really knew what dreams meant in the first place.

So why was she upset?

Because she was afraid of what the dream meant. Because maybe it didn't just have to do with secret thoughts. Because maybe, just maybe, it had to do with secret *acts*—oh, stop it.

She shivered, and blamed the chill that went through her on the wind.

She was just turning the corner onto her own street when she saw a car pull up in front of her house. The door on the passenger side opened and Roberta got out. Instinctively, Ariel drew back into the cover of a clump of barberry bushes. She watched as Roberta turned to say something to the driver, straightened up, swung the car door shut. The car remained stationary until Roberta had gone up the steps and opened the front door of the house. Then it continued down the block toward where Ariel was waiting.

It was a Buick with a maroon body and a black vinyl landau roof. The driver was a man, and there was something familiar about him but the car was past her and out of sight before she could fix his features firmly in her mind. Who was he and where had she seen him before? She couldn't remember.

DWE-628. That was the license number. South Carolina license, and the number was DWE-628.

DWE-628. She didn't have Erskine's memory for numbers. He seemed to remember them effortlessly—telephone numbers, license plates, the frequencies of radio stations. She was good at math but remembering numbers was something else again.

DWE-628. She repeated it to herself, concentrating firmly on it, and when she got to her house she went directly to her room, not pausing for a word with Roberta, not wanting to chance forgetting the number. DWE-628. She got to her room, opened her diary, uncapped her pen, and wrote it down.

DWE-628.

NINE

JEFF opened his eyes. He was lying on his back on a king-size bed in a Days Inn motel just off I-26. The air was cool on his bare skin. He raised his head from the pillow and watched Roberta, who was sitting a few yards away in a teak-and-vinyl armchair reading a book. Smoke rose from the cigarette she held in her right hand. One leg was bent sharply, its foot propped on the cushion of the chair, and one shoulder was also held at a sharp angle; he was reminded of a couple of pictures from Picasso's blue period—the guitar player, the woman ironing. Her body displayed that attitude.

He continued to watch her, enjoying the moment, until she evidently felt his eyes on her nude body and turned to meet them. "Look who's awake," she said.

"I guess I was sleeping."

"No kidding."

"What time is it? Was I sleeping long?"

"It's past two. I already had my shower."

"I never even heard the water running."

"Well, you wouldn't have heard World War Three," she said. "You were really out. I'll never understand why sex wakes women up and puts men to sleep. Whoever worked out the natural order of things seems to have screwed up there, wouldn't you say?"

"It's handy for men who work a night shift. They go home, make love, and the little wifey gets up and starts in on the housework."

"Trust you to see the bright side. The silver lining. Incidentally, who *cares* if every cloud has a silver lining? You still can't get a peek at the goddamned sun through it."

"I keep forgetting what a literal-minded sort you are. What are you reading?"

"The Bible. What else do you do in a motel room? Just commit adultery and read the Bible."

"Do you think of this as adultery?"

She turned toward him, crossed one leg over the other. "Well, what else would you call it? I don't think of it as a sin, if that's what you mean."

"That's what I meant."

"Well, I don't. This book would tend to disagree with me, however. The Living Bible. That's what it seems to call itself. Evidently the good old King James version is the Dead Bible."

"What is it, modern English?"

"Modern and not terribly grammatical." She closed the book, put it down on the lamp table. "If you're going to read a Bible it ought to be full of thees and thous and begats. When it starts to sound like the host of a morning television talk show it loses me completely. The mystery is gone, and then what's left?"

"Like when they took the Latin out of the Mass."

"That's right, you're Catholic. I tend to forget that."

"Lapsed Catholic. And I can't blame it on Vatican Two, either. I was gone before they changed the Mass. We'd better get going, don't you think?"

"I suppose so. You want to take a shower, don't you? Or do you want to carry my spoor back to Elaine?"

"Your spoor. Like some jungle beast."

"That's the idea."

He showered thoroughly but quickly, toweled dry, and emerged to find her already dressed. "And now the gentleman puts on *his* clothes," she intoned, "and the charming couple will be on their way. The gentleman will return to his office—you *are* going back to your office?"

"Yes."

"—while the lady goes back to her haunted house. God."

"It bothers you, doesn't it?"

"More than ever. I'm living in a hostile environment. Getting away from it just makes me aware of how unpleasant it is. I spend a couple of hours with you in this room or one like it and it's neutral, it's uncomplicated and safe. Then I walk through that door and there's a presence in that house that hits me like a two-by-four between the eyes. Haven't you felt it yourself?"

He shook his head. "But I don't have to live with it," he said. "And I haven't really been inside your house except for the first time."

"And you don't have to live with her."

"You mean Ariel."

"Obviously. Who else?"

In the car, heading back into town, he said, "You hardly ever call her by name, have you noticed that? It's always *she* or *her* or *the child.*"

"I'm aware of it."

"Any particular reason?"

"I don't know. It just turned out that way."

"Since Caleb's death? Or before it as well?"

"Before it. Since his birth. Maybe even before that. There's been a gradual change in my attitude toward her."

"Did you love her originally?"

"Yes. Wait, I'm not sure of that. I thought I loved her because we'd adopted her and therefore I was supposed to love her like my own child and therefore I was determined to feel what I was supposed to feel. Once Caleb was born, well, I certainly couldn't deny that I felt something for him I had never felt for her."

"What do you feel toward her now?"

"I don't know. She spooks me."

"What does that mean? Are you afraid of her?"

"We talked about it. I can't get rid of the feeling—"

"That she was responsible for Caleb's death. I know that, and we both know that all it is is a feeling. But let's deal with present time. Are you afraid of her now?"

"I don't know."

"And I don't know what you mean by that."

She turned to him, unhooking her seat belt so she could face him, tucking her right foot under her left thigh. "I don't know means I don't know," she said levelly. "You know the cliché about adoption, don't you? You never know what you're getting."

"I've heard that."

"My mother used to say don't put money in your mouth because you never know where it's been."

"Everybody's mother used to say that."

"Well, I don't know where the child's been. I got her and I don't know what I've got. She's strange, dammit, and it's not a familiar strangeness, it's not my strangeness or David's strangeness, it's something uniquely hers and I don't know what it adds up to. Am I afraid of her? God, I *don't* know. I don't know if I should be or not. Maybe she'll murder me in my sleep. Maybe she'll poison my food. Maybe she just gives off an evil presence, the same as that godforsaken house." She fumbled in her bag, found a cigarette. "And maybe I'm just overreacting to Caleb's death, and the child's normal and innocent, and I ought to take David's advice and lie down on Gintzler's couch and tell him all my nice Freudian dreams."

130

"Is that what you want to do?"

"No."

"What *do* you want to do?"

"I want to keep on keeping on, I guess." She plugged in the dashboard lighter, lit her cigarette when it popped out. "I want to spend as much time as possible with you in nice clean sterile anonymous motel rooms. Incidentally, I want to start paying half."

"You don't have to do that."

"But I want to." She reached into her purse again, counted out some money. He shook his head impatiently. "Then I pay for the room next time," she said. "Agreed?"

"If you insist."

"I insist."

"Fair enough. Who picked out the name?"

"Huh?"

"Who decided to name her Ariel?"

"I did. I picked both names. Why?"

"They're unusual."

"I'm partial to unusual names. I was then, anyway. Odd names and old houses."

"Ariel and Caleb," he said, and frowned in thought. "Ariel and Caliban," he said.

"How's that?"

"From *The Tempest*. You know the play?"

"I must have read it. I took a Shakespeare course in college. Ariel and what?"

"Caliban. Ariel was the airy spirit who served Prospero. Caliban was a primitive type, lived in a cave, something like that."

"I wasn't thinking of the play when I named them. Unless I made some unconscious connection while I was pregnant with Caleb, thinking that it was a name that went with Ariel. Except I didn't, really. I found it in a long list of biblical names in a book on what to name the baby, and most of them were about as appetizing as Ahab and Nebuchadnezzar and Onan. Can you imagine calling a child Onan?"

"Somebody named a canary Onan. I think it was Dorothy Parker. Because he spilled his seed on the ground."

"I'll bet it was Dorothy Parker. Shadrach, Meshach and What's-his-name. They were all like that, or else they were very ordinary, and then I saw Caleb and I was struck by it. What did you say Caliban was? A primitive type? Sort of a noble savage?"

"Hardly that. He tended to lurk and howl. I think he symbolized the evil of man's basic nature."

She laughed shortly. "Then I got them backwards," she said. "Didn't I?"

That night Jeff and his wife played bridge with a couple who lived a block away. Jeff was an aggressive player, his chief fault a slight tendency to overbid, a natural outgrowth of his enthusiasm for the game. One of the things he liked about it, he had often thought, was that it was one of the few things he and Elaine did well together.

But this night the game had lost its savor for him. He played well because he could do so automatically, but a part of his attention was focused inward. He would look at Elaine, seated across the table from him, and he would think of Roberta, and his mind would find it difficult, and a little pointless, to concentrate on jump overcalls and cue bids.

How long could they go on this way? Hurrying off to motels, shutting out the world for an hour or two, rolling together in fitful passion, then washing each other off beneath the shower and slipping back into their separate lives. Sex had always had an electric intensity for the two of them, and now it seemed to possess a special urgency, as if they were calling upon the flesh to solve problems of the spirit. They could shut out the world by locking themselves in a room at the Days Inn or the Ramada; they could shut out their own thoughts by locking themselves into one another.

But they couldn't have sex all the time, nor could they spend eternity behind closed doors. Most of the time they were apart. And most of the time Jeff had his thoughts for company.

More and more, lately, they troubled him.

How could the whole thing resolve itself? Could he leave Elaine for Roberta? He looked at his wife and doubted it. She was as attractive as Roberta, and as bright. She was also rather easy to live with, and it had struck him more than once that Roberta would be hell to live with. Roberta was exciting, but the quality that excited him was bearable only in small doses. He couldn't take her twenty-four hours a day.

Another thing that had struck him was that Roberta wasn't all that tightly wrapped. From what she'd said, he gathered that David wanted her to resume visits to her psychiatrist. Jeff had a fundamental bias against psychiatrists, thought they were rarely much more than witch doctors, but he wasn't sure in this case that David was very far off the mark. Because there was something a bit more than slightly crazy about Roberta, and it often bothered him to face this fact.

Was it also this quality that excited him? He didn't like to think so, and "crazy" might be too strong a term for Roberta's emotional eccentricity, but he couldn't deny that something deep within him responded to that quality in her. Perhaps he wasn't all that tightly wrapped himself, and perhaps her nuttiness touched off a sympathetic vibration in his own psyche. Wasn't there a French phrase for that kind of shared lunacy? *Folie à deux?* Something like that?

On the other hand, just how crazy *was* Roberta? It might help to know where reality left off and her imagination took over. There was no way he could tell what she had or hadn't seen lurking in the corner of her bedroom the three nights before Caleb died. But what about Ariel? Was she some sort of twisted child, some kind of evil creature? Or was she just an ordinary little girl hovering on the brink of puberty, and no doubt being driven slightly whacky by her mother's attitude toward her?

Maybe it would help if he could answer some of those questions. He'd seen Ariel several times lately, but always from a distance and never for any length of time. Once, after he dropped Roberta, he caught a passing glimpse of the child at the streetcorner. Another time, on an afternoon when he and Roberta had not been together, he'd left the office and walked over to Ariel's school. He sat on a bench at a bus stop, a newspaper on his lap, and watched the children leaving school and heading homeward, trying not to be obvious about it lest the police pick him up as a potential child molestor. And he'd seen Ariel then, walking briskly down the street with a boy considerably shorter than herself. Probably the odd-looking little fellow Roberta had mentioned, the one who appeared to be Ariel's only friend.

A third time he'd deliberately parked his car on the route Ariel took to get to school in the morning. He sat behind the wheel, waiting, and felt quite foolish about what he was doing. All the same, something compelled him to wait until the child appeared, wearing a loden jacket over corduroy pants, her bookbag over one shoulder. She walked right past the car and never glanced in his direction, while he studied her and tried to read something in the shape of her face and the way she walked.

Her appearance was unusual, certainly, with her long pale face. But he by no means disliked the way she looked.

While no one would be likely to call her pretty, he sensed a quality about her which might well ripen into beauty. He would have liked a longer look at her, but in a matter of seconds she was past him and on her way.

How could she have killed Caleb?

A few days later he and Roberta were in another room at the same Days Inn. This time their coupling, though intense and almost desperate, seemed somehow perfunctory, as though it was something they had to get out of the way, some essential prelude to conversation. Although his climax was as powerful as it had ever been, it left him vaguely unsatisfied, like an orgasm reached by masturbation.

This time sex didn't make him sleepy. He sat up in bed and kept changing position, trying to get comfortable. Roberta once again sat on a chair, her body arranged in a collection of acute angles, smoking one cigarette after the other and displaying her collection of minor irritations.

The pilot lights on the stove kept going out. He told her, as he'd told her often enough already, to call yet another repairman and have it seen to. She insisted that was pointless. He suggested she get another stove, an electric range, for example. But she liked to cook on a gas flame, she told him, and it was a fine stove, a wonderful stove, and the only thing wrong with it was that the pilot lights kept going out.

And something new to whine about—she was convinced someone was going into Caleb's room and moving things around. In the first place, he couldn't understand why this bothered her. While he wasn't prepared to say as much to her, there was something unhealthily morbid in her whole attitude toward the baby's room. And suppose Ariel did go there, or David, just out of a desire to feel close to Caleb? What was wrong with that?

"But I don't want them in there," she explained, without troubling to say why.

He asked how she knew they went in there. Because the position of certain objects seemed to change from one day to the next. But how come she noticed this? How did she happen to visit the room so frequently herself?

"I'm drawn there," she told him. "The other night—I couldn't sleep, I got up to go to the bathroom, and on my way back I just found myself in Caleb's room. I wasn't even aware of it until I was suddenly standing there with my hand on the light switch. I suppose I was half asleep at the time."

"Do you go there during the day?"

"Of course. I have to dust."

"How often?"

She ignored the question. "I go there sometimes. Why shouldn't I? I'm his mother."

And Ariel was upsetting her. She couldn't shake the feeling that the child was sneaking around the house, skulking on the staircase, spying on her. "The only time I can relax is when she's playing her flute," she said, "because then I know where she is. But how can I relax with that damned music going on?"

"Maybe it's the flute."

"You don't mean that it's enchanted, I hope?"

"You described it as some sort of semi-toy. Maybe the sound of a regular orchestral flute would be less likely to give you chills."

"I think it's what she plays more than the instrument. But I suppose it's possible."

"Suppose she took lessons."

"I've suggested it. Maybe I could suggest it again."

But nothing *he* suggested seemed to have much effect on her, and he came to realize she didn't want to hear his suggestions. She merely wanted to voice her discontent. He felt himself growing increasingly irritated with her, and in a sort of desperation he wound up dragging her back to bed. He was fiercely potent, thrusting at her as if to hurt her, to punish her, to pierce her with his angry penis. But there was no pleasure in the thrusting, and he could neither reach a climax nor lose his erection, and when at last she pushed him away he felt angry with her and with himself.

They had met at the motel, arriving in separate cars, and this time she had paid for their room. Her car was the first to leave the motel parking lot, and he pulled out after her, followed her part way back to the city, then let her get ahead of him. His sexual desire was long gone now, but the tension that had been a part of it had merely taken a different form. He wanted to scream, to beat on the steering wheel with his fists, to swing the wheel hard left and plow across the median strip and take an oncoming car head-on.

He did none of these things. Instead he drove slowly and steadily into town, went to his office, left after a few minutes and had a cup of coffee at the Athenian on Meeting Street. He got back in his car and drove past Roberta's house. Her car was parked in front and there were lights on.

It was mid-afternoon, and there were children walking around the neighborhood, singly and in groups, on their way home from school. He drove up one street and down the next, slowing down periodically to scan the faces of the children he passed.

Then, when they were more than a block away, he spotted them. Ariel and her little friend with the glasses.

He pulled the car to a stop alongside the curb, pressed a button to lower the window, kept the motor running. The two of them were deep in conversation, unlikely to notice him, and he felt driven to stay where he was and get as good a look at the girl as he could.

The two drew nearer. When they were almost abreast of

his car, Ariel turned to look directly at Jeff. Something went through him when their eyes made contact, something cold. She stopped in her tracks. Her mouth was slightly open, her face ghostly pale. Beside her, the boy had stopped when she did and looked now to see what had attracted her attention.

Images flashed on the screen of Jeff's mind. His car, animated, with eyes for headlights, leaping the curb to bear down on the two children. Ariel, nude, her breasts tipped with staring eyes, beckoning seductively to him. The boy, dancing goat-footed like Pan. Images, amorphous ones, of blood, of lust, of death.

Only a few yards separated them. He and Ariel stared deeply into each other's eyes for an immeasurable moment. Then, with an effort, he put the car in gear and pulled away from the curb.

A block away, he had to pull over and stop again. His heart was pounding, his palms too slippery with sweat to grip the steering wheel. He dug out a handkerchief, dried his hands, mopped perspiration from his forehead.

Now what, he wondered, was *that* all about? One look into a child's eyes and he'd been thrown so far off his good reasonable center? But something *had* happened, he had to admit, and he couldn't begin to say what it was. It was as if those damned bottomless eyes of her had functioned as a mirror, showing him aspects of himself he had no desire to see.

Bobbie was overreacting to Ariel, he was still certain of that much, but he no longer felt her perceptions were so entirely out of whack. There *was* something about the child, something very damned unsettling.

Maybe he should tell Bobbie as much. But he knew, suddenly and certainly, that he would not. He would not tell *anyone* what had just happened.

TEN

"ARIEL?"

Erskine was tugging at her arm. She had turned to watch the car drive off and it was gone and she continued staring after it. With an effort she turned to face Erskine.

"That was him," she said.

"Who?"

"Didn't you recognize him?"

"The man in the car? No. Who was he?"

"The Funeral Game."

"Huh?"

"DWE—I forget the number. The license plate."

"DWE-628."

"You didn't notice his face but you memorized his license number? You're really weird, Erskine."

"I didn't even notice his license number. You told me the other day, remember?"

"And it happened to stick in your mind?"

"I remember things like that," he said patiently. "You know that."

"Well, it was him." She was a shade calmer now, but her emotions continued to wrestle inside her. There was fear, and anxiety, and off to one side was a growing sense of anger. "He was the one who dropped off Roberta the other day."

"What was it you said before about funerals?"

"He was at Caleb's funeral."

"You're sure?"

"Positive." They were walking now, bound for Erskine's house. "He even came out to the cemetery. I thought maybe he was studying to be a game-show host. You know, *the Funeral Game.*"

"Great program. How would it work?"

"You know, pick the right coffin and win a prize."

"A free embalming. I think you've got something there, Jardell."

He got carried away with the idea, suggesting various prizes and competitive trials for the program, and Ariel waited him out. Then she said, "You're missing the point. He was waiting for me."

"What do you mean?"

"Sitting there in his car with the motor running. He was waiting for me to come home from school. Then he took a close look at me and I looked at him and he drove away."

"Oh, boy."

"What's the matter?"

"Paranoia strikes again."

"I'm not being paranoid. What do you think he was doing there? He even had his window rolled down so he could get a good look."

"Lots of people roll their windows down."

"Not as cold as it is today. How many cars do you see driving by with the window down?"

"That's a point."

"He was waiting for me."

"Then why did he drive away the minute you turned up?"

"I don't know."

"You're just lucky I was along to protect you, Jardell. God only knows what fate would have awaited you otherwise."

"Be serious."

"Oh, I can't," he said, flapping his arms and making a face. "I can't because I'm a kid, and kids are never serious." He went on flapping his arms and darted on ahead, making horrible bird noises. Ariel shook her head, sighed, and walked on after him. . . .

Up in his third-floor room, Erskine said, "All right, Mr. Funeral Game was looking for you. Why?"

"You mean you want to talk about it? You're done with your imitation of a constipated vulture?"

"You just saw him twice before? At the funeral and when your mother got out of his car?"

"That's right. Maybe I saw him years ago. There's something familiar about him, but maybe that's just because he's got those television looks."

"Same as you and me."

"Funny, funny. Maybe—"

"Maybe what?"

"Maybe he's a detective."

"You've got your television shows mixed up. Why a detective?"

"Maybe Roberta hired him."

"To find out why you don't come straight home from school? Wouldn't it be easier to ask you?"

"She knows I come over here. That's not why she would hire him."

"Why, then?"

"To find out how Caleb died."

"Don't you go to a doctor for that?"

"Not if she thinks Caleb was murdered."

He sat forward, staring at her, and now his eyes looked absolutely enormous. "You think she thinks—"

"She thinks I killed Caleb." The words echoed, caroming off the walls of the little room. She had never spoken them aloud before. She was surprised her voice sounded so calm.

"Did she say anything?"

"Not exactly."

"Then—"

"It's what she thinks. The other day she asked me how I knew Caleb was dead that morning. She was in his room, she was on her way out of the room, and one look at her face and it was obvious somebody had died. I mean, it couldn't have been anything else."

"And you just knew it?"

"The idea was just right there in my head. I looked at her and it was like hearing this voice inside saying *Caleb's dead.*"

"Did you tell her?"

"Try telling Roberta something like that. I don't remember what I told her the other day. I sort of brushed off the question. I said something about not remembering that morning too clearly. I remember it, all right."

"So you think he's a detective."

She shrugged. "What else could he be?"

"And now he's looking for evidence to prove you killed your brother."

"It sounds crazy, doesn't it?"

He studied her, his face thoughtful. She wished he would take off his glasses so she could get an idea what was going through his mind.

"I don't see how he could be a detective," he said. "Or what he could do if he was one."

"Well, who else could he be?"

"Maybe he's a doctor."

"There was already a doctor who examined Caleb."

"Not that kind of doctor. Maybe he's a psychiatrist."

"She used to go to a psychiatrist. I wonder if she's crazy."

"Maybe the psychiatrist's for you."

"Huh?"

142

"Well, he's following you around, right? Maybe Roberta figures you killed Caleb because you're crazy, so she's got a psychiatrist to observe you."

She frowned. "I don't think that's how it works. I think you have to go to the psychiatrist's office and lie down on the couch and talk to him. Or he gives you tests to see if you've got a screw loose. Ink-blots and pictures to make up stories from."

"You sound like you went once."

"No, but I know how it works. From things I've read. And there was that program, it was a special about a teenager with mental problems. Didn't you see it?"

"No. Maybe Roberta found a psychiatrist who makes house calls."

"Maybe."

"Or maybe he's some combination of psychiatrist and detective. Or maybe he's somebody else altogether. Maybe he's an interior decorator and she wants new drapes for the living room."

"Then why would he turn up at the funeral? And why would he be parked and waiting for us today?"

"Maybe he's a pervert with a thing for twelve-year-old girls."

"And dead babies."

"Right. It's one of your standard perversions."

"And he's one of your standard perverts."

"You got it, Jardell. You know what? I'm not a psychiatrist *or* a detective—"

"Just a pervert."

"—but I bet I could *be* a detective."

"What do you mean?"

"I mean I think I'll find out who he is."

"How?"

"I have my methods, Watson."

"C'mon, how?"

He smiled, pleased with himself. "You'll see," he said.

Jeff couldn't sleep.

He kept turning in the bed, trying to find a comfortable position. He had been tired by the time he got into bed and thought sleep would come quickly, but he couldn't seem to unwind. A mental tape kept replaying the scene that had taken place earlier, when he and Ariel had stared so long, and hard, into each other's eyes.

She was just a *child*, he told himself. Awkward, innocent, unformed. And yet, damn it, there was some quality of secret knowledge in her gaze that he could neither pin down nor dismiss out of hand. And now the memory of it wouldn't let him sleep.

Beside him, Elaine's breathing was deep and regular. For a moment he considered reaching for her, seeking release in the warm depths of her flesh. She wouldn't mind that sort of awakening. She always welcomed it, always dropped off to sleep easily afterward.

Perhaps he had a real need for that sort of release. His lovemaking with Bobbie that afternoon had left him frustrated, and maybe that was what was keeping him awake. On the other hand, he was uncertain of his capacity to perform the act. Be a hell of a thing to wake Elaine and then be unable to deliver.

He adjusted the pillow once again, rolled over onto his side, then onto his back once again.

He reached, not for Elaine, but for himself. He stroked himself idly, mechanically, and felt his flesh respond with an urgency that approached pain. He sought to fill his mind with fantasies that had served him in the past, flickering images of anonymous flesh straight from the nether world of pornography.

It was Ariel's face, pale and shining, that kept intruding. And, when his flesh coughed and spat in orgasm, it was her cool eyes that burned in his mind.

They were in Erskine's room Monday afternoon before either of them mentioned the man in the Buick. Ariel had thought of the man on the way home from school, looking over her shoulder once or twice to see if they were being followed, but she hadn't felt like saying anything to Erskine.

Now he said, "Jeffrey D. Channing, 105 Fontenoy Drive, Charleston Heights. Law offices at 229 Meeting Street. Home phone 989-8029. Office phone 673-7038. His wife's name is Elaine and he has two daughters, Greta and Deborah. What else would you like to know about him?"

"Who is he?"

"The funeral man. Mr. DWE-628, and his Buick's a year old, by the way. Your detective. I'll bet I'm a better detective than he is."

"You found out all that about him since Friday? Tell me again." She listened carefully this time while he repeated everything. "A lawyer," she said thoughtfully. "Why would she have a lawyer following me?"

"Maybe she wants to sue you."

"Fontenoy Drive in Charleston Heights. That's not far from my old house."

"And the funeral parlor's in that neighborhood too, isn't it?"

"Right."

"Maybe he popped into the funeral because he happened to be in the neighborhood."

"How did you find all this out, Erskine?"

"I told you. I have my methods, Jardell."

"You're not going to tell me?"

"You're really impressed, aren't you?"

"I just don't see how you did it."

"A magician never reveals his tricks."

"Are you serious? You're not going to tell me?"

"Oh, of course I'll tell you," he said, grinning. "If you'll play the flute for me."

"I don't think I can."

"Well, in that case—"

"Erskine—"

"I'll tell you," he said gently. "You'll play the flute for me someday. You can always play *my* flute, Ariel."

"Gross pig."

"Oink. The first thing I did, Saturday morning, was steal a hubcap."

"From Channing's car? How did you know where to find it?"

"I didn't. You want to let me tell this?"

"Sorry."

"I just took a screwdriver and I went out and stole a hubcap, and *not* from his car. As a matter of fact it was from a car parked all the way over on Savage Street. That's how far I had to walk before I found a Buick with nobody around to see me pry the hubcap off."

"Why a Buick? Oh, because his car's a Buick."

"Good thinking. I brought it home and I told my mother it rolled off a car and the driver didn't notice it but I got the license number. Guess what license number?"

"DWE-something something something."

"628. I told her the driver would probably like to get his hubcap back, and she was really proud of me for being so public-spirited, but she didn't know how to find out who he was. I had to suggest it to her."

"Suggest what?"

"That she should call the Department of Motor Vehicles and tell them what happened. I thought of calling myself, and if I did that I wouldn't have had to actually steal the hubcap, because they wouldn't ask to see it over the phone. But I figured they wouldn't be as likely to cooperate with a kid. I thought of trying to sound grown up. I didn't think it would work."

"Probably not."

"Anyway, she made the call. You know my mother. God

help anybody who tries to tell her it's against policy to give out information, blah blah blah. She got his name and address and a description of the car, and it was the same car, a maroon and black Buick Electra. Then she said she'd drive me out there so I could return the hubcap."

"Did you go?"

"She couldn't take me right away, and I said maybe I'd go by bus instead. I think she was afraid I would get lost, but she didn't come right out and say so, and she just told me to call first."

"So you called them?"

"I pretended to. I looked up the number in the phone book, and that's when I saw the office listing on Meeting Street. Then I went out and walked past the office, just to be doing something, and I kept walking and wound up seeing a movie at the theater on King near George. The Olympia. They really ought to call it the King George. There were two science fiction movies and I got there in the middle of one and walked out in the middle of the other. I left the hubcap under my seat."

"Clever."

"Well, I had to ditch it somewhere. I wasn't going to try putting it back on the car on Savage Street."

"He'll be missing a hubcap and never know it played a part in a larger drama."

"It's a shame we can't tell him. Anyway, I came home and later that night she asked me if Mr. Channing gave me a reward. I said no, and she said didn't he even reimburse me for my busfare, and I said no because I wasn't thinking too fast, and she said that was terrible and she had a good notion to give him a piece of her mind."

"Did she call him?"

"She was getting ready to. Then I managed to tell her that a kid answered the door and took the hubcap, and of course the kid didn't think to give me money, and I didn't really want any money anyway. And she said why didn't

I say so in the first place, and of course I would have if I'd thought of it, but I just mumbled something and went upstairs."

"That's amazing," she said. She thought for a moment. "There were other things you said before. About him being a lawyer."

"It said so in the phone book."

"And his wife's name, and his kids."

"Elaine and Greta and Deborah. I got that over the phone yesterday afternoon."

"What did you do, pretend you were taking a survey?"

"No. I called up and asked to speak to Margaret Channing."

"And?"

"And the woman who answered said there was no Margaret there, and she didn't know of any Margaret Channing in the Charleston area, that her name was Elaine Channing. Then I said Margaret was a kid, and she said her daughters were named Greta and Deborah. For the hell of it I asked her if she had a son and she said she didn't. I thought of asking her if her husband was a pervert but I decided against it."

"Probably wise of you."

"That's what I figured."

She got up, turned on Erskine's short-wave radio, waited for the tubes to warm up. "Jeffrey Channing," she said. "Who is he? Why is he following me around?"

"He wasn't exactly following you. It's more like lurking in ambush."

"Terrific. How old are his kids?"

"What's the difference?"

"Maybe I used to know them. I think I remember where Fontenoy Drive is. It's not far from our old house. Maybe I went to school with Greta and Deborah."

"We could find out."

"How?"

"We could take the bus out there tomorrow after school. Or we could wait for the weekend."

"I suppose so."

"Or there's a faster way. C'mon."

He used the phone in his mother's room on the second floor, dialing the number rapidly, asking to speak to Greta. "This is Graham Littlefield, Mrs. Channing. I'm in Greta's class in school. . . . Hi, Greta. It's Graham. Sure you do. Look, I'm having a party and I wanted to check how old you are. Uh-huh. When's your birthday? And you'll be ten then? Thanks. Oh, by the way, how old is Deborah? Your sister. Right, Debbie. Okay, thanks a lot, Greta. See you tomorrow."

He replaced the receiver and looked up in triumph. "Greta's nine. She'll be ten the eleventh of February. Don't forget to send her a card."

"You're amazing."

"I know. Debbie's the younger one. That's what they call her, not Deborah, and when I called her Deborah Greta giggled. She does that a lot. Debbie's six and a half, going on seven. Why do people say that, do you suppose? *Everybody* who's six and a half is going on seven."

"I guess I didn't know them. They're a lot younger."

"I guess not."

"How come you said Graham Littlefield?"

"Well, I had to say something. Now she'll spend the next few days trying to figure out which kid is Graham. And waiting for an invitation to his party."

"Then she'll read in the paper when you kill Graham and she'll get suspicious."

"When I kill Graham—oh, right, I forgot that conversation. Maybe that's why I used his name. It's easier than killing him. We could still go look at Channing's house tomorrow or Saturday. If you want."

"What for?"

"I don't know. Same reason the bear went over the

mountain, I suppose. To see what he could see."

"Maybe." She was impressed with what he'd found out, and she decided to let him know it. "You're a good detective," she said. "You're really great over the phone. And I never would have thought of that business with the hubcap."

He flushed, pleased. "I have my methods," he said. "C'mon, let's get back upstairs. The radio's on."

He led the way, taking the attic stairs at top speed. . . .

A little later she said, "Erskine? I was just thinking."

"It's a nasty habit."

"So's picking your nose."

"I wasn't picking my nose."

"I know."

"Anyway, did you ever stop and think that people say it's disgusting if you pick your nose, but suppose you *never* picked your nose and you just sort of let all that crud collect in there. Wouldn't that be even more disgusting?"

"That's the grossest and most revolting thing you've said in weeks."

"But if you think about it—"

"I don't want to think about it."

"Anyway, you're the one who brought up nosepicking."

"I'll never do it again."

"What were you thinking?"

"Oh. About you being a detective and all. It was just a thought, actually."

"What?"

"Well, maybe a detective could find out who my real parents were. That's all." She looked away. "It was just a thought that came to me."

ELEVEN

THE Child Placement Service of Greater Charleston occupied a suite of offices on the top floor of a three-story suburban office building on Sam Rittenberg Boulevard. The corporate motto, painted on the frosted glass outer door, was *"Bringing Parent and Child Together."* Jeff read it and thought of alternatives. *"Caveat Adoptor"* had a nice classical ring to it, he thought. Or Roberta's phrase—*"You Never Know What You're Getting."*

In the sparsely furnished waiting room he leafed through a *National Geographic.* Instead of paying any mind to the pictures of Cecropia moths and Trobriand Islanders, he kept seeing Ariel's pale face as he'd seen it Friday from his car. That moment when she turned and met his eyes with her own was engraved firmly in his memory. If he closed his eyes he could see her as he'd seen her then, could recall in all its flavor the sense of *déjà vu* he'd experienced at the time. As if this were a face he'd known before, in dreams or in another lifetime.

Of course he had seen Ariel before—the time he dropped off Roberta, and before that at Caleb's funeral. But this was the first time he had ever truly experienced the child.

The child. That was Roberta's phrase for her, and he was

beginning to understand the usage. There was something curious about her, a quality unquestionably evident even in a brief meeting of the eyes. A sort of transported quality, at once disturbing and compelling.

"Mr. Channing? This way please."

He followed a slender young woman into a sizable windowed office where a thickset woman in her late thirties sat behind a large blond oak desk. She rose at Jeff's approach, introduced herself as Ms. Anne-Marie Craig, and shook hands like a man. She sat down again and Jeff took a chair across the desk from her.

"Now let me make certain I understand the situation," she said. "You're an attorney representing Mr. and Mrs. David Jardell. Is that right?"

"Not quite. My client is Mrs. Jardell."

"The Jardells have separated?"

He shook his head. "But my inquiries are being undertaken on Mrs. Jardell's behalf and without her husband's knowledge."

"I see." Her eyes dropped to a sheet of paper on her desk. "The Jardells adopted a female infant through our agency some twelve years ago. I believe they named her Ariel."

"That's correct."

"And your purpose in coming here—"

"Is to inquire into Ariel's parentage."

"I'm afraid that's impossible. CPS has a policy absolutely forbidding the release of such information. It's a two-way street, Mr. Channing. The natural mother is absolutely prevented from making contact with her child, and the child and his adoptive parents are not permitted to know who the mother is. I'm afraid we're quite strict about that, and I'm sure you can appreciate the advantages of the rule."

"There have been some cases recently challenging that sort of policy."

Ms. Craig nodded briskly. "Several of them, and the

152

courts have ruled differently in different states. There's an argument that an adopted child has a right to information about his or her parentage. Our own policy has been revised accordingly, without altering its basic purpose. When a child reaches maturity, which we define as the age of eighteen, he or she can advise us that he or she—why don't I just say *she* since the Jardell child is female?"

"Fine."

"She can advise us that she wants to contact her natural mother. At this point we release no information. Instead we make an effort to contact the mother ourselves, informing her that the daughter wishes to make contact. If the natural mother is not interested in allowing this, her right to privacy is respected. If the natural mother does want the child made aware of her identity, then we furnish the child with that information. In this particular case, the child will not be eighteen years old for over five years. When the child is a minor, we do not even set about attempting to trace the mother and ascertain her wishes. That's policy, Mr. Channing, and we won't bend it."

He nodded; he'd expected as much. "Suppose what I want, what my client wants, is information *about* the natural parents."

"Information which would not serve specifically to identify them?"

"That's right. The question's a medical one, Ms. Craig. My client's concerned about the medical history of the biological parents and the possibility of inherited predisposition to disease."

"If there were anything of that sort she would have been informed prior to the adoption. You mean some sort of genetic illness like hemophilia or Huntington's chorea? I checked our files before seeing you, Mr. Channing. Our records indicate the natural mother was in perfect health and had nothing ominous in her medical history."

"And the father?"

"We have no data on the father."

"He's unknown?"

"Unknown to us," Ms. Craig said. "He may have been known to the mother but she may have elected to keep that information to herself. Many of our mothers prefer to do that."

He thought of Roberta, keeping the fact of Caleb's paternity from him. Did Ariel's father even know that he'd sired a child?

"So there's nothing known about the father's medical history," he said.

"Nothing, I'm afraid. Is Ariel displaying symptoms of some illness?"

"Not a physical illness."

"Oh?"

"My client is concerned about her daughter's emotional health. She thought if there were any information available about the mother, information not dealing with her identity per se, it might be helpful in evaluating her present condition. If you could tell us anything about her personality, her lifestyle, her background—"

"Excuse me a moment, Mr. Channing." He waited while she disappeared through a door on the left. He sat looking out through the window, watching traffic on the boulevard, until she returned.

"Nothing," she said. "I'm afraid there's no one here who worked at CPS at the time Ariel was born, so no one remembers her mother. Our records don't indicate mental illness or eccentricity of personality or anything of the sort. Is Ariel institutionalized at present?"

"No, she's living with the Jardells."

"Is she receiving psychiatric treatment?"

"No."

"But your client is concerned about her emotional state?"

"Yes."

"Ariel must be on the verge of puberty. A great many children find that stage a stressful one. Sometimes the answer is treatment, sometimes they just have to be allowed to grow out of it. But the problem's rarely hereditary, Mr. Channing. Adoptive parents sometimes like to think a problem is hereditary in order to absolve themselves of blame. Perhaps you could find a tactful way to suggest as much to Mrs. Jardell."

TWELVE

THE lilting song of the flute filled Ariel's bedroom. But she was not playing now. She sat on the edge of her bed listening to a cassette she had recorded earlier. She heard it all the way through, sitting with her eyes closed, her body swaying very slightly with the music. Now and then expressions played over her face in response to something she heard.

When the music stopped she rewound the tape and let it play through a second time. This time she did not give the music her undivided attention. While she listened, she wrote in her diary.

This is very strange. Listening to myself on Erskine's tape recorder. It's like hearing myself for the first time. I can't really hear myself when I play because I have to concentrate on playing.

The reason all of this is happening is I couldn't play the flute for Erskine. He kept saying he'd like to hear me play and I kept saying he wasn't missing much, and finally the other day I dragged the flute over to his house after school and we went up to his room and I tried to play. But I couldn't make it come out right. I could hear the notes in

157

my head but I couldn't seem to find them on the flute.

So he thought of the tape recorder. It's a Japanese one, portable, and you can plug it in or use batteries, and you get half an hour on each side of the tape. He said I could take it home with me and just put it on when I play, and before I knew it I would forget it was even in the same room with me.

"You've been on tape before," he said, and he found a cassette and played it for me, and it was a conversation we had the other day about how he found out I have to be eighteen before I can try to trace my real mother. He had taped it without me knowing anything of it.

When he played the tape I got properly pissed. I don't guess there was anything on it you couldn't play in church but it was the idea of him doing it secretly that bothered me. I told him if he was President he could get impeached for carrying on like that, taping people without them knowing it, and then we would up running some jokes on the subject which took the edge off my pissed-offedness. (If there's even such a word, which there is *now!*)

Anyway, listening to myself talking on tape was weird in the same way that listening to myself play the flute on tape was. That's nothing like I always thought I sounded. Erskine says everybody's voice sounds weird to them because you normally hear yourself differently from the way other people hear you, because of some of the sound being carried to your ears through the bones in your skull. Sounds travel differently through solid objects, he said, which I told him would apply more to his head than to mine.

He said he always figured mine was hollow.

What he should do is get contact lenses when he's older. His eyes are very attractive.

Anyway, tomorrow he can listen to *Ariel Plays the Flute*. He says once that's over and done with I'll be able to play in front of him with no hassle, but I don't know about that.

What's funny is I can play with Roberta in the house and it never bothers me. Of course I don't actually play in front of her. And the fact that I know she's not listening probably makes it easier.

The following afternoon the two of them walked home from school together. Ariel had not brought the recorder to school so they walked to her house to pick it up. The maroon Buick didn't show up. She thought she'd seen the car twice since the time she and Channing had taken a long look at each other, but there had been no confrontation since then.

Roberta's car was gone when they reached the house. "Come on in," Ariel suggested.

"It's okay. I'll wait out here."

"Nobody's home. Roberta's out somewhere. You've never seen my house."

"I can see it fine from here. Just get the recorder and we'll go to my place."

"We always go to your place."

"I'm a creature of habit."

She started for the door. Then she changed her mind and turned around. "The thing is," she said, "I really want you to come in."

"Fuck it," he said. "I don't mind."

"The reason I like you is you're charming."

"I was wondering what it was."

She led him into the house and up the stairs to the second floor. The tape recorder was all packed up in its canvas carrying case. He asked her if she wouldn't like to play it then and there but she shook her head. "Listen to it by yourself," she said.

"You'd be embarrassed?"

"I guess so."

"Did you play it back or anything? Or haven't you listened to it either?"

"I listened to it twice. Two and a half times, actually, and then Roberta came up and said maybe it was a little late for music. Meaning it was driving her crazy. Two and a half times that I listened to it plus the time I played to record it. She didn't even know it was a tape and she said I'd be tired today from playing so long. Oh, and look at this. She gave me this the day before yesterday. *Teach Yourself to Play the Flute.*"

"Is it any good?"

"How would you like it if your mother gave you a book that would tell you how to turn the car radio on and off?"

"Oh."

"It's the worst. If you go all the way through the book you wind up learning how to play *Go Tell Aunt Rhody* and *Be Kind to Your Web-Footed Friends.* Just what I want to sit around and do. The thing is she thinks she's being nice to me. I'm tons more advanced than the book but she doesn't have any idea."

"What song did you say? Not *Web-Footed Friends* but the other one."

"*Go Tell Aunt Rhody.*"

"I never heard of it," he said. "What are you supposed to tell old Aunt Rhody?"

"That her bird died," Ariel said. She sang:

> Go tell Aunt Rhody
> Go tell Aunt Rhody
> Go tell Aunt Rho-o-o-ody
> The old gray goose is dead.

He looked at her. "That's it?"

"There's other verses telling what he died of and how broken-up Aunt Rhody is, but that's it. That's all the

160

notes there are to play in it."

"It's got a nice beat to it," he said solemnly, "and the words tell a story, and you could dance to it. I'd give it about a seventy-five."

They went downstairs and she showed him through the first floor. In the kitchen she poured two glasses of milk and found a package of chocolate-covered graham crackers.

"It's a neat house," he said.

"I hope we don't move."

"Why would you move?"

"Crazy Roberta. She wants to sell the house and move."

"Where to?"

"I don't know."

"Like out of the neighborhood or what?"

"I don't know. She's crazy, that's all. The house spooks her or something. I heard her talking to David and she was saying the same thing on the phone the other day."

"Do you think you would really move?"

"Who knows?" She rinsed out her glass in the sink, turned to him. "Aren't you going to finish your milk?"

"I've had enough."

"Then give me your glass. Roberta's been acting really weird lately."

"How?"

"Oh, giving me strange looks when she doesn't think I'm paying any attention. I'll get a glimpse of her out of the corner of my eye and there's old Roberta studying me like a rare species of insect."

"Ugh."

"Sorry," she said. Erskine had a thing about bugs, and it even bothered him to hear about them. "I'm glad I was adopted. Otherwise I'd worry about going crazy like Roberta. I wish I didn't have to wait until I was eighteen."

"I suppose you could try lying about your age."

"Funny."

"You were going to work on David, weren't you? To find out if he knows anything?"

"I haven't gotten around to it yet."

"Well, don't expect too much, anyway. Even if you find out who your mother is, she'll probably turn out to be just as bad as Roberta. You met *my* mother, don't forget."

Ariel had met Mrs. Wold several days earlier when the woman was returning home from work just as Ariel was getting ready to leave. Mrs. Wold was a tall overbearing woman, her slate gray hair pulled severely back from a bulbous forehead, and she had spoken with the overprecise enunciation of a kindergarten teacher. *"I am so happy to meet you, Ariel. I want to tell you how much Mr. Wold and I appreciate your spending time with Erskine. We are both just so pleased that he finally has a friend. You know, Erskine is a very special child. His health is extremely delicate and that has affected his development in many ways. Believe me, Ariel, my husband and I are both very grateful to you."*

Erskine had been in the room throughout this little speech. Afterward he and Ariel could hardly look at each other.

"Parents are horrible," he said now. "Real or adopted, it doesn't make any difference. Parents suck."

"And what happens when you're a parent?"

He shook his head. "That'll never happen."

"Why? If kids are better than parents, wouldn't you want to have some around?"

"Are you kidding? Actually bring something into your house that's going to *know* what a total shit you are? That would be really stupid, Jardell."

She stared at him. "Erskine Weird," she said.

"Very funny."

"Come on," she said. "I'll show you the upstairs."

"We were already there."

"Have to get the tape recorder anyway. And all you saw was my room. Come on."

"What are you doing?"

"Blowing out the pilot light."

"Why?"

"No particular reason. Come *on.*"

She showed him the master bedroom and he was not surprised by the twin beds. "They had a double bed at the other house," she told him. "But they got rid of it when we moved."

"They actually used to sleep together?"

"No, they took turns using the bed."

"Mine would, if it was a choice between that or sleeping together."

"Well, they slept together once, didn't they?"

"Sure, and look what it got them."

"You."

"Right. So they won't make that mistake again. How about if we screw in their bed? That would be better than blowing out a pilot light." He pointed at a closed door. "What's that, the bathroom? No, the bathroom's down the hall. What's that?"

"Caleb's room."

"The room where he—"

"Died," Ariel said.

"What's it like?"

"Like a baby's room. A crib and a bathinet and a playpen and things like that."

"And the door's kept shut all the time? Does anybody ever go in there?"

"Roberta, sometimes. She sneaks in and out sometimes."

"Honestly?"

"Uh-huh."

"How about you? Do you ever go in there?"

"I used to. I would play the flute for Caleb or tickle him or things like that."

"What's wrong, Ariel?"

"Nothing's wrong. Why?"

"The expression on your face. Like something bad was happening in your mind."

"No. Maybe it was just the lighting."

"I suppose."

"I wasn't thinking about anything besides what I was saying."

"Don't you ever go in there now that the room's empty?"

"It's not empty. All his things are there. The only thing missing is Caleb."

"Well? Don't you ever go in?"

"I'm not supposed to. Roberta says nobody should go in there."

"So?"

She hesitated. "Once or twice when I was all alone in the house. I don't know. It feels funny."

"When you have an old house, there's always rooms that somebody died in at one time or another."

"Any minute now I'm going to start talking about bugs."

"I didn't know it bothered you."

"A little."

"Can we go in there?"

She thought for a moment, then shook her head.

"Open the door and let me look in? Roberta won't know and I won't actually go inside if you don't want. Please?"

She sighed. "Open it if you want. I don't want to look. And promise you won't walk in?"

"Sure.. You want me to cross my heart?"

She turned away and regarded the far wall for a few moments. The door to Caleb's room opened. Erskine said nothing. Then there was the sound of the door closing and Ariel turned toward him again.

"I see what you mean," he said.

"Do you?"

"Yeah." His eyes swam out of focus behind his thick lenses. "Hey," he said, "where's the attic?"

"On top of the house. We were going to keep it underneath but the basement was already there and the two of them would have crowded each other."

"Don't be a cunt, Jardell."

"Oh, charming," she said. "You haven't called me a cunt since the day before yesterday."

"I didn't *call* you a cunt. I told you not to *be* one. Where's the stairs to the attic?" She pointed. "What's it like up there?"

"I don't know."

"You don't go up there?"

"No. There's just things that haven't been unpacked. Suitcases and things."

"But you've never explored up there?"

She shook her head.

He flung open the door and took the stairs at a dead run. She hesitated for only a moment, then trudged up after him.

The attic was unfinished, with no insulation beneath the rafters. Accordingly it was very cold and uncomfortable up there. Ariel would have been perfectly happy to take a quick look around and go back downstairs, but Erskine was in his element. He couldn't get over the fact that Ariel had lived in the house for the better part of a year without once investigating the attic.

"People leave valuable things in attics," he said. "It happens all the time. They hide something and then die before they have a chance to tell anybody where it is. Or it's not valuable when they put it there but it becomes valuable years later."

"Like *True Confession* magazines," Ariel offered.

"Very funny."

But it turned out to be more interesting than she had thought it would. There were no lights, which made things difficult, and the cold certainly interfered with her enjoyment of the project, but it was definitely interesting. The dozen or more Jardell cartons were off on one side, easily ignored once they had been identified. And the other cartons and bushel baskets and heaps of articles were all the debris of previous occupants of the house.

There was a steamer trunk filled with old curtains and drapery, all smelling of must and mold. There was a stack of local newspapers with dates in the forties. There were several cartons of old clothing, all of them smelling as uninviting as the drapes.

And there was the picture.

It was lying flat in a corner and she very nearly missed it. Then she happened on it and just gave it a quick glance, not wanting to waste any time on it, not really wanting to waste any more time in the cold attic. And then she saw what it was.

"Hey!"

"Find something?"

"It's a picture. I think it's a painting."

"Of what?"

"I can't tell. Help me get it over to the window, will you? I want to see it in the light."

"Can't you manage it?"

"The frame weighs a ton."

Together they got the picture over near the window where enough light filtered through to illuminate the painting. It was a portrait. The frame was a massive wooden rectangle with an oval opening. The frame had been gilded, and most of the gold paint still adhered.

The oil portrait was of a woman who looked to be in her

twenties or early thirties. Her perfectly straight light brown hair flowed down onto her bare shoulders. Her face was wedge-shaped, her skin very pale but glowing with vitality. Her hands, narrow and long-fingered, were clasped at her waist, holding a single red rose. Her eyes, small and pale, looked directly out of the picture at the viewer, burning with a passionate intensity.

"I wonder who she was."

Erskine shook his head. "Must be very old." He extended a forefinger, touched the painting where the woman's hair met her shoulder. The surface sported a web of tiny cracks. "All dried out," he announced. "It could be a hundred years old. Maybe older."

"I wonder if she lived here. In this house."

"Maybe. She could have lived here a hundred years ago. Or maybe she lived in England and never saw this house and ten years ago somebody found her in an antique shop and bought her and stuck her in this attic." He giggled. "There's no way to tell, is there? Unless there's a signature on the painting and we can find out something about the artist."

They looked, but there was no signature visible.

"She lived here," Ariel announced.

"Maybe."

"She did."

He looked at her curiously. "Whatever you say," he said. He extended his forefinger again but this time he touched the woman where her cleavage began just above the top of her gown. He moved his finger down over her breasts. "Nicely built," he said.

"You're disgusting."

"I know."

"Don't do that."

"Are you crazy, Jardell? All of a sudden I'm not allowed to feel up a picture?"

167

"Just quit it, okay?"

"Okay, but I think you're nuts."

"Help me carry her downstairs."

"Why?"

"So I can see her better."

"Wouldn't it be easier to get a flashlight and bring it up here? Remember how much trouble we had dragging her over to the window."

"If you don't want to help me, just say so."

"I didn't say that. What's the matter?"

"Nothing," she said. She didn't know what was the matter but the picture was having an effect on her. And she wanted it downstairs in her room.

"I'll help you, Ariel."

"Not if it's too heavy."

"No, we can carry it. If we got it this far we can carry it downstairs."

"Maybe it's too heavy. I'll ask David to do it. Your delicate condition and all."

"You fucking shit."

"I'm sorry. I don't know why I said that."

"You've been weird all day. Have you got your period or something, Jardell?"

She started to giggle.

"What's so funny?"

"As a matter of fact I do," she said, blushing. "But I don't see what that has to do with anything. Can we please take her downstairs now? *Please?*"

Carrying the portrait downstairs to Ariel's room turned out to be less of an ordeal than either of them had anticipated. Once they had the right sort of grip on it the weight was not difficult to manage. They placed the picture on the floor, leaning it up against Ariel's dresser for support. She got a towel from the hall cupboard and wiped all of the dust from the picture and its frame.

The woman's visage, arresting enough in the dimly-lit attic, was positively imperious in a bright room. The woman's gaze was almost hypnotic.

"She's beautiful," Erskine said. His voice was pitched higher than usual, and he sounded as though he was surprised at the beauty of the woman.

"And she belongs in here."

"Not on the floor, though."

"On that wall."

He looked where she pointed. "It would fit there."

"I'll get David to hang her for me."

"You figure they'll let you keep it?"

"Why not? She belongs in this room."

"You keep saying that."

"Look at her," she said. "Who does she look like?"

"I don't know."

"*Look* at her."

He shrugged, studied the painting once again. Ariel tried to watch his eyes but his glasses concealed their expression. Then Erskine wheeled abruptly and scanned Ariel's face. He looked at the painting, then back at Ariel again.

"Oh," he said.

"It's true, isn't it? I'm not just imagining it?"

"She looks like you."

"She really does, doesn't she?"

"The shape of the head, the way the mouth is formed, the eyes. But you don't stare that way."

"Just watch me," she said.

Her eyes burned into his. Erskine held her stare for a moment, then took a step backward and took his eyes away. "Don't do that," he said. "I don't like it."

"All right."

"She really does look like you. It's incredible."

"I know."

David hung the picture for her after dinner. She had been prepared for an argument from one or both of them but none was forthcoming. Roberta had started to ask what she had been doing in the attic in the first place, but Ariel's vague reply that they had just been looking around evidently satisfied her. David at least showed a certain amount of interest in the picture, while Roberta barely glanced at it, merely wondering aloud why Ariel would want a gloomy thing like that on her wall.

David pointed out a few interesting things about the picture. He showed her how the artist had painted the foliage of the rose in such a way that part of the model's hands were concealed. "Hands are sometimes hard to paint," he explained. "A lot of old portraits are the work of amateur artists, gifted people who taught themselves how to paint. They lacked academic training and so they don't always get proportions correct. They don't know much about perspective and they don't understand anatomy. This artist had more of a feel for his subject than most of them. There's a lot of character in her face."

She summarized the events in her diary before going to bed, noting David's comments:

> But he didn't see the resemblance. He looked at how the hands were painted but never noticed who she looks like. But Erskine didn't notice either until he really took a good look at her.
>
> I saw it right away.
>
> No I didn't either. What happened was this: I looked at the picture and I *recognized* her. That's what it was. I never saw her before but I recognized her and it felt strange. I got dizzy for a minute. Then I was looking at her and I realized why I recognized her, namely that she looked like me.
>
> But I recognized her before I knew that.
>
> She is the beautiful stranger.

I'm not beautiful. But she really is beautiful and she really does look like me.

When I look at her I get the feeling she has things to tell me. If only she could talk. But if she really could talk she'd probably just say how boring it was to spend fifty years in a dusty attic.

I wonder how long she really was up there waiting for me to find her. I wonder who she was or is or whichever it should be.

I keep writing a few words and then looking up at her again.

Tonight would have been a good time to ask David about my mother. He was in a good mood, explaining to me about the painting. Then he went downstairs to his study and I thought about going in and sitting on his lap like I used to do, and lighting his pipe for him. But I just didn't feel up to it. I wanted to be alone in my room. Alone with her, I mean.

She put her diary aside, played the flute for a few minutes, then had her bath and went to bed. Her room was quite dark, but for a moment she fancied she could see the eyes in the portrait, beaming down at her in the darkness. Before she could entertain this thought for any length of time she fell into a deep and dreamless sleep.

Sometime in the middle of the night she got out of bed and went to the bathroom. After she had used the toilet she went downstairs to the kitchen. The stairs were silent beneath her feet. Without turning on a light she went through the kitchen drawers until she found a small box that contained five of its original six candles. The candles were four inches long and made simply of ordinary white wax. She took one of the candles from the box and put the rest back in the drawer.

There was an empty applesauce jar in the garbage. She

washed and dried its lid, then lit a match and melted the bottom of the candle enough to affix it to the center of the jar lid.

Back in her room, she positioned her bedside table so that it was centered directly beneath the portrait. She cleared everything from the table and placed the candle in its center. She lit the candle with another match and sat cross-legged on the floor so that her eyes were level with its flame. She folded her hands in her lap and looked up at the portrait.

When the candle had burned to within an inch of the jar lid she blew it out and got back into bed. And fell asleep immediately.

When she awoke in the morning she remembered what she had done but the memory was hazy and she thought it might all have been a dream. But the bedside table was underneath the portrait and there was a jar lid on it with the stub of a white candle on it.

Quickly she got out of bed and placed the candle in her bottom dresser drawer. She returned the table to its usual position beside her bed and restored her lamp and clock to their usual places. She had to hunt for the folder of matches; they turned up underneath her bed, and she put them in the dresser drawer with the candle.

If they knew about this they'd lock me up, she thought. They'd think I was really crazy.

THIRTEEN

THERE was a sound that woke her, a sharp dry sound like a tree branch snapping. Then she was awake, and sitting up in bed, and the woman was in the corner of the room near the window. She was perfectly defined now, her pale face gleaming, her eyes fiery. The shawl covered her shoulders and was draped over her décolletage.

She was holding a rose.

Roberta stared at her, heart pounding, throat dry. The woman's image shimmered, swayed in the darkened room, the pale face glowing as if illuminated from inside. Roberta tried to avert her eyes but the woman's gaze held them.

"Jeff!" she called out. The name echoed in the room and she realized she had made a mistake. "David . . . I meant David!"

There was no response. She tried to cry out again but the two names fought one another and no sound escaped her lips. Roberta looked at the woman's eyes, dropped her own eyes to the rose clasped in her hands. Its petals were red as blood, and drops of blood hung from its thorns.

Again Roberta tried to call out and could not. With an effort she turned her eyes from the woman and looked across at the other twin bed, one hand extended to rouse her sleeping husband. But there was something wrong with the other bed. Roberta couldn't touch the body lying on it because there were rails in the way, as if it were not a bed at all but an oversize crib.

And who was it who lay on top of the bed? David? Jeff?

No, it was a skeleton. Bare bleached bones lying uncovered on the bed, and she wanted to scream, and she looked at the woman and saw the pale face grow larger and more vivid, remaining where it was but seeming to come closer, so close that Roberta could see brushstrokes on the forehead and the sides of the face . . .

Brushstrokes?

Crib rails on her husband's bed?

With a great effort she hurled herself up out of sleep. It had been a dream. Sleeping, she had dreamed an awakening but had emerged only into the dream itself. Now she sat up in bed and of course there was no apparition in the room, no rails on David's bed. He was deeply asleep, his body giving off its familiar night-sweat scent of alcohol, his breathing slow and regular. He had not awakened because she had not made a sound. A dream, all a dream.

She wanted to get up. Drink a glass of water, smoke a cigarette. But the dream had been exhausting and the relief at having escaped from it had a profoundly sedative effect. She heaved a sigh, lay back for a moment, closed her eyes for a moment, and was instantly asleep again.

When she awakened hours later at her usual time, she did not remember the dream. Perhaps she repressed the memory; perhaps she had been so briefly awake and had fallen asleep again so quickly that the dream had had little opportunity to impress itself upon her conscious mind. In any event, she went downstairs and had breakfast and set about the business of the day without any thought of the terror that had interrupted her sleep.

Then, shortly before noon, it came back to her in a flood. She remembered what she had experienced and how it had felt, and her chest and throat constricted at the recollection. She could close her eyes and picture the woman, standing just as she had stood in the dream, her features clear as they had never been during her three appearances immediately before Caleb's death. Then she had been wispy and insubstantial, like the ghost Roberta had assumed her to be. In the dream she looked as though she'd been painted.

Painted!

The brushstrokes she'd seen just before wrenching herself up out of the dream. And the rose she held in her clasped hands.

She ran to Ariel's room, barely aware of the furious creaking of the stairs beneath her feet. . . .

Moments later she was on the phone to Jeff. They had spent the previous afternoon at a motel, an enervating and ultimately unfulfilling afternoon, and had not planned to meet today. But she was insistent. He had to come to the house. Not to pick her up, but to come inside.

When he arrived she sat him down in the front room and told him about the dream. When she had finished he didn't bother to mask his irritation.

"So it was just a dream," he said. "I broke an appointment to get here, Bobbie. I'm sure it was a scary dream, but I can't rush over and hold your hand every time you have a bad night."

"Come upstairs."

"I don't see—"

"Just come with me."

She led him up the stairs and the length of the hall to Ariel's room, then pointed to the picture. The woman's eyes glowed, catching the light in the room, throwing it back at them. "There," she said. "That's her."

175

"It's who?"

"It's the woman I saw last night. It's the same face, the same pose."

"Her shoulders are bare. What happened to the shawl?"

"What difference does it make? It's the same woman. She's holding a rose. She held one in the dream."

"With blood on the thorns."

"Yes."

"Maybe it's colder in your room. Maybe that's why she needed the shawl."

"Damn it, Jeff—"

He approached the picture, examined it closely. "Where did this come from, Bobbie?"

"Ariel found it in the attic. It may have been there for a century or more. David hung it for her the other day."

"And you saw it then?"

"I barely glanced at it."

"But you had a look at it before last night."

"Yes, but—"

He spread his hands. "The defense rests. It's simple enough. If you dreamed a particular face, red rose and all, and then subsequently you saw a portrait for the first time and it was the same face, then you might well have something that indicated something. You wouldn't have *evidence* of anything, certainly, but you'd have food for thought. But you saw the portrait *first.*"

"So?"

"So you remembered it and it sparked your dream. You said yourself that the woman you saw when Caleb died was vague and insubstantial. She probably didn't look like anything in particular. And when you saw the portrait the other night you didn't make any connection because there was no connection to be made. But perhaps there was a superficial resemblance, enough for you to link something up unconsciously, and last night you expressed your perceptions in a dream. You dreamed of the woman you saw earlier, but you fleshed out the apparition by giving her the features you saw in the portrait."

She resisted what he was suggesting. But he went over the argument a second time, and she found herself nodding, allowing the logic of what he was saying.

"I just glanced at her, Jeff."

"The brain takes very vivid pictures even when we don't think it registers anything at all. I could show you a photograph for a couple of seconds and you'd swear you barely saw it and didn't remember anything but the most general impressions. Then, if you were to be hypnotized, you might very well be able to describe that photo as if you were still looking at it. The same sort of thing can happen in a dream."

"I suppose so . . ."

"The portrait's very likely of someone who lived in this house, or of a member of the family, at least. Now if there's such a thing as ghosts . . . let's pretend, for the sake of argument . . . and if that's what you saw when Caleb died, it's not inconceivable that the ghost was a relative of the woman in the portrait. Perhaps you sensed a family resemblance between the two and that was enough to set you up for the dream—"

"I think it was the same woman."

"All right, suppose it was. She lived here and died here and every once in a while her ghost plays a command performance in the bedroom. Maybe you caused her to appear, Bobbie."

"I don't follow you."

"You loved Caleb, you were close to him. That special closeness of a mother for her child. Maybe you had a premonition without even identifying it as such. You sensed that something was wrong with Caleb, that he was in danger, and maybe your unconscious fear conjured up the

177

woman, or whatever, that you saw in the bedroom."

"You're saying I imagined her."

"No."

She lit a cigarette, glanced at the portrait through a haze of smoke. The woman's eyes had been painted in such a way that they seemed to follow one around the room. They held Roberta's eyes now.

"Who'd you buy the house from, Bobbie?"

She had to think for a moment. "A young couple," she said at length. "Why don't I remember their names? I could look it up."

"Don't bother. Had they lived here long?"

"Less than a year. He was transferred to Charleston and they bought the house, and after nine or ten months they transferred him out again so they sold it. They wanted a fast sale and we got a good price. Traphagen, that was the name. Carl Traphagen, and her name was Julie. I don't remember where they were transferred. Somewhere in the midwest, I think."

"It doesn't matter. Do you know who had the house before them?"

"No." She frowned, grappling with a shred of memory. "She was pregnant," she said. "Julie Traphagen. Not enough to show, but she happened to mention it. I wonder."

"You wonder what?"

"I wonder what would have happened to her baby," she said. "If she'd had it in this house."

FOURTEEN

"THAT was him," Ariel said. Erskine looked at her. "The funeral man, the lawyer, *you* know."

"Channing?"

"Uh-huh."

"I didn't see him. Where?"

She pointed down the street. "In his car," she said. "In fact all I really saw was the car. He just drove on by. I don't think he even saw us. Maybe he was at my house."

"Maybe."

"Maybe Roberta asked him over to check out the stove." She hefted the flute. "It's a shame he couldn't stop and say hello. I could have played for him."

"You still haven't played for me."

"I told you," she said. "Today's your lucky day."

She had brought the flute and the tape recorder to school with her that morning in order to save time. Now she was anxious to get to Erskine's house. As soon as they were settled in his attic room she opened her flute case and fitted parts together, then set up the tape recorder.

"I taped this last night," she said. "Then when I played it back I accompanied myself. Listen to this."

She started the tape, sat back on her heels, put the flute

179

to her lips. After the tape had run for a few bars she joined in, hesitantly at first, then with confidence.

It was just so much fun playing along with herself this way. She didn't even have to think about what she was doing. She had played against this particular tape twice the preceding night, and now she was doing it again, but playing entirely differently from the way she had played then. Her musical mood was different, just as it differed from the track on the tape recorder, but all the same everything seemed to fit together just right. Her fingers automatically selected the notes that would fit into the right places, as if all the music was happening simultaneously in her brain and she could sit back and decide what spaces to fill in and what spaces to leave empty in order to make the musical picture take whatever shape she wanted it to have.

She continued playing for ten minutes or so. Then the intensity of her concentration became painful. Her head ached and she had to put the flute down at her side. Erskine reached to stop the recorder.

"That's really far out," he said. "You played two completely different things and made them go together, so that they wound up being parts of the same thing."

"You could tell."

"Sure. I don't understand music, but I could hear what it is that you do." He frowned. "This is no good. We need another tape recorder. Then you could tape back and forth and lay one track on top of the other the way they do when they make records. Of course you wouldn't get professional quality because the surface noise would pile up but at least the music wouldn't just run off in the air and get lost. You see what I mean?"

She nodded. "I don't know if there would be room for a third track," she said. "Let me think." She closed her eyes. "Maybe it would fit in," she said.

"The thing is you could experiment."

"Uh-huh."

"Plus we could keep one recorder here and one at your house instead of dragging them back and forth all the time." He thought it over, then nodded decisively. "What we need is another tape recorder," he said. "I'll get one."

"How?"

"I'll tell them I need one."

"Your parents?"

"Who else, Santa Claus?"

"You just tell them you need something and you get it?"

"Sure. What do you do when you want something?"

"Nothing."

"Does that work?"

"I don't want many things," she said.

The next day he told her everything was taken care of. "They'll get the tape recorder. You can keep the other one in the meantime. I told them you needed it for a project."

"And that's all you had to do?"

"Sure. When I was younger I used to have to throw tantrums, but after you do that a certain number of times you get them trained. I didn't have to scream or kick my feet or anything."

"No carpet-chewing, huh?"

"Nothing like that." He looked up at her. "So we've got you a tape recorder, Jardell. Now what are you going to do for me in return, my proud beauty?"

She giggled.

"Nothing in return, Ariel?"

"I took care of Graham for you, didn't I?"

He stared at her.

"You think he just *happened* to get hit by a car," she said. "That kind of accident doesn't just happen all by itself, you know. I had to arrange it."

"What are you talking about?"

"Well, I concentrated very hard, and I said a little prayer to the woman we found in the attic, and look what happened." She dilated her nostrils, widened her eyes, hit him with an out-of-focus stare. "I have special powers," she announced.

"You're really weird, Jardell."

"Special weird powers."

"You're spooky, did anyone ever tell you that?"

"Weird spooky powers. You said *you* wanted to kill Graham, so I thought I'd help you out. After all, you're getting the tape recorder. I figured I owed you a favor."

"He wasn't killed, anyway. Just hit by a car."

"My powers aren't fully developed yet," she said. "I'm only a child."

"A weird child."

"Look who's talking."

"Graham got a broken leg and three broken ribs and a ruptured spleen. What's a spleen?"

"Something gross. Something yucky and disgusting."

"It's good people have skin," Erskine said, "or all that stuff would show."

That night she hadn't planned to write in her diary. Roberta had gone out after dinner and David was in his den with the door closed, and she'd planned on doing her homework and then watching television. But the homework didn't take long and when it was finished she didn't feel like watching anything on television. Without really being aware of it she got her spiral notebook and her pen and sat down on her bed.

For a while she wrote about her music, about the tape recorder Erskine was going to get. Then she wrote:

> We didn't see Mr. Channing today. I kept expecting to see him. I would look around for him on the way to school and

on the way to Erskine's afterward. And on the way home from Erskine's I kept looking around for his car. There is something about him and I don't know what it is. I'm scared of him but at the same time I like seeing him. I don't understand it.

Graham Littlefield was hit by a car yesterday. He is in the hospital and is not going to die. Broken legs, broken ribs, and a ruptured spleen, whatever that is. I looked in the dictionary and it says the spleen is a ductless gland at the left of the stomach in man, and near the stomach or intestine in other vertebrates. People used to think that the spleen caused low spirits, bad temper and spite.

I suppose having your spleen ruptured would cause all of those things. I suppose Graham's spirits are low and his temper is bad. Mine certainly would be.

A car hit him and drove off without stopping. Some of the kids were saying that he ran into the street without looking, so it wasn't the car's fault, but it was certainly the car's fault for not stopping.

I spooked Erskine. Telling him I had powers that caused Graham's accident. He didn't really believe me, but there was a minute there when he wasn't absolutely sure.

Suppose Graham was hit by a maroon Buick with a black roof?

Except the other kids just said it was a dark car. Nobody got the license number or anything.

I wonder.

I wonder what would happen if I pretended to have powers. Erskine talked about killing Graham and Veronica, and now Graham's in the hospital, and what would he think if something happened to Veronica?

This is crazy why am I thinking about this I should stop it right now—

Suppose I concentrated very hard on Veronica. Suppose I got up in the middle of the night and lit a candle under the portrait and concentrated very hard.

Nothing would happen.

Would it?

She gave her head a sudden shake, dismissing the train of thought. For a moment or two she sat with her eyes closed. Then she resumed writing.

> I have to wait until I'm eighteen to find out who my real mother is. Erskine says maybe there's a way before then if only he can figure it out. I don't think he'll be able to.
>
> It does not seem so important anymore.
>
> Here is what happens. I think about my mother or start to have an imaginary conversation with her. Then I look at Her.
>
> I mean the portrait. *Her.*
>
> I don't know what to call her. I wish I knew her name. Sometimes she is me and sometimes she is my mother. Of course she is neither of us, not really. She could not have been my real mother because the portrait is too old.
>
> But something happens when I look at her.

She closed the notebook, turned to look at the picture. It had an effect upon her which she did not begin to understand. But she did know it suited her to have the picture in her room. As if the woman was back where she belonged.

This must have been her room long ago, she decided. And she got up and walked to her window, drawing back the curtain and looking out at the street below. It had rained earlier, and a streetlamp cast a yellow glow over the wet pavement. She imagined that the woman in the portrait must have stood like this, looking out like this. Of course there would not have been cars then, just carriages pulled by horses. And the streetlamp would have been a gaslight.

184

She left the window, sat on her bed. At least she hadn't gotten up in the middle of the night lately to burn any more candles. That incident had disturbed her for a while, until she finally decided it had been just one step removed from a dream, like walking in your sleep. Nothing to get all shook up about.

She turned, then, and raised her eyes to meet the glowing eyes in the portrait. She did not break her silent concentration until she heard David's footsteps on the stairs. . . .

David was restless. Roberta had gone out shopping, but the currents she'd stirred were still in motion.

She wanted to move. She'd come to his study immediately after dinner, just as he was preparing to settle in with pipe and brandy, and made her little announcement. This house, she explained, had been a mistake. They never should have bought it in the first place. It was a hostile environment, an unhealthy place physically and spiritually, and the only solution was to cut their losses and run. The Traphagens, anxious for a quick sale, had enabled them to buy at a good price. Now, even allowing for realtor's commission and closing costs, they could very likely turn the house over at a small but tidy profit.

And move where, he'd asked.

The question didn't seem to concern her. Back to Charleston Heights, if he liked, or any comparable suburban neighborhood. A year-round beach house on Isle of Palms might be nice if he didn't mind the commuting time. Just so they got out of where they were—that was all she cared about.

That and proximity to Channing, he thought.

He couldn't sit still. He got up, carried his brandy glass through the downstairs rooms of the house. There was, he decided, nothing wrong with this house and a great deal right with it. The three of them ought to be capable of being very happy in it. They'd been a family once, a happy and complete family. Roberta's affair and Caleb's birth had interfered, had changed things, but Caleb was gone now (think of God's will, good and acceptable and perfect) and if only Roberta were herself again—

And there was the problem.

She was seeing Channing. She was behaving curiously, her voice edged with brittle anxiety, her face sharp and drawn. She barely spoke to Ariel, treating her like an unwelcome stranger. And through it all she maintained poor Caleb's room as some sort of morbid shrine, dusting it almost daily, insisting that he and Ariel stay out of it. He'd almost suggested she hang a padlock on the door, only refraining out of fear that she'd take him at his word.

If they were to sell the house, he had thought of telling her, she'd have to let strangers into her precious Caleb's room. You couldn't very well expect a prospective house buyer to leave one of the upstairs rooms uninspected. And, when the house sold, she'd have to clear out the room. The new owners might not want to maintain the room as it was, giving it National Landmark status.

He finished his brandy, but instead of pouring another he set down his pipe and climbed the stairs. They creaked underfoot. Ought to be able to do something about that, he thought, but the sound didn't really bother him. An old house ought to have its repertoire of sounds. They were like gray hairs on an old man's head.

Ariel was in her room, sitting on her bed with her notebook open on her lap.

"I didn't mean to disturb you," he said. "I suppose you've got a lot of homework?"

She shook her head, closed her book. "I'm all finished, daddy," she said. "I was just looking over what I wrote."

"They keep you pretty busy at this school?"

"I don't mind it."

He nodded absently. "I just felt like talking," he said. "Unless you've got something you wanted to do."

"No."

"Some program on television you wanted to watch."

"No."

He sat on the bed beside her, looked at the portrait he'd hung for her. It was disproportionately large for the room, but she seemed to like it and that was all that really mattered. What had Roberta been saying about the portrait? He hadn't been paying much attention, only recalled that she didn't like it and seemed to find it symbolic of everything that was suddenly wrong with the house.

"Well," he said. "What's new, honey?"

"Nothing much."

"School coming okay?"

"Sure."

He put an arm around her and she snuggled her head to his shoulder. He felt a rush of warmth to his chest not unlike the sensation he obtained from swallowing a generous measure of brandy. His voice suddenly husky, he said, "Then everything's okay with you?"

"Everything's fine."

"You like it here, don't you?"

"Sure."

"Better than our other house?"

"Tons better. I love this house."

"How about your school?"

"It's better."

"Better teachers?"

"They're about the same. The kids are better, though."

"And you've got a best friend."

"Erskine."

"I haven't really met him yet."

"Well, he's shy around grownups."

"I was the same way when I was a kid."

"You? Honest?"

"Honest." He gave her shoulder a squeeze. "Something I wanted to talk about with you," he said. "Your mommy's going through a hard time lately. I suppose you've been able to sense that yourself."

She didn't say anything.

"It's the shock of what happened to your brother," he went on. "She's having trouble getting over it. It's given her bad feelings about this house and—"

"Are we going to move?"

"I don't think so. You don't want to move, do you, honey?"

"No!"

He smiled at the determination in her tone. "Neither do I," he admitted. "And I don't really think it'll come to that. It's just something your mother has to go through right now, and we have to go through it with her. She's been short-tempered with me and probably with you, too. She's under a lot of emotional stress and it's very difficult for her."

"How can I help?"

"Just be understanding."

"Okay."

"And if you've got problems of your own, don't keep them bottled up inside you. Bring 'em to me, hear?"

"Sure."

He gave her another hug. "I love you so much," he said. "Your mother and I both love you. You know that, don't you?"

"Sure."

He glanced at his watch. "*Rhoda*'s going on in a minute," he said. "Want to watch it with me?"

"Okay, sure."

"You go ahead downstairs," he said. "I'll be down in a minute."

He walked into the upstairs bathroom while she hurried downstairs. What Roberta had said was true, he noticed—the stairs made no sound when Ariel used them. She weighed less, he thought, and walked lightly.

He didn't really have to use the bathroom. He just wanted a moment alone, so he rinsed his hands and dried them and stood for a moment in thought.

"Your mother and I both love you. You know that, don't you?"

Did Ariel believe it?

Was it true?

He loved her, certainly. And never more than he did tonight.

But Roberta?

He left the bathroom, walked the length of the hallway to the closed door of Caleb's room.

And remembered.

Roberta at the hospital right after she'd had the baby. They were wheeling her to the recovery room and she was still delirious from the anesthetic. People always said crazy things when they were coming out from under anesthesia. It didn't necessarily mean anything.

"David? David, there's something you have to do." And, when he'd leaned forward to catch her words, she'd whispered, "Get rid of Ariel, okay? We have a real baby now so we don't need her anymore. Okay? You get rid of her. You take her back where she came from and I'll bring the real baby home from the hospital. Okay, David?"

It didn't mean anything. That's what he told himself now and what he had assured himself at the time. People said crazy things under such conditions, and she was delirious and had no idea what she was saying.

"Your mother and I both love you. You know that, don't you?"

He stopped to pour a glass of brandy and fill a pipe, then joined Ariel in front of the television set. They were still watching *Rhoda* when Roberta returned, barely acknowledging their greetings. She brushed past them into the kitchen, set down a bag of groceries, then swept past them to carry the rest of her purchases upstairs. The two of them went on watching television. David was on the point of saying something to Ariel, something about having to understand her mother's behavior, but he couldn't find a sentence that would improve the situation. He took a small sip of brandy instead and drew contemplatively on his pipe.

It was perhaps ten minutes later that they heard Roberta scream.

FIFTEEN

SHE managed to get hold of Erskine in the morning before the first bell rang. "Listen," she said, "you have to tell me something."

"What's the matter?"

"Just tell me one thing. You remember when you were over at my house?"

"Which time?"

"The first time. When we found the picture."

"So?"

"And you went into Caleb's room."

"So?"

"What did you do in there?"

"Nothing. Why?"

"What did you *do?*"

"Nothing, I said. I didn't even go inside, I just looked from the doorway. Maybe I went in a step. Why?"

"Did you touch anything?"

"No."

"Swear it."

"Ariel, what's the *matter?*"

She wanted to hit him. "Swear it," she said. "This is important. Did you touch anything or didn't you?"

"Jesus," he said. "I solemnly swear I did not touch a thing in that room. Is that okay or do you want me to hunt for a Bible?"

She relaxed. "You really didn't."

"I just *said* I didn't. What's going on?"

"I'll tell you later."

"Hey, wait a minute." He grabbed at her coat. "What's it all about, Jardell? Hang on."

But she wrenched free from his grasp. "Later," she said. "After school."

Several times in the course of the day he tried to get her to explain but each time she put him off. She wanted to wait until there was more time. As they walked from school to his house he was elaborately casual, not even deigning to refer to the incident. They talked about other things. Then, when they were in his room, while he recovered his breath from his headlong charge up the attic stairs, she explained.

"Somebody did something in Caleb's room."

"Did what?"

"I don't know exactly. It was hard to understand because she was so excited. Took his fish mobile down. Pulled some of his decorations off the walls. You absolutely swear you didn't touch anything?"

"How many times do I have to swear? Don't you take my word all of a sudden?"

"I'm sorry," she said. "But she came home last night and I guess she went into his room and she gave out with a scream like the world was coming to an end and then she tore downstairs and started yelling. She wanted to know why I'd been in his room and I said I hadn't been in there, which was true, the last time I went in Caleb's room was ages ago. Before the time you went in there."

"You weren't in there since?"

She hesitated for an instant, then shook her head. "No,

not since the time you opened the door. Remember I didn't even want to look inside?"

"I remember. You turned your head away."

"Right. I haven't been in there since. I'll stand outside the door once in a while but that's all. Listen. I just thought of something. Was the fish mobile hanging over his bed when you were there?"

"How do I know?"

"I thought maybe you would remember one way or the other."

"I barely remember what the room looked like, for God's sake." He shifted uncomfortably in his seat. "I wasn't really interested in looking at anything. I just wanted to get an idea what it felt like. You know, standing there and looking at the crib where it happened."

"Where what happened?"

"You know, where he died. That's all. But I didn't notice anything, really."

"Some of the wall decorations were on the floor. And the mobile was all broken. You would have noticed things like that, wouldn't you?"

"Maybe. I suppose so."

"She thought *I* did it. She was screaming like an insane person. If David hadn't been there I think she would have tried to kill me or something."

"What did you say?"

"I told her I didn't do it. What else could I say? I don't think she believed me. She had to pretend to but I don't think she really believed me."

"Weird." He chewed on a knuckle. "What do you figure happened? You didn't really think I did it, did you?"

"I didn't know. I thought maybe you would fool around like that not knowing it would cause her to have a fit. But if you say you didn't—"

"I swear I didn't, Ariel."

"I believe you. Maybe she did it herself. I'll tell you something, I think she's crazy enough."

"Why would she do it?"

"Why do crazy people do things? I don't know."

"Maybe David did it."

"Sure. He's just the type. Maybe the bogeyman did it."

"That's a good idea," he said. "I should have thought of that myself. Maybe the bogeyman did it."

"Always a possibility."

"Maybe Graham Littlefield did it. He strained himself tearing the room apart and that's how he ruptured his spleen. Then the Funeral Man hit him with the car as a punishment."

"We'll have to tell that to Roberta . . . Maybe Veronica did it."

He shook his head. "Not Veronica. Maybe Aunt Rhoda did it."

"You mean Aunt Rhody."

"Right, Aunt Rhody. Maybe the old gray goose did it."

"No, the goose is dead."

"That's the way it goes. And maybe the fucking wind did it, did anybody have the brains to think of that?"

"That's what David said. But it couldn't have happened that way. Everything was tossed around, the way Roberta described it. It would have taken a hurricane. No, somebody actually went and did it. Roberta thinks it's me and if it wasn't me it must have been the house."

"Huh?"

"I told you she's crazy. 'The house is evil and it makes things happen.' Quote unquote. You wouldn't believe how crazy she is. Your parents are a pain in the ass—"

"No kidding."

"—but they're not crazy the way she is."

"Well, maybe she's right. Maybe the house did it."

"Sure . . . Maybe—"

194

"Maybe what?"

She squeezed her hands together. "Maybe I did it," she said softly.

"You . . . ?"

"Maybe in a dream," she said. "Maybe in my sleep."

"I don't think that makes any sense, Ariel."

"Don't you? I don't know if it does or not. Sometimes I do things in my sleep that are weird."

"You mean in a dream?"

"Not exactly."

"Then how?"

"I can't explain it."

"Well, what kind of things do you do?"

"I don't want to say."

"Great."

"I just don't want to say, all right? Nothing worth talking about. Just weird things that I do during the night."

"Now I'm really getting interested."

"Well, don't. And I have strange dreams. I don't know. Maybe I got up one night to go to the bathroom and I went into Caleb's room and did something and then went back to bed without knowing it. And when I woke up in the morning I didn't remember anything about it. That's possible, isn't it?"

"I suppose so. But why would you do that?"

"I don't know."

"Then—"

"Well, somebody did it. Roberta said—"

"Maybe she did it herself," he suggested.

"Who, Roberta?"

"Why not, if she's as crazy as you say. You just said it was possible. And that makes as much sense as maybe you did it in your sleep. Maybe *she* did it in *her* sleep."

"Yeah."

"Let's see what's on the radio, huh? I'm getting a headache from this conversation."

"Okay," she said. . . .

And later she said, "Channing, the Funeral Man. Remember how we thought he was a detective?"

"Before I found out he was a lawyer."

"I thought he was investigating me for murdering Caleb. I don't know if I really thought that. But she thinks I killed him. She really thinks that."

"Well?"

"Well what?"

He cocked his head, interested. "Well? Did you?"

"What?"

"Did you do it?" he said patiently. "Ariel Jardell, you have sworn to tell the truth, the whole truth, and nothing but the truth. Did you, Ariel Jardell, murder your innocent baby brother?"

"Oh, sure," she said. "I did it in my sleep." They looked at each other for a moment, and then they both began to laugh.

SIXTEEN

IN Dr. Reuben Gintzler's office one sat on neither couch nor chair. The diminutive psychiatrist provided his patients with a tufted yellow chaise lounge, an uncomfortable piece of furniture on which one could not quite sit and not quite lie down. Roberta had occasionally entertained the thought that this was all according to the man's master plan—he wanted to keep you off-balance. At other times she decided he was not so much calculating as he was oblivious to such matters.

She was on the chaise now, had been on it for half an hour. She'd been guarded at first, her monolog punctuated by long silences, but then her guard had slipped some and she'd let herself run off in several directions at once, talking about the state of her marriage and the death of her son, about Jeff and Ariel and the picture from the attic and the mysterious attack upon Caleb's room. She found herself tugging at a conversational thread, drawing it out until it hit a snag, then switching abruptly to another and repeating the process.

She became silent now, her eyes lowered and half-lidded. There was no sound in the room but the ticking of Gintzler's wall clock, a Regulator pendulum-type in an unvarnished oak case. Clocks-like that had hung in schoolrooms when Roberta was a girl, and she wondered if they were there still. Perhaps they had all been rescued to tick out their lives in shrinks' offices, letting neurotics know when their fifty minutes were up.

"Mrs. Jardell?"

She turned to look at Gintzler. He was poking at a pipe with a wire cleaner, running it through the stem and shank. He never smoked the pipes, only played with them incessantly.

"You are very scattered today," he said. "Your thoughts run all over the place. Your son, your daughter, your husband, your lover. You came here as if you were at a crisis, and indeed you behave as though this were so, but instead you discuss a great many areas of concern without touching on any crisis. I wonder why."

She shrugged, said nothing.

"I wonder what really bothers you, Mrs. Jardell."

"All of the things I've been talking about."

"Oh? I wonder if this is really so. You have mentioned so many unrealistic concerns. Ghosts which form in the corners of rooms. An old black woman who mutters occult secrets in dialect. A painting which seems to have some arcane significance. A mysterious spirit which haunts your gas range and extinguishes its burners. A flute which evidently is not to your liking musically. A curious force, no doubt a poltergeist, which rearranges articles in your dead son's room. Stairs which creak, windowpanes which rattle. It would seem—"

"It would seem as though I'm crazy," she said. "So I guess I'm in the right place."

"It would seem as though you are using all of these phenomena to mask what is really bothering you."

"And what would that be?"

"Can't you tell me, Mrs. Jardell?"

And then she was talking about Ariel again, talking about Jeff's attempt to learn more about her parentage, defending her desire to know Ariel's ancestry. "Environment isn't everything, is it?" she demanded. "Don't genes count for anything? They determine what a person looks like. Why shouldn't they have a lot to do with what's on the inside?"

"This is a recent concern, Mrs. Jardell?"

"I don't think so."

"I have never heard you allude to it before."

"No."

"But now your natural son has died and you react by showing increased concern for your daughter. You mask this concern by saying it is for her character. You are afraid to worry about Ariel's possibly dying because that is unthinkable. To think it might cause it to happen. We do not speak the word cancer because that might cause us to have it, and so it is with other unmentionable topics. So your mind rejects the notion that Ariel might die as your son died, and instead you worry that there is something wrong with her, just as perhaps you worry now that something was wrong with your son, that some genetic flaw you passed on to him led to his being taken from you. You are shaking your head. Are you so certain what I suggest is unsupported by the facts?"

"Yes."

"There is guilt involved, you know. You betrayed your husband with another man. That guilt was always present, even though you have never permitted yourself to experience it, to deal with it. Perhaps there is a belief within you that your son was conceived in guilt, that his magical death was your punishment for adultery."

"That's crazy."

"Perhaps it is illogical. What we believe is not always what we ought to believe. Perhaps you feel guilt over Caleb's death—"

"No, I don't!"

"You feel you should have been able to prevent it—"

"No."

"You even feel you caused it."

"I feel *she* caused it."

"Yes, so you have said. But of course that makes no sense. I feel you have erected a whole superstructure to support this delusion in order to keep yourself from fearing for your daughter's life. You—"

"Dammit, she's not my daughter!"

The vehemence of her outburst surprised her. Around her the silence became heavy, oppressive. The clock ticked some more of her hour away. She lit a cigarette, dropped her lighter back into her purse. Calmly now, she said, "Did you ever happen to read a book called *Helter-Skelter?* About the Manson family?"

"Why do you ask?"

"Did you read it?"

"I am familiar with the book. I have never read it."

"He had children with most of those glassy-eyed little girlfriends of his. Charles Manson did. Of course it was always tricky to know just who fathered which child because all of those people did everything to everyone, they behaved like animals. But there were quite a few children born. And according to the book most of the children wound up being placed for adoption after the arrests were made and the Family broke up. The authorities just swept up the children and offered them for adoption."

"And?"

Her eyes were intense. "Can you imagine? A man and woman decide to adopt a child and without having the slightest idea they take the daughter of two murderers into their home. Can you imagine that? Can you?"

"Mrs. Jardell . . ."

Her hands were shaking. She couldn't seem to get hold of herself.

"Mrs. Jardell. You are not seriously suggesting that perhaps your Ariel was one of those children? Because the dates are wrong. And surely those children would have been placed with families in California, or at least in that part of the country. You can't suspect—"

"Oh, Christ," she said. "Don't order a straitjacket just yet, all right? I know she's not one of those kids. I was just giving an example of what could happen."

"And what is it that you think could happen, Mrs. Jardell?"

"I don't understand."

"What could happen now? What is the threat?"

She tried to concentrate. "You think I'm afraid that Ariel might die."

"Your son was born out of adultery and he died. Now you have resumed the affair. And now you expect punishment for it."

She thought of telling him that the affair wasn't going all that well, that she and Jeff seemed to be more bound up in compulsion than carried away with passion.

"Tell me about Ariel, Mrs. Jardell."

"Tell you what? I've told you everything about her."

"Tell me why you are afraid of her."

"Because I think she's dangerous."

"To whom?"

"To me."

"Do you really believe she killed your son?"

She closed her eyes, sighed heavily, opened them again. "No," she said. "No, of course not."

"Why not?"

"Because it's impossible. Because she loved Caleb. She

used to go into his room and play with him. She played that horrible flute for him. That might have driven him crazy but it couldn't have harmed him, could it?"

He said nothing.

"No, of course not," she said, answering her own question. "Then why is it so easy for me to see her as a murderess? What is there about her that makes me want to put her in that role?"

"Is it something in her?"

"Do you mean it's something in myself?"

"Do you think that might be what I mean?"

"How do I know what you mean?"

Again he let the silence build around her. She felt very weak now, very tender and vulnerable. Was it all her inner problem, something that came from within her own mind? Was it her fault for worrying that everything was her fault? Was it ultimately that simple, and that ridiculous?

He said, "You see, Mrs. Jardell, it is not a simple matter of taking an aspirin for a headache. This is part of something that has been manifesting itself in various ways in your mind for as long as I have known you. From time to time you rush to me as if for emotional first aid, and always it is the same underlying problem. You cannot take an aspirin for it, you cannot put a bandaid on it. It is involved in your feeling for your own parents, rooted in some childhood experiences of your own we have barely gotten a hint of."

"I barely remember my childhood, doctor."

"And do you suppose that what you fail to remember no longer exists? We deal with things by forgetting them, but it does not work as well for us as we might like." He seized a pipe, twisted it apart. "Of course you can go on this way. You can come to me once or twice a year, when your mind drives you here. I can chat with you for an hour, skimming the surface of your anxiety, and I can give you an occasional prescription for Valium."

"Or?"

"But you know the answer, Mrs. Jardell."

"Therapy."

He nodded. "A regular program of regular appointments which you will keep and which will become part of your schedule. A program dealing not with the intermittent manifestations of your problem but with the problem itself, the problem that lies deep in you."

"How long would it go on?"

"Two years. Perhaps longer."

"And how often?"

"Twice a week. Once a week is possible, but twice is better."

"Twice a week for two years."

"Very likely."

"But it might run longer."

"That is possible, yes."

Her eyes challenged him. "And what'll it do for me? There are no money-back guarantees in this sort of thing, are there? You can't sue a shrink for malpractice."

He did not answer.

She lit a fresh cigarette, filled her lungs with smoke and thought involuntarily of her own mother. Her mother's hands, grotesque with signs of age. Her mother's body, wasted in the last stages of her disease.

She took another drag on her cigarette.

"I just don't know," she said.

"I suggest you think about this, Mrs. Jardell."

"Oh, I'm sure I will."

"It is true there are no guarantees. But I can give you a negative guarantee. This problem will not vanish of its own accord. There has been some deterioration since I last saw you. Your problem is getting worse, not better."

"I've been under a strain."

"Yes."

She thought of Jeff. The two of them in his Buick, speeding west on a section of the Interstate. Just leaving everything behind.

But you couldn't run away from things. They tagged along after you like old shoes tied to a honeymoon couple's rear bumper—

"The time, Mrs. Jardell."

His words brought her around. They never lost sight of the time, did they? They always knew when your hour was up.

She got to her feet.

"If I could have some Valium," she said. He looked at her for a moment, then nodded and reached for the prescription pad.

SEVENTEEN

ETTA Jellin had been in the real estate business for half a century. She'd gone to work fresh out of high school as a secretary to an up-and-coming young realtor. Within three years she'd become his wife, and a couple of years after that she had her broker's license and worked as his partner. For the dozen years of her widowhood she'd gone on operating the King Street office herself, managing the rental properties Sam had left her and specializing as always in downtown residential property.

"Why, David Jardell!" she said. "How nice. You're looking well."

He thanked her and returned the compliment, thinking that she was indeed looking well. But then she always did. In all the years he'd known her, Etta Jellin had remained the same, fat and saucy and always possessed of a good humor and a shrewd glint in her eye.

"Have a seat," she said. "I don't believe I've seen you since you lost your son. I was awfully sorry to hear about that."

"Yes," he said. "Thank you."

"I didn't go to the funeral. Last one I went to was my

husband's. The day I buried Roy I said, by God, I'm not going to another of these affairs till I go to my own. Which some folk doubtless feel is long overdue. Well, I'm sure we can find a fitter subject for conversation. How's that house I sold you? Bricks still staying one on top of the other?"

"Oh, it's in good shape."

"Would I sell you a bad one? Those old homes will outlive us all, my friend. They were built in saner times than our own. I swear I'd hate to hold mortgage paper on some of what's being built nowadays. The banks'll write thirty-year paper on some of these cardboard boxes, and you just know the houses won't last the thirty years. House'll be long gone before the mortgage is anywhere near paid off."

"It's true."

"But don't shed tears for the bankers," she went on. "Inflation the way it is, land prices rising the way they are, they'll be able to foreclose on the empty lots and come out ahead of the game." She leaned back in her swivel chair. "Lazy old afternoon," she said. "What brings you here, David?"

"I wanted to get the benefit of your professional expertise."

"Oh?"

"Let's suppose I wanted to sell the house," he said. "What could I figure on netting for it?"

She looked him over carefully, her dark eyes narrowing. "You didn't move in but less than a year ago."

"I know."

"They go and transfer you? Or did you find something else out of town?"

"Nothing like that, Etta."

"Then why in tarnation would you want to sell the house?"

He forced a smile. "I'm not saying I want to," he said. "I just wanted to know what it would amount to in dollars."

"If you're looking for cash, I know some awfully good sources of second-mortgage money, David. It's none of my business to pry and I'm not prying, but if that's what it is don't be ashamed to say so, for the Lord's sake. You shouldn't ever sell real estate because you need cash, not unless you're in the business and that's what you do for a living. Always borrow on it if you can. Every year the dollars get cheaper and the man who's in debt is that much ahead of the game."

"Cash isn't a problem, Etta."

"Then what on earth—?"

"Let's say it's personal."

She looked at him thoughtfully, then swung her chair around and rolled it over to a gray filing cabinet. "Just to refresh my memory," she said, leafing through a drawer of file folders. "Let me see now. Uh-huh. All right. I thought I remembered the house well enough. Peddle enough properties and they tend to merge when you get along in years but I still have a good memory for houses and a tolerable one for figures. You paid sixty-seven thousand five hundred according to what I've got written down here."

"That's right."

"House was listed at seventy-five, you offered sixty-five, and you and the seller settled at sixty-seven five. I think that's how it went."

"That's exactly how it went."

"And you want to know what you'd get selling it . . . depends, depends how anxious you are to sell. And how anxious somebody is to buy it. You might list it today at seventy-five and sell it tomorrow, if just the right person happened to come along and he wanted it badly enough. Or if you were willing to put it on the market today and sit tight for up to a year, then you could be fairly certain of getting the seventy-five or close to it sooner or later. But if you want a fast sale and you don't want to count on getting lucky, then you're going to take a loss."

"How large a loss?"

"Somewhere between fifteen and twenty thousand dollars. Plus my six-percent commission."

He winced. There was no way he could sell the house and sustain that sort of loss. His total equity in the house was only a little over fifteen thousand in the first place. If he sold that cheaply they wouldn't be able to move into another house.

"I guess I paid too much," he said.

She shook her head. "You paid a fair price, is all. You found just the house you wanted and paid no more than fair market value for it. If you're willing to wait for a buyer like yourself to come along I'd say you'll get your money out of it, except for commission and closing costs. But if you want to sell in a hurry, well, it's going to cost you. And that's especially true when you're dealing with older homes in town. They're unique. Each of them is one of a kind. The charm of the house, the prestige value of the particular block, the special feeling a given prospective buyer gets from the house, all of these intangibles determine how fast the house sells and what price it brings, and you can't get them down in dollars and cents and put them on the card in black and white."

"I see."

"You didn't overpay and you didn't wind up with a house you're going to lose money on. Unless you want to unload it in a hurry. Real estate's not the stock market, you know. You can't call your broker and be sure of having money in your hand in four days' time. It doesn't work that way."

"I know."

"Why do you want to unload the place, David?"

"I don't."

She stroked her chin. "Your wife's notion? You'll have to

forgive me but her name slips my mind. My memory's better for prices and addresses than it is for people's names."

"Roberta."

"Of course. She wants to move?"

"Yes."

"Because of what happened to the boy? Pshaw. I'm a fat old woman, David, and that's a fine thing to be because you can say whatever comes to mind and not give a damn how it goes over. Now it's a tragedy when a baby dies and only a fool would say otherwise, but it's a far cry from being the end of the world. She was not the first woman on earth to have a baby and God knows she was not the first woman on earth to lose one. If she's going to run around the block every time something in her life takes a nasty turn, she'd be well advised to sleep in a track suit. It's a hard life and it doesn't get easier the more you see of it. All you get is used to it."

"It's not that. Or maybe it is, when all is said and done, but that's not how Roberta sees it."

"How do you mean?"

He hesitated, groping for words. It was hard to explain her feelings, especially in view of the fact that they didn't make any sense to him.

"The house disturbs her," he said finally.

"It disturbs her?"

He nodded. "It makes her uncomfortable. She acts as if it were a person instead of a thing. I don't know how to describe it. She's going through a difficult time emotionally, it's obviously a result of losing the baby, and she's reacted by putting all the blame on the house." And on Ariel, he thought. But the house could be disposed of.

"She think maybe it's haunted?"

"It's as if she thought that," he said. "Of course she's intelligent, she's an educated woman. She doesn't literally believe in haunted houses—"

"Oh?" The dark eyes sparkled. "*I* do. Of course I'm not educated and I daresay I'm not terribly intelligent either, but—"

"You believe in ghosts?"

"I don't know if I believe in ghosts exactly. I believe houses get to be haunted, and I suppose it's ghosts that haunt 'em. An old house like yours, a house on that street, it's more likely to be haunted than not."

"You're not serious?"

"'Course I am."

"You actually believe—"

"Oh, I don't believe in anything. I especially don't believe in astrology. Know why?"

"Why?"

"Because I'm a Sagittarius, and every Sagittarius knows astrology is a lot of hooey." She lay back her head and cackled at her own joke. "I believe and I don't believe, both at once," she explained. "In just about everything, from ouija boards clear through to the Virgin Mary. There's such a thing as haunted houses. You go into your neighborhood, into any of the good old blocks south of Broad Street, and I'd say three houses out of five are likely to be haunted."

"Then you think that Roberta's right?"

"You really want to know what I think?" She sat forward, planted an elbow on her desk top, rested her chin in her hand. "I think houses pick up some of the vibrations of people who've lived in them, and especially people who died violently in them. That's the theory behind ghosts. Somebody dies suddenly or violently and the ghost doesn't know it's time to go on to the happy hunting grounds. Anyway, ghosts or vibrations or *whatever* you want to call it . . . certain people are just more sensitive to the feeling of a haunted house than others. And certain states of mind make a person more or less sensitive. Your house has been standing over a century. The odds are pretty strong that more than a few people died in it, and it's a safe bet that one of them somewhere along the way died in some sort of abrupt fashion. As a matter of fact—" She straightened up. "What's the number of your house again? Forty-two?"

"That's right."

"I wouldn't be surprised if Grace Molineaux lived there."

"Who on earth was she?"

"Before your time," she said. "Before *my* time, if you can believe it. It must have been in the eighties or early nineties. I remember people still talked about it when I was a girl."

"What happened?"

"I'm trying to remember. Now I'm not sure I'll get this entirely accurate. It seems to me she was a widow with small children. Was it three young children? I think so. It's usually three in stories, whether it's three little pigs or three bears or three wishes." She rocked back in her chair and looked up at the ceiling. "I seem to recall she was married to a ship's captain who was lost at sea and left her a young widow. With however many children, but let's say there were three of them. And one night they were all murdered in their beds. The children, that is . . . and it wasn't three, it was four. I'm remembering it now. They were smothered in their sleep, the four of them."

"By their mother? I'm sorry, I didn't catch her name."

"Grace Molineaux. What it was like is Lizzie Borden. Did she do it or was it a prowler? Now I myself wasn't around at the time, David. I'm not quite that ancient. I'm going back to a childhood recollection of conversations about an event that took place before I was born. I believe everybody thought she did it but had no proof. And she came from good family, good old French Huguenot stock, and people sympathized with her over losing her husband. So she was never charged with the murders."

"And she went on living alone like Lizzie Borden? While children taunted her with rhymes?"

"If she did, it wasn't for long. She killed herself. They found her hanging from a rope. Or did she take the gas pipe? It's one or the other, it seems to me. Either way she killed herself."

"Which amounted to an admission of guilt for the murder of her children, I gather."

"Do you suppose it did? You could also take it that she was despondent. Had nothing to live for what with her husband and kids all gone. They argued it both ways but it seems to me I grew up more or less taking it for granted that she killed those babies."

"And it happened in our house?"

"Might have." She shrugged majestically. "I knew which house it was when I was a child," she said. "It was pointed out to me. I recall that it was a big old red-brick house and it seems to me it was on that block and it might have been the same house you're living in today. But they might have pointed out the wrong house to me or my memory might be at fault or any of a hundred other things. You could find out if you wanted."

"How?"

"Check the deed registry in the county clerk's office. Nate Howard'll help you out if you mention my name. He's an old friend. Wait a moment, that might not help. I think Molineaux might have been her maiden name and the house would have been registered to the sea captain. Or maybe not. Now if you were to go over to the *Post-Courier* they'll have back issues into the last century, and they could probably help you."

"I don't think it's worth the trouble, do you?"

She shook her head. "No," she said. "I frankly don't. But

if Grace Molineaux lived and died in your house, well, it kind of adds up, don't it? A woman grieving for a child is going to be sensitive to the vibrations of a woman who lost four children under the same roof. Unless you don't believe any of that crap in the first place."

"All of a sudden I'm having trouble figuring out what I believe and what I don't believe."

"Well, congratulations! I think somebody said that's the beginning of wisdom."

"You mean there's hope for me, Etta?"

"Hope for us all, or so I'm told. Want some advice from a fat old lady? Your Roberta's having a bad time. That's perfectly natural. Be surprising if she weren't, all in all. You go home and tell her the house is listed for sale. That way she'll think you're taking some steps to solve the problem. It'll be that much of a load off her mind. Meantime I won't list the house at all. Or I've a better idea. I'll list it, but I'll put it on the card at ninety-five. Nothing against your house, it's a fine property, but the fool hasn't been born yet who's going to pay ninety-five thousand for it or even ask to go through it at that figure. And if he turns up, well, maybe you wouldn't mind making that kind of a profit on the transaction, or would you?"

"Not at all."

"Fine. So the house'll be listed, and if Roberta ever happens to check you won't turn out a liar. But it won't sell and you won't have to move and as soon as she works things out in her mind and comes to terms with her life, then you can take the house back off the market. How does that sound?"

"It sounds good, Etta."

"Just because a house is haunted is no reason to move out of it," she said. "The hell, it's less lonely that way."

Later that day he felt vaguely dissatisfied and wondered why. It seemed illogical that he should be bothered at deceiving Roberta; the deception was harmless enough, and was designed to help put her mind at ease.

Perhaps it was the story Etta Jellin had told. It was preposterous that such a solid earthy woman could actually believe in haunted houses, and her belief became all the more convincing for her general air of no-nonsense earthiness.

> *Grace Molineaux took a pillow*
> *And planted her kids beneath a willow.*

Not terribly good, he thought. *Willow* was all too obviously there just to rhyme with *pillow*. The bit about Lizzie Borden might also be doggerel, but at least it was good doggerel.

> *Grace took a pillow and gave a shove*
> *And smothered her kids with mother's love*

That was better. A shame he couldn't share it with Roberta, but if one thing was certain it was that he could not say Word One to Roberta about Grace Molineaux and her claim to infamy.

Not that he felt there was more than a chance in a hundred that the woman had actually lived in their house. Of course it was possible, just as it was possible that Grace herself was the subject of the portrait Ariel seemed to be so fond of. Under normal circumstances that was the sort of thing Roberta would have enjoyed believing.

But circumstances had not been normal for quite some time now.

No, this was something he couldn't possibly risk mentioning to Roberta.

W EIGHTEEN

HEN Ariel got out of bed that morning her night table was centered under the portrait of the woman with the rose. Its top was empty except for the jar lid. The candle stub had burned down to less than half an inch. A burnt match lay in a pool of congealed wax at the side of the candle.

She moved quickly, putting the candle away, returning her table to its usual position, replacing her clock and lamp on top of it. Then, hesitantly, she looked up at the portrait.

Evidently she had awakened in the middle of the night to go through the candle ritual again. But she couldn't remember any of it. As far as she could recall, she hadn't even dreamed during the night. The last thing she recalled was lying in bed on the verge of sleep.

Maybe she had gotten up in the middle of the night to go to the bathroom. Sometimes that happened and she'd go and come back and be half asleep, barely able to remember it the next day.

But this was different, wasn't it? Whatever woke her, whatever got her out of bed, she'd evidently gone through a whole ritual with the candle, moving furniture and lighting a match and doing God-knew-what while the candle burned. She looked at the portrait again, trying to learn something from the woman's compelling gaze, but it didn't help. Her memory was blank and it frightened her.

Was that all she had done? Just light a candle and go through some mental hocus-pocus number?

Or had she left her room?

She dressed and left it now, walking directly to the bathroom, hurrying past the closed door of Caleb's room. She washed up, brushed her teeth, used the toilet. In the hallway, she cocked her head and listened. David and Roberta were both downstairs.

She walked to Caleb's door, stood outside it for a moment. Her hand settled on the doorknob, hesitated. She turned the knob, drew a breath, opened the door.

The room was untouched. Everything was as it had been when Roberta last straightened it. Caleb's fish mobile remained in place over the crib.

Relief. Whatever weirdness she'd been a part of last night, at least she hadn't done a number on Caleb's room.

She closed Caleb's door and went downstairs for her breakfast.

While Jeff Channing had known Etta Jellin for years, it never occurred to him to turn to the realtor for information about previous occupants of the red-brick house on Legare Street. Instead he did what his legal training had taught him to do, searching the house's title. He'd done this sort of thing any number of times in connection with real estate transactions, and there was no particular difficulty now in tracing the ownership of the house down through the years since it was built in 1822 by a Colonel Joseph Warren Clay.

The house had changed hands half a dozen times during the nineteenth century. A man named James Petersmith had bought it in 1903. His children had sold shortly after the 1929 stock market crash, and since then the house had never remained in the hands of a single owner for longer than seven years. Several owners had bought and sold the place within periods of less than a year.

A curious history, he thought. Americans were a mobile lot, certainly, especially since World War Two. He recalled reading somewhere that twenty percent of the nation's families pulled up roots and moved every year. But homes in Old Charleston didn't tend to turn over quickly. The sort of people who were attracted to them tended to stay put for a while.

Maybe there *was* something about the house, something vaguely disquieting that made its occupants sufficiently uncomfortable to sell and move on. The Traphagens, who had sold to the Jardells, had been transferred to another location, and no doubt other residents had had similarly sound reasons for moving. But it seemed a fair assumption that at least a few of the house's recent owners had been made uneasy by the night sounds and had shrunk from the damp. Perhaps they'd seen things in the corners of the bedrooms too. Perhaps their noses had wrinkled at the smell of gas when the stove's pilot lights had refused to stay lit. After a while people could weary of rationalizing the peculiar and just get out . . . unless, like himself, a person was concerned about one of them and was drawn in, out of curiosity and concern, to probe further, regardless of realistic skepticism . . . in spite of it . . .

Odd, too, that no one had even gotten around to replacing the old gas range. Odd, for that matter, that so many owners had made so few changes in the old house.

Odder still that the portrait had lain unnoticed for years until Ariel came on it. You would have thought some previous owner would have cleaned out the attic.

By the time he left the Deeds Registry, Jeff had covered a sheet of paper with names running all the way back from Traphagen, Carl and Julia, to Clay, Colonel Joseph Warren. He scanned the list, unsure that it represented anything beyond busywork. The subject of the portrait in Ariel's room might be on the list, and if so hers was very likely one of the first six or eight names on it. But it seemed even more likely to him that some recent tenant had picked up the portrait at an auction or garage sale, then stowed it in the attic and forgot it at moving time. The painting needn't have anything to do with Bobbie's house; indeed the woman it depicted might well never have been within five hundred miles of Charleston in her life.

Fool's business, he thought. And it wasn't as if he didn't have anything better to do. He'd been letting his work slide shamefully lately, staying away from the office for long stretches every day and finding himself incapable of concentrating during those rare hours that he did spend at his desk. The informal title search he'd just conducted was the first genuine legal work he'd done in far too long.

It was, no question, getting to him and he didn't know just what to do about it. His inability to work was just a symptom, and not the worst of the lot. His mind was acting strangely, hurling uncomfortable thoughts at him, leaving him anxious and jumpy inside however calm the exterior he managed to present to the world. His perceptions were askew, his judgment unreliable.

He kept a lid on this most of the time. When Bobbie had shown him the portrait, he'd been strong and logical and reassuring, the apostle of pure reason.

Yet he'd looked at the portrait and had seen, instantly, Ariel's face. Ariel as an adult, strong and seductive, pale face shining and damned eyes burning hypnotically as they had burned when they had held and looked into his. That was what he had seen—but he had given no sign, and a later glance told him, all reasonably, that the portrait was merely a portrait, the woman in it merely a long-dead flower of the south.

Sometimes it seemed obvious to him that the only answer lay in breaking things off with Bobbie once and for all. The hours they spent in interchangeable motel rooms, for all the frenzy and heightened tension, were increasingly unsatisfying, leaving him time and again with a feeling not unlike a hangover, dry of mouth, short of breath, determined never to touch the stuff again. That he elected to continue the affair sometimes seemed to him the clearest evidence of all that he was indeed losing his grip on things, that he was truly losing his mind.

And yet something inside him kept insisting that Bobbie was the core of his life, his destiny—she *was* the mother of his dead child . . . they'd shared life and death, after all— that the hours he spent *away* from her were unbearably flat and lifeless. Just the other night he'd been sitting in the basement recreation room with Elaine and the girls, watching something unmemorable on the tube, glancing from time to time at the wet bar and the knotty pine walls and the recessed lighting, then at his wife and daughters, then once more at the oversize color television set. The good life in the suburbs, he had thought, and all of it hollow, pointless, and he found himself yearning to be away from all of this, away from it and from them forever, alone somewhere on an island or in a city or off in the middle of the desert with Bobbie—her pull was that strong, however much she upset him.

There was a time, he thought now, when that might have worked. When she was pregnant with his child, that would have been the moment for them to turn their backs on everything and just go. But instead it was the moment that had just gone, and he had stayed with Elaine while she had stayed with David, and Caleb was born and died and—

Well, fool's business, he told himself, was better than no business at all. He left the Deeds Registry, strode on foot to his office and past it, and headed for the newspaper offices.

Erskine was waiting for her when school let out. "Well, we're on our way," he said. "Got busfare?"

"Oh."

"Nice day for an expedition, isn't it? Sunny, not too cold out."

"Maybe we should forget it."

He looked at her.

"Well, I haven't even seen him around the past few days," she said. "Maybe Roberta just had to see him for some reason or other, and then we happened to see him a few times out of coincidence."

"Some coincidence."

"It's possible."

"Why would she be seeing some lawyer, anyway?"

"Maybe to get a divorce."

"From David?"

"Well, who else is she married to, birdbrain? Of course from David. She'd be glad to get a divorce from me but you can't divorce children. It doesn't work that way. The only way she can get rid of me . . ."

"What were you going to say?"

"I was going to say the only way she'll get rid of me is by killing me, but I don't want to say it too loud. I wouldn't want to give her any ideas."

They walked as they talked, heading automatically for the bus stop on Meeting Street. Erskine pointed out that Channing had been at the funeral, that he had been cropping up in their lives too frequently for his connection to be merely professional.

"Oh, I know," Ariel said. "I just don't know if I feel like

going all the way out there, but it's all right. I'm going, aren't I?"

"It's just a bus ride and a walk."

"And a bus ride back."

"Right. Maybe we'll see his kids. Greta and Debbie."

"That'll be a thrill. Which was the one you talked to?"

"Greta. She's the older one."

"Right, and you told her you were Graham. You can show her your spleen."

"You always tell me *I'm* gross, Jardell."

"Well, look who taught me. Maybe she'll be cute and you can make out with her."

"She's all of nine years old, remember?"

"Well, tell her you're Graham and you can pretend she's Veronica."

"You must have taken a weird pill today, Jardell."

On the bus, he said, "Speaking of Veronica, she wasn't in school today."

"So?"

"I wonder what's wrong with her."

"The poor little thing probably has the sniffles."

"Maybe."

"Of course if you want to send her a get-well card, go right ahead. What's the big deal that she stayed home from school today?"

He shrugged. "Just that I was thinking," he said. "That conversation we had, and then Graham got hit by a car and now Veronica stayed home from school."

"That doesn't make any sense."

"I suppose not."

She thought of a candle stub centered beneath a portrait —but that was crazy. She hadn't done anything. She hadn't even thought of Veronica in days.

"Graham got hit by a car," she said.

"I know."

221

"And Veronica probably has a cold or a stomach ache. Or maybe she just stayed home to go someplace with her mother."

"Maybe."

"Talk about *me* being weird today, Mr. Erskine Wold. You could make money giving weird lessons."

Investigation is a simpler process when you know what you're investigating. If Jeff had had the benefit of David's conversation with Etta Jellin, he'd have been looking for material on Grace Molineaux from the start. Instead he had to spend several hours in the newspaper files, scanning endless yellowed issues of last century's newspapers for anything he could find relating to various occupants of the brick house on Legare Street. He came on the stories of several persons who had died in the house and made copious notes on each, having no way of knowing whether or not he'd found what he was looking for.

When he hit Grace Molineaux, he knew he was home.

The story was much as Etta Jellin remembered it, with a few exceptions. Grace Duprée Molineaux's four children, three boys and a girl ranging in age from four months to five years, all died within a three-week period in September of 1882. The youngest, a boy, was the first to go, dying in his sleep on the night of the fifth. The girl, a three-year-old, died six days later, and her eighteen-month-old brother perished the same night. The oldest boy failed to wake up on the morning of the twentieth.

The newspaper coverage was guarded. The first death was unremarkable—infant mortality was high in those days. Jeff missed the initial story, a two-line squib on a back page. But when the boy and girl died in the same night, and only a week after the first death, the coincidence drew journalistic attention.

The fourth death was the clincher. Reading between the lines, Jeff could easily determine that public opinion suspected the Molineaux woman of smothering her children while they slept. Without suggesting as much, the anonymous author of one news story hastened to point to extenuating circumstances, showing that Grace was under a strain. She was a young woman who had married a man twenty years older than herself. Jacob Molineaux, a heavily-decorated hero of the Confederacy, had given her four children in as many years, only to be lost at sea weeks before the birth of his youngest son. Grace's own father had died a matter of months earlier, and a favorite cousin had killed himself at about the same time in remorse over heavy gambling losses. All of these tragedies, cited ostensibly to show that the loss of her children was by no means the first blow Grace had suffered, served to imply that, if indeed she had murdered her children, she had done so out of stress-induced emotional instability.

Perhaps for lack of evidence, perhaps in deference to her family background and her husband's war record, no charges were brought against Grace Molineaux. Her name disappeared abruptly from the newspapers, only to reappear just as abruptly on November 4th, when the newspaper reported her sudden death as a result of gas inhalation.

She had been found, it was reported, in the kitchen of her Legare Street home. While suicide was not mentioned, in keeping with the newspaper's evident view of decorous journalism, the inference was inescapable.

She killed her kids, Jeff thought. Maybe the first one did die of crib death or some nineteenth-century infant malady. That was certainly possible, but somewhere along the line Grace had snapped, and she'd certainly murdered the other three children, and when she found she couldn't live with herself she put her head in the oven and turned on the gas.

Could it be the same stove? The one Roberta cooked on, the one with the eccentric pilot lights? Was her restless ghost haunting the stove, leaving it only to appear in the upstairs bedroom with a baby in her arms? Lord, was this Jeff Channing, man of laws, thinking this way . . . ?

His head was reeling by the time he left the newspaper offices. His nostrils were full of the musty smell of ancient newsprint. He'd been unable to find a photograph of Grace Molineaux, but he had no doubt that she was the woman whose portrait hung in Ariel's room. He had no grounds for this belief. There was no evidence that Grace had ever had her portrait painted, or that her appearance had been anything like that of the woman in question. But he only had to remember the expression on that face, the look in those eyes, to be sure the likeness was that of Grace Molineaux, madwoman, murderess, and suicide. Good Lord . . .

He did not return to his office, did not even consider returning to his office, but walked instead to where he'd left his car, got into it and drove around. He passed the house on Legare Street three or four times, returning to it compulsively, staring at its brick-clad bulk as if it might reveal itself to him. Roberta's car was parked at the curb, but he had no desire to stop for a word with her. He couldn't tell her what he had learned. She was under a strain as it was, having a tough time emotionally and—

Just like Grace Molineaux, he thought.

And pushed the thought aside, and drove aimlessly around, trying to think if there was any further direction his investigations might take. Could he possibly establish whether the painting was of Grace? It occurred to him that there might be a way. Even if the painting was unsigned, a comparison of the style with that of various local portraitists of the time might establish who had painted it. Painters frequently kept records, and historical societies tended to preserve records of that sort. A little creative research might clear things up.

For that matter, a little further research in the newspaper files might be time well spent. He already knew as much as he wanted to know about Grace Molineaux, but it occurred to him to wonder what effect her house might have had on persons who had occupied it after her death. He already knew the house had changed hands at an unseemly rate. Had there been a disproportionate number of deaths? Was unexplained infant mortality a legacy of Grace's?

Or had other people sensed something and moved away, before *their* lives were affected by whatever permeated the damp old walls? Maybe the house had been waiting all these years, waiting for the Jardells . . . A house *waiting?* The defense better rest . . .

He drove around until he tired of aimless driving, then found a main avenue and headed north. It was getting on toward dinner time. Time to leave both the nineteenth century and the cloying streets of Old Charleston. Time to get back to his own time, his own house, his own wife and children.

Until, on his own block just two doors from his own house, he saw them.

Erskine and Ariel.

The bus heading back into the city was two-thirds empty. Ariel and Erskine sat all the way in the back. Erskine had his legs draped over the back of the seat in front of them.

"I almost ran," he said.

"Why run?"

"No reason. Just blind panic. When he drove up and saw us I thought we were going to be in trouble."

"We didn't *do* anything."

225

"I know. I'm not saying it makes any sense. I just figured he'd be pissed off. We looked at his house and talked to his kids."

"Just one of his kids."

"Just Debbie. Greta had to practice the piano. She's only nine. Isn't that young for piano lessons?"

"Some kids start taking when they're seven. I wonder if she's any good."

"You could play duets, Jardell. Ladies and gentlemen, for your listening pleasure, the piano artistry of Miss Greta Channing and the flute wizardry of Miss Ariel Jardell. For their first selection, your ears will be treated to . . . to what?"

"*Go Tell Aunt Rhody*, I suppose. We used to live in a house like that one. Erskine, what if we're moving back?"

"To the same house?"

"To one like it. To any other house. I really don't want to move."

"Don't worry about it."

"Right."

They were silent for a moment. Erskine burped and Ariel clucked her tongue reprovingly. He took his feet down from the seat in front of him and yawned elaborately.

Then he said, "You were very cool. Just staring back at him when he stopped the car."

"Well, it never occurred to me to run. I was surprised to see him, but after all it's his house. I guess he has a right to go there."

"Weren't you scared?"

"No."

"Not even when he stopped the car alongside us?"

"No."

He glanced at her. "I get the feeling you sort of like him," he said. "He can be your new boyfriend."

"Well, he's not bad-looking."

"Huh?"

"He's not. I think he's handsome."

"Oh, come on, Jardell. He's like you said in the beginning, he looks like a television emcee. Remember the *Funeral Game*?"

"That doesn't keep him from being good-looking. It bugs you, doesn't it?"

"What bugs me?"

"That I think he's handsome. It really bugs you."

"You can think Dracula's handsome if you want. I don't give a fuck."

"Really bugs you."

"Just cut it out, Jardell. That lah-di-dah singsong teasing shit."

"Hey, calm down."

"You want to think he's handsome, that's fine with me. The big dumb shit's old enough to be your father."

"Two children," Jeff explained. "A boy and a girl. About, oh, twelve or thirteen years old. The girl's the taller of the two. A very long, pale face. The boy's very small with thick eyeglasses."

"What about them, darling?"

"I saw them out front," he said. "Just as I was driving up. I hadn't seen them before."

"You know this neighborhood. The only constant is change. People move in and out all the time, and the number of children—"

"I thought they might have come here. To the house, I mean."

"What made you think that?"

"I don't know. The way they were walking. There was something sort of furtive about them, as if they'd just broken a window of ours or something like that."

"You got this impression just watching them pass by?"

He shook his head, dismissing the thought. "If you didn't notice them, there's nothing to talk about," he said. "Maybe Debbie or Greta saw them."

"Jeff . . ."

"What?"

"Are you feeling all right, darling?"

"Of course. Why?"

"You seem under a strain. I wonder if you haven't been working too hard."

He nodded, seeming to weigh the thought, while inside him he fought to keep from laughing. Crying. Working too hard? He wasn't working at all. If he was under a strain, it certainly had nothing to do with work.

"Maybe you're right," he said. "I guess I've been pushing lately. I'll have to try taking things a little easier."

She nodded, moved closer to him, slid an arm around his waist and laid her head against his chest. Reflexively he put a protective arm around her. His wife, he thought, hearing the words in his mind. His wife, the mother of his children. "Elaine the fair, Elaine the beautiful, Elaine the Lily Maid of Astolat . . ."

He hugged his wife close, closed his eyes, and saw Bobbie's face grinning mockingly at him, one eye squinched shut in a lewd wink, the inevitable cigarette drooping from the corner of her mouth—the face flashed and was gone, and then it was Ariel's face, burning with an unholy knowledge . . . then melting into the face in the portrait, the face of Grace Molineaux . . .

He opened his eyes, and he was standing in his own house with his arm around his wife, inhaling the fragrance of her hair.

Easy, boy, he told himself sardonically. You've been working too hard. You must be under a strain.

That night Ariel went to her room directly after dinner. She tried to play the flute but the music didn't want to come and she gave up on it. She did her homework, then sprawled on her bed with a book and tried to get lost in it. But her mind kept wandering away from the words on the page and after a while she closed the book and set it aside.

She looked up at the portrait.

"Old enough to be your father."

She hadn't reacted openly to Erskine's words, even though the impact was like getting hit between the eyes with a fist.

Jeffrey Channing was old enough to be her father. And he'd come over to the house to talk to Roberta, and had turned up at Caleb's funeral, and had then taken to lurking in his car, spying on her and . . . Suppose he *was* her father? Suppose thirteen years ago Jeffrey Channing had an affair with someone, maybe with a girl much younger than he was, for example. She got pregnant, but he was married and couldn't marry her. The girl had the baby, and she put it up for adoption, or maybe she died in childbirth, but *anyway*, the baby wound up getting adopted by David and Roberta Jardell . . . And then years later Jeffrey Channing found out about it, he was a lawyer and he would know how to investigate that sort of thing . . . In between he'd had two children of his own, Greta and Debbie. And they didn't know about Ariel, and neither did Mrs. Channing. What was her name, again? Erskine had found it out and she ought to be able to remember it, but it wouldn't come to mind. Well, it didn't matter. Anyway, they didn't know about Ariel. (Elaine, that was Mrs. Channing's name.) They didn't know, and her fa—Jeffrey Channing wanted to take an interest in his . . . in her and learn a little about her without anybody finding out his secret. Maybe Roberta herself didn't know who he really was. If he was a lawyer, he probably had some clever way or other to explain what he was doing.

Father.

She tested the word, let it echo in her mind. Part of her wanted to believe that this handsome well-dressed man was indeed her father. Another part couldn't regard the notion as anything more than a seductive fantasy. At least it made for a harmless mind-game . . . Ariel Channing . . .

Twice now they had exchanged long glances, their eyes sort of locked in a wordless stare. Both times he had been behind the wheel of his Buick while she had been walking with Erskine. Both times something had passed between them, something special . . . was the look they exchanged a father's and daughter's?

It was exciting and upsetting and a little crazy. After a while she ran a tub, took a bath, making the water hotter than usual and adding some of Roberta's bath salts. She lay back with her eyes closed, soaking for a long time in the hot tub. Then, drained, she dried off and went to bed.

She lay in bed exhausted but unable to sleep. She began touching herself, as if to reassure herself that she was there, as if to read her features as a blind person might. She touched her face, her shoulders, her breasts. She touched between her legs, then put her hand to her face and breathed in her own scent.

Images bombarded her. At one point she saw Channing standing alongside the woman in the portrait. They were dressed like the man and woman in *American Gothic.* Instead of a rose, the woman was holding a baby. For a moment the baby was herself, and then it was Caleb, and then it was a rose again, a rose that wilted until a drop of blood fell from its petals.

Ariel slept.

Jeff couldn't sleep. After an hour's tossing and turning he gave up and got out of bed. In the living room he tried to concentrate on a magazine but couldn't make sense of what he was reading. He tossed it aside and tried to make sense out of the afternoon.

Had he really seen them?

It was hard to believe he had seen two children who looked like them. Their appearance was too distinctive and he had had too good a look at them to have been confused in that fashion. Of course it was possible that he had fancied a resemblance where none existed. He'd been tired, emotionally exhausted, and he could have seen two children who really looked nothing like Ariel and her friend and his imagination could have connected the dots.

Or there might have been no one there at all. No boy and girl walking past his house. People under a strain sometimes saw things that weren't there. It was not comforting to admit that possibility where one's own self was concerned, but it was not a possibility which could be categorically denied.

Finally, it was possible that he had seen precisely what he had thought he had seen. But what on God's earth had sent them wandering through his neighborhood? It was miles from where they lived. Assuming they had a reason to be in Charleston Heights, was it sheer coincidence that put them in front of his house on his return?

Or had they come looking for him?

He put his head in his hands, pressing against his temples, trying to make his thoughts run along logical lines. There ought to be some way to make sense of all this and he couldn't seem to latch onto it. Was all of this linked to pressure resulting from his affair with Bobbie? Or did it somehow tie in with what he had learned about the portrait?

He closed his eyes, and his mind filled with Grace Molineaux's image. It flickered and was gone, replaced, for God's sake, by a vision of Ariel. He wanted to open his eyes, but half afraid that should he do so he'd discover her standing there in front of him.

He opened his eyes. He was alone in the room, and he reacted to this discovery with a mixture of relief and disappointment.

NINETEEN

IT was impossible to say what woke her. Roberta was sleeping soundly, deep in Valium-induced dreamlessness, when some force propelled her up out of sleep. She was suddenly sitting up in bed with her eyes open.

In the other bed, deep in his usual brandy stupor, David grunted and rolled over onto his side. Across the room, beside the window, stood the woman in the shawl.

She was as formless, as imperfectly defined, as on the first night Roberta had seen her three nights before Caleb's death. Her pale face loomed in the dimness, and all the rest of her was shadowy and indistinct, shifting as if tossed by air currents in the room.

Was it a dream? She had dreamed this woman's appearance once. Was she dreaming now?

"What do you want?"

Had she spoken the words out loud or merely voiced them in her mind? The apparition did not react, nor did David stir. He slept on, unaware.

"Who are you? Why are you here?" She listened as the words seemed to reverberate off the walls, shaking loose windowpanes like strong wind.

The woman turned her face a little more directly toward Roberta. There was something in her eyes, something Roberta thought she ought to be able to read.

Then, like smoke, the woman melted away and was gone.

Roberta put her fingertips to her breast over her heart and felt its insistent beat. She forced herself to take slow deep breaths.

She got up.

Caleb's door was closed. She hesitated before opening it, afraid of what she might find. Perhaps this *was* a dream, she thought, and she decided to be on the lookout for any inconsistencies in Caleb's room which might indicate that she was indeed asleep and dreaming.

She opened the door. The room was undisturbed, with everything in its proper place. The only thing missing, she thought, was Caleb—and the thought, catching her at a vulnerable moment, brought a rush of grief that very nearly knocked her off her feet. She clutched the doorframe for support and managed to keep her balance.

There was no question *now* that she was awake. But for how long? . . . She left Caleb's room, closed his door, and went back to the bedroom for her robe. There was only one cigarette left in the pack on the night table, and when she got it out she saw that it was broken in the middle. She went downstairs for cigarettes, and even before she reached the bottom of the staircase she could smell gas escaping.

She went into the kitchen. All three pilot lights were out. For a moment she worried that it might be dangerous to light a match, but the burners themselves were shut off, and how much gas could escape from the pilot lights? Not much, she was sure. David had said so. She was just extremely sensitive to the odor.

She lit the pilots, opened a fresh pack of cigarettes, smoked two of them in the living room. Why, she wondered, had the woman in the shawl appeared after all this time? What did it mean?

She crushed out her cigarette, mounted the stairs, winced at the sound they made underfoot. The house was listed for sale now, according to David, but so far nothing had happened. There'd been not a single call, no one coming around to be shown through the place.

And when that happened, she thought suddenly, would she take them through Caleb's room? How would she explain a nursery with no baby in it?

Ariel's light was on. She noticed it when she reached the top of the stairs, a sliver of light beneath the child's door at the end of the hall. Had it been on before? She hadn't noticed one way or the other.

Why was the child awake? It was the middle of the night. She started down the hall, slowed, stopped.

She turned instead to the bathroom, where she took two little blue tablets from the Valium bottle. She gazed at them for a moment, the two of them an inch apart in the palm of her hand. Without having swallowed them she could already anticipate how they would smooth things out inside her.

She filled a glass with water, swallowed the pills.

In the hallway, she glanced once again at Ariel's door and the light that was visible beneath it. The light seemed to flicker, as if it were not an electric light at all but a gas flame, or perhaps the flame of a candle.

Maybe the Valium was already at work, she thought, distorting her perceptions. She took a hesitant step toward Ariel's room, then changed her mind. No need for a confrontation with the child, not at this hour, not after what she'd been through already. Let her stay up all night if she wanted. Just so Roberta got some rest herself.

She returned to her room, settled herself beneath the covers. Her sense of smell, she decided, was especially acute tonight. The gas in the kitchen had been far more pungent than usual, and now the alcoholic perspiration that David gave off was stronger than she remembered it. Perhaps it was a heightened sensitivity of hers that made her see the woman in the shawl on this particular night.

She lay back, closed her eyes. A couple of thoughts began to move into her consciousness, but the Valium took hold quickly and she slid away from them.

She awoke in the morning with what felt like a hangover. Her breakfast was coffee and cigarettes, an excessive amount of each, and they set her nerves on edge. She went to the medicine cabinet, hesitated, then took a Valium. What the hell, they were medicine. Otherwise why would Gintzler have prescribed them for her?

Around ten-thirty she called Jeff at his office. He wasn't in and she declined to leave a message. She called again at eleven and a third time at eleven-thirty, and each time his secretary assured her that he was out. The third time she said, "This is Mrs. Jardell. I'm sure he'll talk to me."

"But he's not in, Mrs. Jardell," the woman said. "He may be in shortly, or he'll probably call in for his messages. Shall I have him call you?"

"Please."

She had no appetite for lunch but forced herself to make a cheese sandwich and managed to eat a little more than half of it. She drank some more coffee, smoked several cigarettes, and swallowed another Valium on her way out the door.

It was cold out, and the wind had an edge to it. She drew her car coat around her and walked purposefully south and east. At the Battery, she walked through the little park and stood with her arms propped on the railing, looking out over the water. She was alone. There was no one fishing from the shore, only a few scattered persons on the park benches. A few hundred yards out on the water, a cruise boat carried passengers taking a tour of the harbor.

It was restful at the railing, restful looking out over the water. Here, away from the house, she could dismiss the pools of anxiety that floated on the edge of consciousness. She didn't have to let herself be aware of them. Instead she could relax in the Valium's embrace, going with the flow, letting herself relax. Sometimes she would feel her mind beginning to drift, and at those times it was necessary to drag herself abruptly away from those areas that didn't bear thinking about. Each time she made herself return to the peace of the harbor view like a meditator returning to his mantra, embracing it with something like relief.

When she turned from the harbor view, her eyes fastened on a black woman seated on a bench halfway across the park. She was leaning way forward, trying to feed something to an apprehensive squirrel. At first Roberta thought it was the woman she'd talked to before Caleb's death, the woman who had spoken so knowingly of haunts.

She wanted to avoid her entirely, then realized she'd come here hoping to encounter the woman. She made her way toward the bench, only to discover when she'd come within fifty yards of the woman that she was someone else altogether, a stranger, years younger and a good deal taller and more robust than the woman to whom she had spoken.

She turned from the woman and headed home.

At four o'clock she finally reached Jeff. She had called on returning to the house, thinking he might have tried her in her absence, but his secretary reported she had not heard from him. When she did reach him, he was short with her, almost brusque. She tried to tell him about the woman's appearance in her bedroom and he didn't seem to be paying much attention.

"I was hoping to see you today," she said.

237

"I was tied up. Running around all over the place."

"Maybe tomorrow—"

"I don't think so, Bobbie."

She hesitated, unable to leave it at that. "I *need* you," she said. "I'm having a tough time right now, Jeff. I feel as though I'm cracking up. I'm holding myself together with little blue pills and I have a feeling there's a point when they stop working."

"I'll try to call you."

"Can't we see each other?"

"Listen, I can't make plans," he snapped. "How do I know what I'll be doing tomorrow? I might be dead tomorrow."

"What are you talking about?"

"We could all be dead tomorrow," he said. "Maybe we'd be better off."

She was left holding a dead phone in her hand, shaking her head in wonder. He had never said anything remotely like that before. Nor had she ever felt the way she was feeling lately.

She felt all shaky inside.

Was it time for a pill? You were supposed to wait four hours. Had it been four hours? Not that the pills could have little Swiss watches ticking away inside of them. Four hours was the standard medical interval, wasn't it? Four hours, two hundred forty minutes, fourteen thousand four hundred seconds—there was nothing magical, was there, about that particular span of time?

She laughed at her own rationalization. And went upstairs to take a Valium.

The pill grabbed hold almost immediately, as if the mere act of swallowing it engendered a psychological easing of tension even before the tablet could dissolve and enter the bloodstream. With its assistance, Roberta was able to concentrate on preparing dinner. While it was cooking Ariel came home, carrying her horrible flute, and David arrived moments later. For once Roberta was glad to see them, glad for company in the house.

The meal went well enough, she thought. She and David had a drink before dinner. You weren't supposed to drink when you were taking Valium, she knew, but she didn't think one would hurt. It did make her the slightest bit woozy, but its effects had vanished by the time dinner was over.

Afterward she cleared the table, did the dishes. Now a few hours of television, she thought, and you'll have gotten through another day, and that's not so bad, is it? She could just take them one at a time, and next week perhaps she'd start seeing Gintzler again. Or maybe not. Maybe she didn't need therapy.

She couldn't concentrate on the television.

Twice she got up, walked to the closed door of David's study. Both times she made herself turn and walk back to the television set.

The third time she knocked briskly, then opened the door. He was sitting like some sort of English gentleman with his pipe and his brandy and his book. He frowned at her, and she saw that his eyes were already slightly glazed. He was drunk, she thought.

"What?" he said. "What do you want?"

Drunk. No time for a conversation, least of all a heavy conversation. Say something trivial, she told herself. Something about trouble with the car, something that won't lead anywhere, and then go back to the television set and numb yourself out until it's time for bed.

Instead she said, "Could you come in the other room for a minute? I think we should talk."

Ariel started the tape recorder, picked up her flute to play along with the track she had recorded earlier. She put

239

the flute to her lips and waited, but instead of playing she merely sat and listened to the music. After a few moments she set her flute aside.

It had been a funny day. For some reason Erskine had been getting on her nerves, and she didn't think it was anything he did. It was just her nerves.

On the way to his house after school, she had seen Jeffrey Channing three times. The first time Erskine didn't see him. The car passed them without slowing down, and she just got a glimpse of him behind the wheel before he was out of sight. Another time his car crossed an intersection as they were approaching it, and it was Erskine who pointed it out, reading the license number as the car disappeared from view. The third time, Channing drove slowly past them when they were on Erskine's block. Erskine said, "Don't look but it's him again," and of course she looked, and her eyes locked with his but only for a moment because although he was driving very slowly he was still going faster than they were.

Several times that afternoon they looked out of Erskine's third-floor window, and once she thought she saw his car parked directly across the street, but it was already growing dark by then and it was hard to be sure. And on the way home she kept looking nervously around, trying to spot him, but she was unsuccessful.

She kept wanting to tell Erskine the thought that had come to her, that Jeffrey Channing might be her father. But she was afraid he would think she was demented. And she was having more and more trouble deciding how she felt about the man. If he was her father she wished he would stop playing tag in his car and come right out and talk to her, and if he wasn't her father she wished he would disappear altogether, because then he was either working for Roberta or was some free-lance pervert and she didn't want to have anything to do with him.

The other thing that bothered her was Veronica. Veronica still hadn't come to school, and somebody said something about her being in the hospital for tests. Something about her blood, and maybe it was nothing, but on television programs whenever anybody went into the hospital for routine blood tests you knew they were going to die of leukemia or something equally horrible before the hour was out. And if she and Erskine hadn't had that stupid conversation about killing people she'd just be vaguely sorry for Veronica, if indeed there was something seriously wrong with her, but they *had* had that conversation, and the two people they mentioned were Graham and Veronica, and Graham had a ruptured spleen and Veronica had whatever she had, and it was creepy.

Really creepy.

She drifted to the music, reached for her flute, put it aside without sounding a note. She glanced at the portrait, then heard something that made her tune down the volume on the tape recorder.

Roberta and David. In conversation, their voices raised to an unusual level.

She turned the music up again, deciding to ignore them. But something made her go to her door and open it. She could hear them a little better now. She hesitated, then walked silently to the staircase and went down halfway, seating herself on a step.

She heard Roberta insist that they have the conversation some other time, that David was drunk. She heard David say loudly that he wasn't drunk, that no one could blame him for drinking anyway.

She heard Roberta protest that the *child* would hear. She heard David reply that the *child* had a *name*, that the child's name was Ariel, and that a decent mother would call her child by name. Besides, he added, Ariel wouldn't hear anything. She was playing her flute, and couldn't Roberta hear it?

They were both silent for a moment, and Ariel listened to the tape of her music. You could hear it clearly.

Then she heard Roberta say that she could hear the music, all right, if you wanted to call it music. And then there was a long exchange that she couldn't follow, and then she lost interest and thought of returning to her room, and then abruptly David was shouting again, accusing Roberta of having an affair with . . . Jeff Channing.

Ariel was stunned. She tried to listen to what was said next but her head was reeling and she had trouble taking it all in. There was a lot said, a lot shouted, but the one thing that stayed with her was David's accusation. Roberta and Channing, Roberta and Channing—her head was spinning with it.

Then he wasn't her father. He was Roberta's lover. But maybe he was both, maybe he had started sleeping with Roberta after he had tracked down the Jardells and found they adopted his daughter. Maybe . . .

The possibilities suggested themselves infinitely. She stood up, felt dizzy for a moment, then managed to turn and make her way silently up the stairs. Roberta and David continued their argument below her but she was no longer able to pay them any attention.

If he was her father, why did David think he was sleeping with Roberta?

If he was Roberta's lover, why was he following Ariel?

She couldn't begin to make sense of it.

The argument left Roberta drained, exhausted. It ended inconclusively, of course, with David returning to his study while she stationed herself in front of the television set and waited for him to go upstairs to bed. When he finally did she gave him time to pass out, then made herself watch another reel or two of the late movie. She was tired, could have fallen asleep at any time after the argument, but the longer she stayed awake the greater the chance of sleeping uninterrupted until dawn.

Just for insurance, she took an extra Valium before retiring.

And woke up in the middle of the night in spite of everything. Woke from a sound sleep, woke with no warning, and saw the woman in the corner of the room.

Her features were a little more sharply drawn this night, as they had been on her second appearance before Caleb's death. And she was carrying something, and just before she vanished she turned toward Roberta, and the object she was holding flashed. Roberta couldn't tell what it was, only that it flickered brightly at her.

Then the woman was gone.

Roberta felt herself drawn back into sleep. She was tired, had awakened incompletely, and still had the drug circulating in her bloodstream. She wanted to lie down and drift off.

Something made her get out of bed. She walked to Caleb's room and stood outside the closed door. Her hand was reaching for the doorknob when she glanced to her left and saw the sliver of light underneath Ariel's door.

She strode the length of the hallway, flung the door open. Ariel was sitting stark naked on the edge of her bed, her hands folded in her lap. A candle was burning on her night table below the portrait she'd dragged down from the attic.

The child seemed to be in a trance. It took her a long moment to react. Then she recoiled, folding her arms in front of her little breasts, shrinking away from Roberta.

"It's the middle of the night," Roberta said. "What's the matter with you? What do you think you're doing?"

"I couldn't sleep."

"What's this crap with a candle?"

"I—"

"And you're naked. You'll freeze, Ariel. What's the matter with you?"

"I don't know."

"Put out that candle. Get some pajamas on and go to sleep. Do you hear me?"

The child stared at her. She looked helpless and confused, Roberta thought, and for a moment the impulse came to reach out to her, to hold her and hug her and tell her everything would be all right. But she couldn't do it and the moment passed.

"Put out that candle," she said. She swept out of the room, drawing the door shut after her. On the way back to her own room she paused just long enough to take a pill. Just one pill this time.

TWENTY

SIX years earlier there had been a rash of break-ins in Charleston Heights and environs. Somewhere in its course Elaine Channing had become nervous about being home alone at night, and Jeff had decided she ought to have a gun around the house. He didn't suppose she'd be very likely to use it, but felt it might give her a feeling of security.

The gun he'd bought was a .25-caliber automatic, nickel-plated, a tiny gun that could slip easily into a pocket or evening bag without causing a bulge. Elaine had refused to have anything to do with it, and it had stayed ever since, fully loaded, in the bottom left-hand drawer of the leather-topped kneehole desk in the living room, along with the original box of shells and a spare clip. The drawer was locked to keep the gun out of the children's hands—Greta had been only three when it was purchased—and the key in turn was kept in the center drawer, in a little box with postage stamps and paper clips.

That morning Jeff was drawn to the gun like iron filings to a magnet. There was no conscious thought involved. He rose, showered, ate a good breakfast, and the next thing he knew he was unlocking the bottom drawer, scooping up the little gun and dropping it into his jacket pocket. He stowed the spare clip in another pocket, closed the drawer, then opened it again and retrieved the box of shells, placing it in his briefcase.

He drove to work and was at his desk by nine. He went through a stack of letters, glanced over his list of calls. None of it made any sense.

After a while he drew the gun from his pocket, turning it over and over in his hands. Funny how he'd taken it from the desk without even thinking about it, as if he'd been led to it by some force or will stronger than his own.

How cool the metal was.

He took the clip out, put it back in, flicked the safety catch off and on, jacked a round into the chamber. He laid the barrel of the weapon alongside his forehead, noting again how cool it felt. Like a cold cloth on his forehead. Like his mother's hand, checking to see if he were running a fever.

It was hard to believe such a little gun was truly lethal. He took experimental aim at the wall calendar, at a glass ashtray on top of one of the filing cabinets, at the silver-framed photograph of Elaine and the girls. Each time his finger gave the trigger a tentative caress.

He placed the gun on the desk and sat looking at it. Something had led him to it, and not so that he might cool his brow with it. The gun was a machine for killing. Whom, he wondered, was he supposed to kill?

He sat for several moments, considering this question. Then, with a sigh, he got to his feet and returned the gun to his jacket pocket.

"Don't look now, Jardell, but we're being followed."

"Huh?"

"He's just creeping along behind us. Our favorite Buick. Good old DWE-628. Why don't you turn around and give him the famous Jardell stare?"

"I don't want to."

"What's the matter?"

"It's creepy," she said. "Why's he following us?"

"He always follows us. Especially since we turned up at his house."

"Maybe it was a mistake, going to his house."

"Well, it seemed like a good idea at the time. Besides, who expected him to turn up there?"

She frowned. "Maybe I'll just go home to my house today."

"Why?"

"I don't know."

"Maybe he's following us because he heard you were a musical genius. He wants to sign you to a recording contract."

"Sure."

"Or he's a white slaver. He's going to chloroform you and fuck you five hundred times and ship you to Argentina where they'll make you do it with Shetland ponies."

"Or he's from the Legion of Decency and he heard that there's a gross pig named Erskine Wold who ought to be arrested."

"*He* could probably get arrested for what he's doing, as far as that goes. It's against the law, isn't it?"

"What, following people?"

"Well, bugging little kids. We could call the cops from my house."

"And tell them what?"

"That this man keeps following us all the time. I could tell them the license number. I wouldn't have to say that we know who he is because we did a little investigating. They might not like that part. But if we gave them the license number they could pick him up and give him a hard time."

"Roberta would have a fit."

"Roberta?" He stared at her. "What's she got to do with it?"

"Nothing."

"Come on, Ariel. Why'd you say that?"

She shook her head. "No reason," she said. . . .

When the two children entered the Wold house, Jeff circled the block and parked five houses down the street. He shut off the motor, left the key in the ignition. After a moment he took the gun from his pocket and gazed at it as if he were seeing it for the first time. It seemed to him to be an object of considerable artistic merit, its proportions mathematically perfect, the angle of butt and barrel evidence of its designer's brilliance. With a fingertip he stroked its gleaming nickel surface. He tilted it in his palm, seeing himself reflected in its mirror surface.

If he were going to kill himself, how would he set about doing it? He held the gun first to his temple, then with the barrel in his mouth, tilting it so that it pointed up through the roof of his mouth.

You would have to take careful aim, he thought. The gun fired a small-caliber steel-jacketed slug that would not expand upon impact. To do the job properly, you would have to put a bullet directly into the brain.

When he withdrew the gun from his mouth he felt as though he had passed through some sort of ordeal. The taste of metal lingered on his tongue. He breathed deeply, in and out, in and out.

He looked at the Wold house. He thought of Grace Molineaux, and he thought of Bobbie and Elaine, and finally his thoughts centered on Ariel. It was difficult for him to think about Ariel because his thoughts were never very clear on the subject. There was something hypnotic about the child, something that clouded his thoughts.

He extended a hand, adjusted the rear-view mirror so that he could see his face in it. He kept glancing at his reflection and immediately looking away, not liking what he saw. Each time he met his own eyes in the mirror, a pulse worked in his temple and he felt something throb at the base of his skull.

But he couldn't avoid looking into the mirror.

An answer presented itself. He took the little gun from his pocket, braced himself against the seatback, leveled the pistol at the mirror. His eyes closed involuntarily as he tightened his finger on the trigger, but he willed them open and was staring wide-eyed at his reflection as he fired.

The gunshot was deafening in the enclosed car. The mirror shattered and the slug ricocheted, starring the window on the passenger side, rebounding into the back seat. Jeff sat motionless for a moment, then touched his left forefinger to the barrel of the gun. It was quite warm. He reached up to remove a few stray shards of glass from the mirror frame and let them fall to the floor of the car.

No one seemed to have heard the shot. He inhaled deeply, breathing in the smell of cordite, listening to the ringing in his ears. He felt calm now, and pleased with himself. It seemed to him that he had confronted a problem head-on and solved it.

TWENTY-ONE

ERSKINE'S new tape recorder was larger than his old one, with a more powerful speaker. They sat listening to a cassette Ariel had made. She had played her flute while one of her tapes ran on the original recorder, and now she was hearing the result, a flute duet in which her two voices sang one against the other, blending yet remaining distinct.

At first she had trouble concentrating on the music. She couldn't get her mind off Channing, and twice she went to the window and checked to see if his car was there. But then she managed to slip into the music and get lost in it.

They were sitting side by side on Erskine's bed. Just as she was fully caught up in the music he slipped an arm around her and she felt his fingers take a tentative purchase inches from her breast. She could feel the urgent pressure of his hand through her sweater. She tensed the muscles in her legs, trying not to lose the flow of the music, trying to will his hand from her. The hand stayed where it was. She twisted her upper body away from him to dislodge the hand but it held on and began to crawl like an insect toward her breast.

"Stop it," she said. The hand at least stopped moving. "I said stop it."

"Aw, Ariel . . ."

She stood up, crossed to the recorder and pushed the stop button. "I don't want to hear any more now."

"It sounds good."

"Maybe. I wish you would cut that out."

"I wasn't doing anything."

"It's hard to concentrate on the music when I've got hands all over me. I don't like it."

"Sorry."

"How would you like it if someone was grabbing you all the time?"

"I'd love it."

"You probably would."

"Want to grab me, Ariel? Grab me here."

"You're disgusting," she told him. She went to the window again, eyes searching for Channing's Buick. "That was creepy before," she said.

"I touched your sweater, for God's sake. What's so creepy about that?"

"I mean the way he was following us. He never did that before."

"Maybe he thinks we're agents of a foreign power."

"Be serious."

"Want to put the music back on? I'll sit on my hands if you want."

She shook her head. "I don't feel like listening to it. I don't know if it's any good."

"It sounded good to me."

She shrugged.

"You can't even tell which part you recorded first," he said. "It's even tough to tell where one part begins and the other leaves off."

"Not for me it isn't."

"Well, you're the one who played it, Ariel. That makes a difference."

"I suppose."

"You're in a terrific mood, Jardell. You're a lot of fun to be with."

"I'm sorry."

"What's the matter? That creep Channing?"

She shook her head.

"What?"

She thought of the argument the night before. Channing was Roberta's lover and the knowledge confused her, but it was not something she was prepared to share with Erskine, not just yet.

Anyway, that wasn't the only thing that was bothering her.

She sat down beside him. "We're moving," she said.

"What?"

"I heard them talking the other day. He went to a real estate agent and put the house on the market. Pretty soon I guess somebody'll buy it and we'll have to look for a new place to live."

"You're kidding."

"I wish."

"Where are you going to move?"

"I don't know."

"Maybe she's got her eye on one of those mansions on the Battery."

"I don't think so."

"You think she wants to move out of the neighborhood?"

"I said I don't know." She looked at her lap. Her little hands had hardened into fists and she studied them, then opened them and placed them palms-down on her knees. "He said they wouldn't even look at houses until they found a buyer for ours. And he told her it would take time before they found a buyer who would pay a fair price. But the house is up for sale and anybody who wants it can just come along with a suitcase full of money and I'll have to move."

She looked at him and then had to look away because she could tell his face was a mask composed to keep back tears. If she went on looking at him she was likely to start crying herself and she didn't want to cry.

"I'm not moving," she said.

"Maybe they'll stay in the neighborhood, Ariel. There's plenty of places for sale. The Moeloth house right across the street's for sale. Move in there and we could run a phone wire across the street between the two houses. I bet we could even work out a pulley system to send things back and forth."

"I'm not moving anywhere," she said. "Not across the street, not anywhere."

"What are you going to do?"

She didn't answer immediately, and when she did her voice was softer and carried less conviction. "I don't know," she said. "I'll think of something."

"Get a lawyer to block the sale. Maybe your friend Channing can make himself useful."

"Sure."

"You know what you could do? You could live here."

"What do you mean?"

"Here," he said, gesturing. "This house. You could have my old room. My parents suck but I don't suppose they're any worse than David and Roberta."

"They couldn't be."

"So?"

She looked at him. "You're serious."

"Sure."

"They'd never let me do it, Erskine."

"Sure they would. They never let up about how glad they are that I finally found a friend."

"I know. I only spend time with you out of charity. I'm going to take a tax deduction for it."

"Shut up. The thing is, if they're so glad you're my friend, why wouldn't they let you move in?"

"*Your* parents might. Or I could just move in quietly and they wouldn't notice."

He giggled. "My father could live in the same house with you and not notice you were there. At dinner you could ask him to pass the salt and he'd pass it and *still* not notice. But my mother would catch on sooner or later. She's sharp."

"Mine would never go for it, David and Roberta."

"Can't you get unadopted? And move in here?"

"I don't think so," she said. She went to the window again, just to see if the car happened to be around, and she couldn't see it. "Anyway," she said, "I don't want to move out of my house. I like it there."

"I know you do."

"I want to live there forever. I knew that the minute I saw it and every day I like it more."

"I know."

She sat down heavily. "I don't know what to do."

"Want to listen to the music some more?"

"No. Maybe I'll go home."

"It's still early."

"I know. I'm in a weird mood."

"Want to play a game? Cards or Boggle or something?"

"No."

He touched her arm lightly. "Listen," he said, "don't panic or anything, okay?"

"I guess."

"We'll think of something. Maybe nobody'll want to buy your house."

"Are you kidding? A house like that? Somebody'll buy it."

"Yeah." He brightened. "Maybe my father'll buy it."

"Your father?"

"He'll buy it for us."

"Sure," she said. "Just tell him you need it, like the tape recorder. 'Daddy, I sort of need Ariel's house.' Perfect."

"Don't laugh," he said. "It might work."

It was cold when she left Erskine's house, with a wind blowing up that chilled her the minute she got outside. She had her bookbag hitched over her shoulder with the strap cutting into her. The bookbag was heavier than usual, weighted down with one of the tape recorders. She was carrying the other one.

A car's engine turned over as she left the house. About the time she reached the sidewalk, the car was pulling away from the curb several houses down the street. She was only faintly aware of it until it braked to a stop alongside of her.

"Ariel!"

She turned. It was the Buick, and Jeffrey Channing was leaning across the front seat, rolling down the window on the passenger side. There was a small hole in the window, she noticed, with lines radiating out from it like the spokes of a wheel.

"Come here, Ariel."

He knew her name. Well, of course he would know that. If he was Roberta's lover or lawyer or whoever he was, he would surely know her name. He'd been following her, after all. Small surprise that he knew who he was following.

"You're Ariel Jardell," he said.

And you're Mr. Jeffrey Channing, she thought, but decided against letting him know that she knew who he was. She merely nodded, and took a tentative step toward the car, moving from the sidewalk to the narrow strip of lawn between sidewalk and curb.

"Get in the car, Ariel," he said. He let the door swing open and smiled at her, a tight smile that stopped short of his eyes. He was definitely a handsome man, she thought, and wondered that Erskine couldn't see it.

Old enough to be her father . . .

"Get in, Ariel. I'll drive you home."

"I live close," she said.

"I know where you live."

"I don't mind walking."

"It's cold out. I'll give you a ride."

"No, I sort of think I'd rather walk."

"Get in the car," Channing said. There was a taut quality in his voice that she recognized. Roberta's voice had that tone to it at times when she was having trouble holding herself together. If he was really Roberta's lover, maybe he learned it from her. Or maybe she got it from him.

"Get in the car, Ariel."

Suppose she ran. Suppose she turned around and ran up the path to Erskine's door. They would let her in and Mr. Wold would call the police.

And tell them what?

"Ariel—"

"Why were you following us?"

"Why were you and your friend at my house the other day?"

"Your house?"

"On Fontenoy Drive. I saw you there, Ariel."

"Oh," she said. "We went to visit a friend of mine from my old school. Her name is Linda Goodenow."

"You were at my house."

"I didn't know it was your house. Honest. We were visiting my friend Linda. You can ask her if you don't believe me."

He looked at her for a moment. Then suddenly his face

257

brightened with a smile. "I believe you," he said, moving to pat the seat beside him. "Now hop in and I'll give you a ride."

"I don't—"

"Don't you know me, Ariel?"

"No."

"You don't recognize me?"

"I don't know who you are."

"I'm a friend of your mother's."

"My mother?"

"That's right."

Her heart pounded in her breast. "Do you mean it? Are you telling me the truth? You really know my mother?"

"Of course."

"You know who she is? Is she alive? Does she live here in Charleston? You really know her?"

"Get in the car, Ariel."

"Are you going to take me to see her?"

He smiled again for an answer.

Who was he? Her father? Roberta's lover? Some combination of lawyer and detective? It didn't matter. He knew her mother and was taking her to meet her. It was hard to believe but it was true. It *was* . . .

She got into the car.

TWENTY-TWO

"**W**HERE are we going?"

"For a ride."

But she already knew that. He had driven out of the neighborhood down streets she did not know, and it was hard to tell whether he had a destination in mind or was just letting the car find its own way. She was sitting next to the door now, her right hand on the handle. All she had to do was wait until he stopped for a light or a stop sign and then open the door and hop out.

"Are we going to see my mother?"

"Your mother," he said, like an echo.

"Are we?"

"You'll be home in time for dinner, Ariel."

"Home?"

"With your mother and father."

Her heart sank. Of course! Like a fool she had believed what she'd wanted to believe. Erskine had said the man was old enough to be her father and she had believed he *was* her father. And he'd mentioned knowing her mother, and she'd believed he meant her real mother when all along he was talking about Roberta. Unless—

"You mean Roberta."

259

He nodded. "Your mother," he said. "I have my own name for her, you know."

"You do?"

"I call her Bobbie," he said. His voice was very soft, tender, and Ariel could imagine him murmuring love things to Roberta—to *Bobbie*—and the idea stirred something in her.

"Where are we going?"

"I told you. For a ride."

"I want to go home."

"Where's that?"

"You know. On Legare Street."

"You can't go home again, Grace."

"My name is Ariel."

"There's no time left, Grace. The captain's lost at sea and all your little ones have died in their beds. Did you smother them as they slept, Grace?"

Oh, God, he was crazy. That's why he'd had that tightness in his voice, just like Roberta. He was as crazy as she was. Maybe even more so.

Why was he calling her Grace? And what was he talking about? . . . Little ones, smothered in their sleep . . . he was talking about Caleb!

"I want to go home," she said.

"Miles to go before you sleep, Grace."

"I want to get out of here." Why was there no red light, no stop sign? He was driving too fast. If she jumped out she might break an ankle or a leg.

"Why did you come to my house, Grace? You should have stayed in the attic."

God, she was in the car with a lunatic. And he thought she had killed Caleb, that must have been what he was going on about. Roberta must have been crazy enough to tell him that, and he was crazy enough to believe it, and now she, Ariel, was crazy enough to have gotten in the car with this nut.

And he was going to kill her.

She felt a coldness settle on her chest. He was going to kill her, she was going to die. It was punishment, retribution, she couldn't escape it.

Because didn't she deserve it?

For Caleb's death. For lighting candles and writing in her notebook. For playing the flute.

For Graham Littlefield's ruptured spleen. For Veronica Doughty.

For blowing out the pilot lights.

For going to his house on Fontenoy Avenue. For sneaking down the stairs last night and spying on David and Roberta.

For hearing her own music. For having dreams, and for what she did in her sleep.

For the mess in Caleb's room. For the painting on her wall and the expression in the woman's eyes. For creaking stairs and rattling windowpanes.

For her eyes. For the shape of her face, and her cool paleness.

For being adopted—

He said, "I can't get away from you, Bobbie."

"I'm not Bobbie."

He didn't seem to have heard. "I can't shake loose. Nothing seems to work anymore. Bobbie, Grace, Ariel—you're so many different women I don't know who you are. Lilith? Astarte? Mother Eve?"

There were shards of glass on the floor of the car. Bits of a mirror, and she raised her eyes and saw that the rear-view mirror had been broken.

He stopped the car.

She looked around. They were in the country, with no

houses in sight, no other cars passing them. If she got away from him here, how would she even find her way back home? And it was a cold night. She could freeze to death, wandering around and not knowing where she was.

She huddled against the door, not looking at him.

For a long moment he said nothing, nor did he move from behind the wheel. With an effort she turned her face to look at him. He had both hands on the wheel and was looking straight ahead, and she saw a tear gathered at the corner of his eye. His face was drawn and he looked as though he had been awake for days and days.

He said, "It's all over now."

"What is?"

He looked at her. "Everything has to happen over and over," he said. "You died a hundred years ago, Grace. Did I know you then? Was I your captain, lost at sea? Or was I some secret lover the world never knew of?"

If only he would say something that made sense . . .

"Who would have thought you'd be back? Last time you killed yourself but this time you won't do it, will you? Will you?"

He reached into his pocket and brought out a tiny silver gun.

Oh, God, she thought. The gun terrified her and she couldn't take her eyes off it. It looked like a toy, a shiny little cap gun, but somehow she knew it was real. Had a bullet from the gun shattered the mirror? Had another one made that little hole in the window and cracked the surrounding glass? She sniffed the air, trying to detect the odor of gunpowder, but smelled only her own fear.

She tried the door. It wouldn't open, he'd locked the doors by pressing something on the dashboard. She tried to raise the button to unlock the door but she couldn't budge it.

Oh, God . . .

He turned the gun toward her. She didn't want to look at it but couldn't keep her eyes from the black hole in its muzzle. He kept the gun pointed at her for a moment, then reversed it, first placing its muzzle against his temple, then sticking it into his mouth. At first she willed him to press the trigger, then found herself praying that he would not.

Maybe it was a toy—

As if he'd read her mind, he suddenly took the gun from his mouth and swung it around, aiming at the window of the rear door on her side of the car. He squeezed the trigger, and the gunshot was the loudest sound she'd ever heard in her life. The gunpowder smell reminded her of descriptions of Hell—fire and brimstone and the reek of sulfur. The window was much more severely shattered than the one beside her, and the bullet had made an irregular hole the size of a half dollar.

She turned to look at him again. He was still holding the gun but it was hanging loosely in his hand, pointed at the seat between their bodies. The act of firing it had drained some of the tension from his features. His breathing was slow and deep.

She looked at him and felt herself gathering strength. She thought of how she'd felt last night, after she'd perched on the stairs listening to David and Roberta argue, thought of the unfamiliar feelings she'd experienced later in her room. And the portrait came into her mind, and she made her eyes like the eyes of the woman in the portrait, and with each breath she drew she felt herself growing stronger.

His grip tightened on the gun. He was pointing it at her again.

She moved toward him, ignoring the gun now, no longer afraid of it. Her eyes caught his and held them. She put her hand on his knee, ran it up along the inside of his thigh. She felt a quivering in her loins, a melting, a rush of warmth.

The gunpowder stench was lost in a heavier scent of musk. Her hand was between his legs now, holding him, and her other hand was under his coat, pressed against his side, clutching at him, and she was leaning into him, her head tilted up and back, her lips slightly parted, her eyes burning bright.

His shoulders stiffened and he tried to draw away from her. She continued to flow toward him, her mouth reaching for his, and she watched with satisfaction as his eyes glazed and his lower lips trembled. He made a sound, a sigh or a sob, and then his shoulders drooped in surrender even as his arms went around her, clutching her to him.

Afterward she sat on her side of the car. There was a lingering pain in her loins, and she could tell that her arms and legs would be sore from the awkwardness of their coupling. She had a headache, too, a dull pulsing in her right temple, and her throat was dry and scratchy.

For all of that, she felt good.

He was still holding the gun but she was not afraid of it anymore. He had never released his grip on it, and at times she had been aware of it, the cold metal pressing against the nape of her neck while their bodies tossed together. Now he was turning it in his hands, studying it as if he had never seen it before.

He looked from the gun to her, his jaw slack, his eyes deeply troubled. "My God," he said.

"I want to go home now."

He was turning the gun over and over in his hands, looking first at it and then at her.

She thought of the portrait and gathered strength, thought of the fire that had burned where now she felt only a dull ache.

"Put the gun in your pocket," she said. "I want to go home."

He did nothing at first. Then he nodded slowly to himself and dropped the gun into his jacket pocket and turned the key in the ignition. . . .

When she got home Roberta told her she was late. "We were worried about you," she said.

"I was over at Erskine's."

"I called there and his mother said you had left. That was a long while ago."

"I left something in the schoolyard and I had to go back for it. It's not that late, is it?"

"It's late. I was starting to worry."

Why would Roberta worry about her? What did Roberta care?

"Nothing to worry about," she said. "I'm fine."

TWENTY-THREE

THE next day was a Saturday. Roberta slept later than usual, waking up groggy with a Valium hangover. She had awakened during the night in spite of the pills she'd taken before retiring, then took more pills to get back to sleep. As a result the Valium blurred the memory of the brief interval when she had been awake. She knew she had seen the ghost for the third successive night, but that was about as much as she could recall.

When she got downstairs, David showed her the morning paper.

She had trouble taking it all in. But the paper screamed out its news and David kept filling in the blanks for her, telling her what he had learned from the radio news. Some twelve hours previously, Jeffrey Channing had shot his wife and his two young daughters to death. Then he had attempted to set fire to their house, but the fire had evidently gone out of its own accord. After lighting the fire he had gone to his car, where he had placed the barrel of his gun in his mouth and fired a single shot into his brain. Death, according to reports, had been instantaneous.

That afternoon Ariel sat in her room trying to read a novel about a teenage girl's struggle to overcome compulsive overeating. She couldn't seem to focus on the story. She put the book down and switched on Erskine's tape recorder to listen to the duet tape.

She turned the volume high, and for a while she was able to lose herself in her own music, but then the volume made the music sound wild and out of control and it bothered her. Once she had adjusted the controls she found herself unable to get back into the music.

She let it play, got out her diary, uncapped her green pen.

Why do I keep thinking he was my father?

I know better. He was Greta and Debbie's father and they're dead now. He killed them. I wonder if they knew what was happening. It said they were found in their beds, but were they asleep when he did it? Maybe he killed them first and put them in their beds.

I wonder if they saw the gun first and thought it was a toy.

It's not my fault!

He would have killed me. He followed me and he made me get in the car and he had the gun along and he meant to kill me. He even pointed the gun at me.

Then he put it in his mouth. That's how he killed himself finally, with the gun in his mouth.

How could he do that?

It's not my fault. I didn't do anything but save myself.

I am all alone in the house now. David was up first and then when I got up I heard him telling Roberta. I was on the stairs. They didn't even know I was there. He went out and then I thought she was on the phone or something because I was in my room and I heard her talking. I went halfway down the stairs again and discovered she was talking to herself. About David and me and about him and about wasting her life.

I couldn't understand most of what she was saying. It's really weird, hearing a person talk to herself. It's like they're a character in a play. You don't expect anybody to do that in real life.

A lot of things happen that you don't expect.

I wanted to get something to eat but I didn't want to see her, so I came back up here and waited until she left the house. When her car pulled away I went down and had breakfast.

She even left the dishes in the sink. Something she never does. I washed them and put them away. Don't ask me why. She'll never notice anyway.

Last night I was afraid to go to sleep. I was afraid of what I would dream. But all that happened was I had a wonderful dream of music. I dreamed a whole piece of music from beginning to end, and I remember part of me knowing I was dreaming and knowing that when I woke up I would be able to play the entire piece.

Then when I did wake up I didn't even remember the dream, and then I did, but I couldn't remember anything about how the music went. Maybe I'll dream it again and it'll stay with me.

I didn't tell Erskine what happened. I called him this morning to tell him that Channing killed his family and himself, but he told me instead. He read the paper. I thought of telling him about being in the car with him but not what happened, but instead I decided not to say anything. What is the point of telling anybody?

Erskine is with his parents today. An old aunt of his mother's is sick and they are all three of them driving up to visit her. Erskine just about had a fit when he found out that was how he would be spending the day. First of all he hates his aunt. She is ugly and terrible and tends to pinch him, which he detests. Plus she lives in the country outside of Georgetown and there are always bugs and crawly things in her house. I said there wouldn't be bugs this time of year but he says in her house it makes no difference and they are there year round.

Plus we were going to check out flutes today in the pawnshops on Commercial Street that he knows about. We want to see if I can play a regular flute and if I like it, because with multiple tracks and all it might be interesting to use different flutes. We want to see if I like another flute as well as I like my flute and we want to find out how much they cost.

Either we'll go after school during the week or wind up waiting until next Saturday.

It helped to keep moving. Roberta had discovered that as soon as she left the house. The Valium took the edge off things, making them easier to bear, and activity kept her body busy so that she didn't live so completely in her mind.

The marketing had to be done, and today she threw herself into it with a vengeance, getting caught up in the deliberate mindless routine of pushing a shopping cart up one aisle and down the next. She liked having to make simple meaningless choices, accepting this brand-name item and rejecting that one, saying yes to this soap powder and no to that liquid bleach. It all had a calming influence upon her, suggesting that there was indeed order in the universe, that life flowed upon certain predictable currents.

If there was order, surely there was also chaos. What could be more chaotic than what Jeff had done? She could see now, although she had not seen it at the time, that he had been acting strangely, that he had been under severe mental and emotional strain. But murder and suicide, slaughtering his family and then taking his own life—

She loaded the groceries into her car, drove to the beauty

parlor. It was the routine things that kept you going, she thought. The shopping, the hair appointment, the household chores. Getting dinner on the table, getting the beds made. She hadn't made her bed this morning, hadn't even done up the breakfast dishes.

She braked at a stop sign, ducked ashes from her cigarette. The ghost, she thought, had come to warn her of Jeff's death. She had first seen it three nights in succession before Caleb died. Then it had not appeared again until it had made another trio of appearances. Perhaps, she thought, there was pattern in everything, order even in chaos.

She wouldn't have to see the ghost again. It had come three times and Jeff was dead and it would not come again, and soon the house would be sold and she would never have to wake up again to see that damn woman hovering in the corner of the room.

At the beauty parlor she had an impulse to have something wildly different done to her hair. She felt the need for a change. But she decided to give herself until her next appointment to think about it.

There was no rush. And by then they might even have a buyer for the house.

When she turned into Legare Street she wanted to keep right on driving, to zoom past that looming old mausoleum and never set foot in it again. No more creaking stairs, no more sounds in the walls, no more cold damp brick underfoot, no more windowpanes rattling in the wind.

She pulled up in front of the house, killed the engine. Their next house, she thought, would damned well have a driveway.

It took her several trips to empty the car of groceries. She thought of calling Ariel to help but it was easier to do it herself than to shout over the flute music that filled the entire house. When the last bag was stacked on the kitchen counter she sighed heavily and leaned against a cupboard, trying to catch her breath. She listened to the music and shuddered. How could the child get that much volume out of a tinny little flute?

She began putting groceries away, but before she had emptied a bag the kitchen started to oppress her. She decided she needed a cup of coffee and a cigarette and went to the stove to put the kettle on.

And of course the pilot light was out. All three stove-top pilot lights were out, and the oven pilot as well. It seemed to her that the gas smell was heavier than it had ever been and she worried that this time it might be dangerous to light a match.

It took her two matches just to light the oven pilot. The first went out as she probed within the oven, but the second did the job. She closed the heavy oven door gently to avoid extinguishing the pilot again, then lit the pilot lights for each of the three pairs of burners. Then she tried each burner to make sure they all worked properly.

She put the kettle on.

Damned old house. Crazy house, with a stove that turned itself off and on according to its private whims. Crazy old house with music cutting through walls and ceilings like a sword slashing a silk shawl.

She stood at the counter, feeling the damp floor through her shoes, and measured instant coffee into a mug. David's breakfast dishes were washed and put away, she noticed, and she was sure she had left them undone. Of course a kitchen that could blow out pilot lights of its own accord might wash dishes by itself if it felt like it.

She felt herself smiling at the thought. No, the child must have washed the dishes. Unless the ghost had taken to walking by day.

The ghost . . .

She could remember more clearly now. She had awakened sometime in the dim middle of the night, waking from a sleep she felt must be too deep for her to have been dreaming. And the woman, wrapped in her shawl, was in her usual position in the corner of the room. Although the drug she'd taken had clouded her mind, she felt her visual perception was good . . . the woman was more clearly defined than she had been the night before.

Once again, the woman had turned just prior to her departure, turned to show Roberta what she was holding. The night before Roberta had perceived something that flickered. This time she had gotten a better look, and the woman had been holding—what?

A mirror.

Yes, yes, she remembered! The woman had held a mirror, and had extended it toward her for an instant before fading and disappearing. It had flashed and flickered, reflecting light that was not there, and Roberta had recognized it as a mirror because she had looked into it and seen—

And seen herself.

God, she remembered it so clearly now! She breathed deeply, trying to come to terms with the memory, and placed her palms on the kitchen counter for support.

And then she felt it.

That sudden touch of cold air on the nape of her neck. She recognized the sensation immediately but tried to find an explanation for it. Was it a trick of the mind, touched off by her recollection of what she had seen last night? No, it was real enough. Well, could she have left the front door open on her last trip with the groceries? But she distinctly remembered kicking it shut. Of course the latch might not have engaged, and perhaps the wind—

No.

There was something behind her. Something behind her. Ariel, she thought, and as before she could feel those pale little eyes on her, touching her like cold damp hands.

But that was impossible. The music, the horrible wailing of the flute. It was going on, as loud as ever, so loud her skull was pulsing in time to it.

And now the teakettle whistled.

She made herself stand absolutely motionless. With very economical hand motions she inched upon the drawer in front of her. Her right hand slipped inside once the drawer was a couple of inches open, and she groped around until she managed to find one of the long knives and retrieve it very carefully from the drawer.

The child was upstairs playing her hellish music and someone was standing behind her. Not David. David didn't sneak up on people.

Someone. Or some*thing*.

She tightened her grip on the knife. Please, she thought, let it be an overactive imagination. Let it be the house making me crazy, let it be the shock of Jeff's death, let it be a reaction to too much Valium, too much excitement, too much stress, too much of everything—

The teakettle went on whistling, contending with the music of the flute. She couldn't just stand there forever. Sooner or later she had to turn around.

She turned.

And Ariel stood framed in the doorway, her little eyes staring, her mouth open.

Roberta screamed. The teakettle whistled, the taped flute played on, and she screamed and screamed.

TWENTY-FOUR

ROBERTA'S funeral was held Monday afternoon. Erskine was there, of course, accompanied this time by his parents, but he and Ariel didn't get a chance to talk. Tuesday he came to the house but there were other people around. Ariel didn't really talk to anyone else either, although she participated in various conversations. She got through them with her mind turned to another channel.

She didn't even write anything in her diary. The night of the funeral she read through several earlier entries before putting the book away in a drawer.

Then finally Erskine came over Thursday after school. David was home, reading a book and smoking his pipes, and he didn't object when she asked if she and Erskine could go upstairs.

When they were in her room with the door closed they were nervous with each other at first. Erskine kept walking around, picking things up and putting them down again, and she wished he would just sit down.

"Well," he said. "How long'll you be out of school?"

"I'll be back Monday."

"So you wind up missing a week, huh? Listen, don't

sweat it. You didn't miss anything so far."

"I wasn't worried."

"They never teach anything anyway."

"I know."

"Tashman's giving us a test next week. And I can get your homework assignments tomorrow so you can do them over the weekend if you want."

"Thanks."

"If you don't feel like it they won't hassle you. Veronica was in school today and they told her don't worry about making up the work she missed."

"How is she?"

He shrugged. "She looks all right. I don't know if she's really sick or not. I wish I knew one way or the other. It's hard to have sex fantasies about someone when you think they might be dying."

"That's really creepy."

"Well, I feel creepy today," he said. "I don't know what's wrong. Why don't you play the flute or something?"

"I can't."

"How come?"

"Not until Monday. It was the same thing when Caleb died. David says it's a way of showing respect. I didn't understand it about Caleb because I used to play for him all the time, but she hated my flute so I guess it makes sense."

"I guess."

"Even if it doesn't, I don't want to argue with him. We had this long conversation the other night. I think maybe he was drunk. Does your father get drunk?"

"Never."

"David was talking louder than usual, plus he would be cheerful one minute and sad the next. It was a little weird. He talked about Roberta and he talked about God's will, and how maybe Roberta was for the best. And how it's just the two of us now and we have to take care of each other."

"Does that mean you get stuck with all the housework?"

"We're going to get a cleaning woman. Roberta used to have help with the heavy cleaning once a week but we'll have someone come in every day. At least that's what he said. I guess she'll do the cooking, too. We haven't had to cook anything so far. People brought tons of stuff to the house after the funeral. Plus there's all the groceries Roberta bought the day she killed herself."

"Oh."

"Anyway, I don't feel like playing music. I haven't felt like it since she died."

"What do you feel like doing?"

"I don't know."

"Do you figure they really loved each other?"

"David and Roberta? No." She reconsidered. "He told me they did. He also said she loved me, and I know she didn't. Or maybe she did some of the time. When she wasn't crazy."

"Why did she kill herself?"

"*I* don't know. Why did the *Funeral Game* man kill his family and himself? Why do people do things like that? Because she was crazy, I guess. It was really weird."

"What happened exactly?"

"I'll tell you if you give me a chance. I was up in my room and I heard her come in with the groceries. And then the next thing I knew the teakettle was whistling and I came downstairs because it just went on whistling and didn't stop. I had the tape recorder going and the teakettle wasn't blending with it too beautifully, and I thought maybe she put the kettle on and went out again and forgot it."

"So?"

"So I went to the kitchen and there she is standing like a statue with her back to me. And the teakettle's screaming away like mad and old Roberta's standing there as if she's frozen. I didn't know what to do. It was crazy."

"And?"

"And just as I was ready to go turn off the kettle myself, she turned around. Except it was more like a lion or a panther springing . . . I mean, turning around all in one motion. And here comes the worst part. She had a knife in her hand."

"Come on."

"I'm not kidding. A carving knife with a blade this long."

"Sure, and the next thing you knew she cut your head off with it. Come *on*, Jardell."

"That's what I thought she was going to do. I swear I did. That's how she was holding it. And you never saw anything in your life like the look on her face. She was completely crazed."

"Honest?"

"No, I'm making the whole thing up. Of *course* it's honest."

"We always talked about crazy Roberta but I never knew she was really that far gone."

"Nobody knew. I couldn't believe it when I saw her like that. I thought she was going to kill me."

"What did she do?"

"She just started screaming. That's all. Just opened her mouth and screamed her head off."

"What did you do?"

"What do you think? I got out of there. I just grabbed my coat and ran."

"Out of the house."

"I would have run out of the state if I knew the way. I just took off like a maniac. I got all the way over to your house before I remembered you weren't home."

"Where was I? Oh, right. Visiting Aunt Claire."

"Then I didn't know what to do. I wanted to go to the

movies but I didn't have any money with me so I couldn't. I wound up at the library. I couldn't find anything very interesting but each time I started to go home I thought of Roberta and went looking for another book."

"And while you were at the library—"

"She was killing herself."

"How did she do it, exactly?"

"She had these tranquilizers and I guess she took a lot of them first. Then she closed herself up in the kitchen and shut the door and everything and turned the gas on."

"You mean the stove?"

She nodded. "She shut off all the pilot lights and then turned on the stove and the oven. And I think she put her head in the oven, or maybe I'm mixing it up with Sylvia Plath."

"The one who wrote those poems named *Ariel?* I'll have to get that book one of these days."

"Don't bother."

"Well, just to see what it's like. I thought she killed herself in her car."

"No, she put her head in the oven."

"Are you sure? I read something about her. I thought she sat in her car in the garage with the motor running."

Ariel looked at him, then at the portrait on the wall. "I'm pretty sure it was the oven," she said. "Anyway, we don't have a garage."

He stared hard at her, his eyes protruding behind his glasses. Then he said, "Who found her? David?"

"Uh-huh. They'd taken her away by the time I got home."

"Jesus. Ariel? How do you feel about it?"

"Weird."

"Yeah."

"I don't *know* how I feel about it, if you want to know.

279

I suppose it'll take me a week or so before I figure out how I really feel."

"I know what you mean."

"I mean, will I miss her? We didn't get along very well but maybe I'll wind up missing her all the same. How can I tell for sure?"

"You'll have to wait and see."

"That's right."

He studied her. "You've changed," he said.

"How?"

"I don't know exactly. You seem older."

"Really?"

"You even look different. Your face." He nodded at the portrait. "More like her."

"You really think so?"

"Yeah . . . Ariel?"

"What?"

"You didn't do it, did you?"

"Didn't do what?"

His eyes drew away from hers. "You didn't just happen to kill her, did you? Like in a dream?"

She stared at him.

"Just kidding," he said.

"Oh, *sure*," she said. "Sure, that's *just* what I did. First I smothered Caleb in his sleep, never mind that I happened to love him, and then I took a car and ran over Graham, and then I fixed it so Veronica got leukemia—"

"Is that what she's got?"

Her eyes flared. "I don't *know* what she's got. But whatever it is I gave it to her, right? And then I shot Debbie Channing and Greta Channing and his wife, I don't remember her name—"

"Elaine."

"I don't *care* what her name was. Then I shot her, and then I put him in his car and shot him, and then I made

Roberta take pills and put her head in the oven. What kind of a person do you think I am?"

"Ariel, I was kidding!"

"You're supposed to be my friend. How could you say a thing like that?"

"I said I was kidding."

"That's no way to kid."

"I'm sorry. Ariel? Don't be mad."

"I'm not mad."

"Yes you are."

"Only dogs get mad."

"Well, don't be angry."

She didn't say anything.

"Ariel?"

"I'm not angry," she said. "It's okay."

"Are you sure?"

"I'm sure."

He reached for her hand. At first it lay lifeless in his. Then she returned his squeeze and both of them relaxed.

"Hey, Ariel?"

"What?

"How do you make a dead baby float?"

"What?"

"I said, how do you make a dead baby float?"

"I don't know what you're talking about."

"It's a riddle. How do you make—"

"A dead baby float. I don't know."

"You give up?"

"All right, I give up."

"Well, it's easy," he said. "You take one dead baby, two scoops of vanilla ice cream, some chocolate syrup—"

"Gross," she said.

"—and some soda water, and a maraschino cherry—"

"Utterly gross and disgusting," she said, but then she started to giggle, and for the life of her she couldn't stop.